CW

getting over
garrett delaney

getting over

garrett delaney

ABBY McDONALD

CANDLEWICK PRESS

Copyright © 2012 by Abby McDonald

First edition 2012

Library of Congress Cataloging-in-Publication Data

McDonald, Abby.
Getting over Garrett Delaney / Abby McDonald. — 1st ed.
p.   cm.
Summary: Seventeen-year-old Sadie Allen has spent the last two years pining for her best friend, Garrett, but when he heads off to literary camp for the summer without her, she decides to kick her unrequited crush for good, with the help of her co-workers, another boy, and her own summer twelve-step program.
ISBN 978-0-7636-5507-5
[1. Love—Fiction. 2. Friendship—Fiction. 3. Summer employment—Fiction.] I. Title.
PZ7.M4784174Ge 2012
[Fic]—dc23   2011018621

12 13 14 15 16 BVG 10 9 8 7 6 5 4 3 2

Printed in Berryville, VA, U.S.A.

This book was typeset in Sabon.

Candlewick Press
99 Dover Street
Somerville, Massachusetts 02144

visit us at www.candlewick.com

DISCLAIMER

You have to understand: I've been madly, hopelessly, *tragically* in love with Garrett Delaney for two years now—ever since the fateful day when I looked up from my list of the Top Ten Couples of All Time and saw him sauntering into the local coffeehouse.

(And before you say that fourteen-year-olds aren't capable of real love, well, my Couple Number Four, Romeo and Juliet, were barely out of junior high when they first met, and nobody doubts the burning force of their passion.)

But back to Garrett. There he was, all long limbs and faded corduroy pants, his dark blond hair falling carelessly over cloudy blue eyes. He stood in the doorway, a battered leather satchel slung across his chest, and right then I knew. He was the one I'd been waiting for, sent by

the heavens to make my life infinitely better and exqui-
sitely painful all in one fell swoop.

Because it was fate—don't try telling me otherwise.
How else can you explain the fact that Totally Wired—
usually half full at most with study fiends and hard-core
cappuccino addicts—was packed solid with baby-yoga
moms and their bawling brats, meaning that I, Sadie
Elisabeth Allen, was sitting next to the only free table in
the entire room?

Never mind that my BFF Kayla was stuck late at viola
practice, so I was waiting there alone. No, the real reason
I know that Garrett and I were destined to meet is that out
of all the trashy, uncool books I could have brought along
(this being the Judith Krantz era of my sexual education),
I happened to pick a battered old copy of Pablo Neruda
poetry my dad had given me, so that when Garrett col-
lapsed into the chair beside mine, he looked over and lit
up with a crooked half smile that to this day still does
strange things to my stomach.

"*Twenty Love Poems?*" he asked while I tried not to
choke on my cheesecake. The teen boy god was looking
at me. The teen boy god was *talking* to me! "Neruda is
my favorite. I love his surrealist work."

He waited patiently while I took a gulp of my mocha
whip and tried to register this new reality where cute boys
actually made intelligent conversation with me instead
of just shooting spitballs into my hair all through third-
period bio. Maybe Kayla was right: maybe high school
really would be different.

"Did you know he wrote only in green ink?" I replied

at last, reciting the only factoid I knew about Neruda. I took a breath, thanking the Gods of False Advertising that I was wearing a padded bra, which could, maybe, possibly make me look *at least* sixteen. "He said it was the color of hope."

"Really? That's cool." He gave me an admiring look. "I'm Garrett. I just moved to Sherman."

"Sadie," I managed. "Hi!"

"Sadie," he repeated, and my name—which had always seemed like such an old-lady name to me, up there with Gertrude and Ada—suddenly sounded glamorous and exotic. "So, Sadie, tell me what the hell you do for fun in this town."

He grinned at me like we were in this together. Friends, partners, future class couple. Prom king and queen. And in that glorious instant, I could see it all stretching out in front of us, like those cute couple montages in all those romantic-comedy movies Kayla and I love: Garrett and me fooling around with old video games in the arcade; Garrett and me snuggled up in a listening booth at the record store; Garrett and me lying out by the riverbank, holding hands, making out. . . .

So what if I couldn't play arcade games and the nearest record store had closed down the year before? I looked over at him and knew that this was the start of my own real-life love story. Move over, Elizabeth and Darcy (Couple Number Six); make way, Scarlett and Rhett (Couple Number Nine)—there was a new entry on that list, and our names were Sadie and Garrett.

TWO YEARS LATER . . .

CHAPTER ONE

"Hey, birthday girl!"

I sit up so fast I get a head rush, the world tilting from blue sky to gray bleachers and back to the lush grass of the empty football field. It's the first week of summer, and there's nobody here but Garrett, heading my way with a knowing grin on his face and both hands hidden behind his back. He's in his usual uniform of faded corduroy pants and a crumpled button-down shirt, this time over an old Clash T-shirt that I can't help noticing hangs against his torso just so. Fifty percent prep, twenty percent punk, thirty percent old-school British indie rock, and one hundred percent gorgeous—that's Garrett for you.

"Close your eyes." He stops a few feet away, the setting sun shining through his hair like some kind of halo.

"And no peeking."

"Is it a kitten?" I clap my hands in excitement, my bracelets jangling. "A unicorn? A kitten-unicorn hybrid?"

"You wanted a kitti-corn?" Garrett teases. "Why didn't you say so? They had them at the store, but I just figured, you know, your allergies, and those wings flapping around . . ."

"But all the other girls have one!" I laugh. "And ponies are so last season!" There's a thud as he collapses on the ground and I open my eyes to find him smiling at me.

"Sorry, I failed. Will you ever forgive me?" He presents me with a package.

"Forgiven." I give the package an exploratory shake. Garrett never just takes the store gift-wrap option or grabs a roll from the closet at home. This time, he's created wrapping out of pages from old books, the paper yellowed and fading at the edges. "I love getting older," I muse as I carefully begin to peel the layers away. "You're closer to death, but there are presents."

"They should put that on a Hallmark card." Garrett laughs. "And file it under Consumerist Celebrations."

"Is there any other kind?" I quip. The last layer of paper flutters to the ground, and I'm left with my bounty: a bundle of *Paris Reviews*, an old-school mix CD, and a beat-up copy of a Kerouac novel, *The Dharma Bums*.

"Thanks!" I beam, turning the book over in my hands. "This is awesome! I've wanted to read this for ages — ever since you told me about it."

Garrett smiles. "Let me know what you think. I left some notes in the margins for you. I can't wait until we do our own big road trip," he adds. "Nothing but open highway, all the way to California."

"Staying in seedy roadside motels . . ." I lean back on my elbows, slipping into our well-worn refrain.

"Living off diner food . . ."

"Stopping to see the world's biggest ball of yarn."

"No way," he protests. "None of that tourist trash. We're going to see the *real* America." He sprawls out beside me, carelessly flinging one arm over his eyes to block out the sun.

I watch him for a moment, shadows falling across those perfect cheekbones. I should be happy, I know—with my gifts, and Garrett's daydreams of our awesome plans—but there's one thing wrong with this picture. With every picture.

He's not mine.

I don't understand it, either. We're supposed to be together. I knew the day we met that it was fate! But I guess even fate finds a way of destroying your hopes and dreams, leaving your heart dashed on the cruel rocks of life—just ask the poor souls in all those Greek myths. See, it turns out I wasn't entirely right about me and Garrett back then. Not the friends part, because despite my fears that he'd show up on the first day of school, get sucked into the vortex, and never speak to a lowly freshman girl again, that's exactly what we turned out to be: buddies, pals, BFFs. Everything except the only thing I ever really wanted us to be.

In love.

And it kills me. Mom says I exaggerate, but I'm

not even kidding about this. You can die of a broken heart—it's scientific fact—and my heart has been breaking since that very first day we met. I can feel it now, aching deep behind my rib cage the way it does every time we're together, beating a desperate rhythm: *Love me. Love me. Love me.*

I sneak another look at Garrett, lying out on the grass beside me. He yawns, stretching a little as he does; his shirt rides up, revealing a whole inch of pale-golden stomach.

Be still, O heart of mine!

I stifle a familiar sigh of longing. It would be one thing if he was completely unobtainable—gay, for example, or madly in love with some other girl—but I have no such comforting reason why we can't make it work. No matter which girl he's dated—and there have been plenty—he's stayed just as close to me. Closer, even, since I'm the one who gets to listen to all his deepest, darkest fears and secrets, the one who brings over pizza and root beers after the (inevitable) breakup.

For two long years, we've been inseparable. And for two long years, I've been desperately waiting for more.

Garrett can never stay still for long, and sure enough, after a couple of minutes, he sits up, restless. "So, you ready for the next part of your birthday? We've got a whole night o' fun ahead of us."

"As long as it includes sugar and caffeine," I reply lightly, as if I haven't just been meditating on his delicious abs.

"Done and done."

I stuff my goodies into my own beat-up leather satchel and head back toward the parking lot, my frayed jeans dragging on the grass.

"Did you pick your classes yet?" he asks as I curl my fingers into my palm to make up for the fact they're not wrapped around his.

"Not yet," I admit. "The short-story class sounds kind of fun. . . ."

"It will be—you'll love it," Garrett insists, enthusiastic. "And your short fiction is getting really great; you've improved so much this year."

"Thanks." Praise from Garrett is praise indeed. "Then short stories it is!"

I think again of the fabulous summer ahead of us. Six weeks together at an intensive writing camp in the woods of New Hampshire—who could ask for a more romantic retreat? Sure, there are eight-hour days of classes scheduled, but those will fly by. It's the nights I'm looking forward to the most. Snuggling together around the campfire, walking in the moonlight down by the lake . . . It's the chance I've been waiting for—I just know it. We're still waiting on our acceptance letters, but Garrett knows one of the instructors through his parents and swears we're a lock.

We reach his old Vespa, parked in the middle of the concrete. "Hey, Vera," I coo, stroking the metal. "How are you feeling?"

"Temperamental as ever." Garrett hands me the cherry-red passenger helmet.

"Aww, she's just messing with you." I knock three

times on the metal for luck as I climb on board. It's stupid, I know, but tradition. The only time I didn't knock, Vera threw a mechanical temper tantrum and gave out on us somewhere past the last gas station but before the creepy abandoned development on the outskirts of town. We froze on the side of the street in the rain until my mom came to pick us up—armed with "I told you so" and a lecture on road safety and organ donation.

"You think she'll make it through another year?" I ask, tucking my hair into the helmet.

Garrett feigns outrage. "You'll have to pry Vera from my cold, dead hands!"

I laugh. "You might want to rethink that metaphor, with all those road-safety stats my mom keeps leaving out for you."

"Hush, child," he scolds me, climbing on in front. "Where's your sense of adventure?"

"I'm plenty adventurous!" I protest, wrapping my arms around him. Never mind adventure. This is the part I love the most: the excuse to hold him tight for as long as our journey takes. "Just remember who you drag along to all those foreign movie nights in the city."

"You love them." Garrett starts the bike, and slowly, we start to ride away. "Don't even try to deny it!" he calls over the noise from the engine.

So I don't. Because I do love them.

And him.

Totally Wired is busy when we arrive, the evening cappuccino crew jostling for position with the summer college crowd buried behind their textbooks. We head for our regular table in back, the one under the wall of old rock-show posters, peeled and fading. "The usual?" Garrett asks.

"Yup!" I hurl myself down on the cracked leather bench. "Here, I think I've got . . ."

Garrett waves away my crumpled dollar bills. "Are you kidding? It's the day of your birth. Your money's no good to me."

He heads for the counter while I settle back and check out the scene. This place is the closest Sherman, Massachusetts, comes to having a hangout of any kind: the lone beacon of coolness in a line of generic drugstores, take-out places, and bland clothing outlets. I live in the cultural wastelands, I swear. After years of praying to the Gods of Cultural Experience, I've had to accept that this town is a lost cause; when they opened a strip mall outside of town with, *gasp,* a Chipotle, it was all kids in school could talk about for a week. No, if we want culture, we have to drive for it: forty miles to the nearest college town or a couple of hours east to Boston, where Garrett and I gorge on Indian food, arthouse movies, and the sweet, sweet mildewy scent of used bookstores.

But I have to admit, as lone beacons go, Totally Wired is great. The bare brick walls and steel pillars and weird art are like something you'd find in Brooklyn, or Chicago maybe, and there's always a cool song playing. If you ask, the baristas will tell you the band and the album and how this new stuff isn't as good as the release from a few years ago, when they had a different bass player and the lead singer hadn't sold out.

"Hey, kid." LuAnn snaps her gum as she clears the table next to mine. At least, I think her name is LuAnn; that's what it says on her old-school diner name tag, but I'm always too in awe of her to ask if it's for real. "Cute shoes."

"Oh, thanks," I mumble. "They're only from Target."

"Still, you're working them." She winks and struts away in her pink 1950s sandals that match her floral-print sundress. I look down at my red sneakers, feeling a glow of pride. Fashion compliments from the resident vintage queen are gold dust; LuAnn is always showing up in crazy ensembles, with her long red hair in pin curls or a severe wave. She can't be more than a few years older than me, twenty at the most, but she has this aura of awesome confidence I can't even begin to mimic. Not that I'd ever try.

"Make a wish." Garrett returns, depositing a tray with our drinks on the table and presenting me with a cupcake adorned with a single candle.

"You didn't have to!" I protest, but inside, I'm beaming. Red velvet: my favorite.

He remembers.

"Sure, I did. It's a momentous day. You're seventeen now. You can do . . . absolutely nothing you couldn't already." Garrett makes a face, then laughs. "Still, we have to celebrate. You're all grown up!"

I grin. "As long as there's no singing," I warn him, then blow out the candle. "You'll get us barred for life."

Garrett blinks. "Are you saying I can't sing?"

"I'm saying the last time you broke out in a chorus of Radiohead, half the neighborhood cats went into a frenzy." I scoop a fingerful of frosting from the top of the cupcake. After all, what is cake if not a vehicle for frosting?

"Yum." Garrett reaches over with ink-stained fingertips and does the same before I can slap his hand away. "Ow!" He sticks out his tongue, covered with sprinkles. "So what did you wish for?"

I shrug. "The usual: world peace, winning the Nobel prize . . . Meeting Justin Beiber . . ." I add with a laugh.

"Aiming high. I like it."

"A girl can dream." I busy myself with the cupcake, hiding my lie. The truth is, I wished for the same thing I always do, when I let myself wish at all.

Him.

A group of girls comes chattering along the aisle next to us, fourteen or fifteen years old maybe, heading back toward the bathroom. They're loud and excited. "Ohmigod, we *have* to see that movie!"

"I know—he's so cute."

"Do you think he did that flying thing, or was it all a stunt guy?"

"No way, he wouldn't do something like that!"

Garrett and I share an amused roll of the eyes. "God, someone needs to lock them in a room and teach them about real culture," Garrett murmurs conspiratorially. I giggle. "I'm serious!" he says darkly. "A whole generation raised on plastic pop stars and movies with happily-ever-afters."

"The only way they'll ever discover great literature is if someone makes a Disney sing-along," I say. "*Anna Karenina:* the dance-off."

He snorts on his coffee, and I feel a surge of pride at my quip. The girls move on.

"So what did your mom get you?" Garrett settles back in his seat.

"No idea." I pour half the canister of sugar into my coffee, the only way I can stand it so black and strong. Garrett says those ice-blended syrupy things are milk shakes with delusions of grandeur—kid stuff—so I switched to the hard stuff ASAP after we met. "She was talking about some big surprise for when I get back tonight."

"Maybe she's finally caved on the car," he suggests. "You left out that list of used models, right?"

I fix him with a dubious look. "We're talking about the same woman, right? Tiny, incessantly organized, insanely overprotective?"

"OK, maybe not," he agrees. "But she's got to let up sometime, right? You're a junior now. It's not like you can ride around on the bus forever."

I grimace. "Don't remind me." In case you hadn't noticed, I'm not a senior. Not anywhere close. In my many disagreements with my mom, this is the sorest spot of all: that despite the fact I turned seventeen today, I'm still only heading into my junior year of high school. Such is the fate of those of us born on the school-year borderline. Sure, Mom has psychology reports in her corner—and believe me, she quotes them all the time—about how it's better to be the most advanced, intelligent, mature kid in your peer group, instead of the underdeveloped wisp in the class above with lower reading scores and a way smaller chest, but honestly, I'd take that boob-related insecurity in a heartbeat rather than feel so out of place and *old* all the time.

"Knowing her, she's probably booked us for another mother-daughter bonding retreat." I sigh. "A workshop on realizing our full potential or some other bleak hell." This is what I get for having a real-live life coach as a mother; the last time, it was "Seven Steps to Actualizing Your Inner Awesomeness," none of which turned out to include room service or cable TV. Some retreat.

Garrett gives me that famous half smile, but this time, it doesn't quite reach his eyes. He's toying with the handle on his coffee mug, and now that I'm sitting right across from him, I can tell something's not right. I have a radar for his moods, and this one isn't exactly a bundle of sunshine and bunnies.

"What's up?" I ask. "Are you OK?"

"Sure. Fine. Hey, did you see that documentary on Warhol and the Factory scene?" Garrett gulps his coffee, looking casual as ever, but I know him too well.

"Nope. You're not distracting me that easy. Spill," I order, setting my elbows on the table and fixing him with a look. "I mean it. You're holding out on me."

He exhales. "It's nothing. I mean, it's your birthday; you don't want me to get into it."

"Garrett!" Now I'm starting to worry. "What's going on? You know you can tell me anything."

A pause, and then he says the words I've been longing to hear, the ones second only to "I love you" and "I can't live without you."

"I, um . . . It's me and Beth. We broke up."

CHAPTER TWO

"You what?" I gasp. Talk about a birthday miracle: I offered my wish up to the universe, and it delivered! OK, so Garrett hasn't swept me into a passionate embrace and sworn he can't live without me, but still, this is a start.

"When?" I ask, struggling to hide my joy. "Why didn't you say anything?"

He looks awkward. "It was just last night. I mean, we've been fighting for a while, but . . . I don't know. I didn't want to spoil your birthday with all my breakup drama." He keeps playing with his coffee cup, looking embarrassed.

"Garrett! What happened? Did she cheat on you? Did you finally get sick of her reading *Cosmo* all the time? Did she throw one tantrum too many?" Garrett has a thing for redheads, and drama club girls at that. I've thought about dyeing my hair and nearly auditioned for the spring play, but somehow, I don't think even that would make the difference. "Wait. I'm sorry," I say, reminding myself that I'm supposed to be the supportive friend here—rather than, you know, filled with wild hope and rapturous expectation. "The most important thing is, are you OK?"

He nods, reluctant, but something about the way he presses his fingertip into the sugar grains on the table brings me back to earth with a jolt. He's genuinely hurt here, and even I wouldn't wish that on him, however thrilled I am about the circumstances behind said pain. "I guess it was inevitable?" he asks. "I mean, she's graduated now. And things haven't exactly gone smooth these last few months."

"You mean, because she's crazy," I point out.

"No! Beth is just . . . complicated. High maintenance . . ."

"Crazy," I finish, shaking my head. "The girl would throw a fit over anything."

You may think I'm a teeny, tiny bit biased when it comes to the character of Garrett's girlfriends, but trust me, this isn't even me being blinded by jealousy and unrequited longing. After tagging along on countless third-wheel movie nights and after-school hangouts, I can safely say that Beth Chambers is a high-strung, temperamental bitch. And I can—say it, I mean. Finally!

"You're so much better off without her," I reassure him fervently. "I don't know why you dated her in the first place."

Let alone for five months. Five whole months of agony, watching him moon all over her, every kiss like a tiny dagger to my heart.

Garrett gives me this wistful smile. "Because she's beautiful." He sighs. "And unpredictable. And being around her inspired me to write the most amazing poetry. . . ."

I bite my lip. OK, so we're not quite done with the tiny daggers just yet. "But it didn't work out, right?" I remind him. "There was a reason you broke up with her."

He nods, resigned. "She wanted commitment. You know, that we'd stay together in college. She made it into an ultimatum, like if I couldn't promise her that, then there was no point in even trying." Garrett's voice is heavy, and even though this is the news I've been waiting—hoping, praying!—for ever since they first hooked up at Lexie Monroe's party, I can't help but feel a pang for him.

"You did the right thing," I insist. "Really, you won't regret it."

Garrett, alas, isn't as convinced. "I don't know. I cared about her," he says quietly. "I still do. I know she could be . . . difficult, but when we were together, just the two of us, it was amazing."

"But she gave you the ultimatum," I remind him gently. "And who could give that guarantee, anyway?"

He manages a smile. "I know. I'll feel better soon. I hope. See?" He rolls his eyes. "This is why I didn't mention it—I didn't want to drag you into my relationship angst. Not today."

"What are best friends for?" I bounce up. "Come on,

no more moping around here. There's a *Before Sunrise* box set with our name on it."

He pauses. "Are you sure?"

"Hmm, let me think about that." I pretend to ponder. "An evening with Ethan Hawke and pizza. Oh, the tragedy!"

Not to mention snuggling up with Garrett on the conveniently small couch.

Garrett finally cracks a smile, genuine this time. "We're gonna party like it's your birthday," he raps, badly, slinging an arm over my shoulder as we head toward the exit.

"Eww, no, stop!" I hit him.

"Gonna talk about Descartes like it's your birthday."

"I'm officially disowning you," I tell him, putting distance between us. Garrett just sings louder.

"Gonna sip root beers like it's your birthday."

I catch LuAnn's eye as we pass. She grins, and I blush. "I can't take him anywhere," I tell her as Garrett makes lame white-boy gang signs.

"You know we'll stay out past eleven o'clock 'cause it's your birthday!"

"And you call yourself a poet."

By the time Garrett drops me off back home after our movie marathon—and a whole tub of peanut brittle—I've managed to convince him that breaking up with Beth is the best thing that's ever happened to him. I definitely know it's the best thing that's ever happened to me. Finally, the Gods of Unrequited Crushes are on my side: Garrett is single, just in time for us to head off to lit camp together. I can see us now: days spent pushing each other to dizzying literary heights, nights spent sneaking away for romantic rendezvous under the stars.

After two years of agony, destiny is on my side once more!

"Remember, no more moping around, reading her old love letters," I order Garrett as I hop off the Vespa and tuck the helmet under the backseat.

"Yes, ma'am." He laughs.

"See you tomorrow?" I ask. "We could spend the day reading out by the river."

"Sounds good." Garrett revs the engine. "Give me a call in the morning, OK?"

I watch happily as he rides away, Vera spluttering all the way back down the street, a flash of red against the green of the shady oak trees and overgrown front lawns. Me and mom live on the older side of town, where the streets are full of rambling colonial houses and leafy backyards, but Garrett's family is across town in one of the newer developments by the lake: the crisp mock-Tudor houses full of plush cream carpets and sofas that get smudge marks just from looking at them.

"Hey, Sadie."

The voice comes from across the street, and I turn to find Kayla sitting on her front porch steps in a pretty print blouse and cutoffs. She waves. "Happy birthday," she adds. "It *is* your birthday, right?"

"Yup, thanks!" I call back, but neither of us crosses the road. After a childhood of sleepovers and playdates, our friendship kind of faded out after we started high school. We still get along fine, but it's clear we're different kinds of people. After I met Garrett, I got involved with the lit magazine, while Kayla turned out to be one of those perky, cheer-filled girls, wearing bright bands in her blond ponytail and gossiping over celebrity breakups. She's been dating a varsity basketball player named Blake for a year now, and sometimes, when Garrett drops me off at home late at night, we pass his blue pickup truck, parked two blocks over, the windows steamed up inside.

I'm just deciding whether to go over and say hi when that very truck pulls around the corner, some rock song playing loudly through the open windows. Kayla bounces up. "Have fun!" she calls, smiling, and then hurries toward the truck. Blake leans over to open the passenger door; Kayla hops in, kissing him for a long moment before he slings one arm around her shoulder and they drive away.

I watch them go, feeling a curious pang of envy. Not because I harbor a secret love for monosyllabic jocks — I would die of boredom spending even an hour with Blake. I've met him in passing a couple of times, and sure he's cute (in a hair-product-and-tan kind of way), but the guy has nothing to say. Not even a little; not even a teeny, tiny bit. *Nothing.* Garrett and I talk for hours, about everything under the sun: politics, philosophy, religion. He challenges me to think about the world in a whole new way. That's real love: when you're intellectual equals. The Ted Hughes to my Sylvia Plath.

18

"OK, all right!" Clearly, Mom realizes that tampering with my library collection is an intrusion too far. She puts a soothing hand on my shoulder and backtracks. "They're still boxed in the garage. We can go get them back."

"Thank you." I sigh with relief. "And, um, thanks," I add, not wanting to seem like a completely ungrateful brat. "For all of this. It's a . . . nice thought."

She smiles. "I promise, just a few days of the new system, and you'll be convinced. It's the first thing I do with my clients. And look, I even made you a wall chart with space for your personal goals and achievement schedule!"

I sigh. "Thanks, Mom."

It was inevitable, I guess. For years now, she's been just itching to get her hands on me: to turn me into one of her little clones, following their checklists and seven-step plans that she hands out like a grade-school teacher passing around paint-by-numbers sheets. She used to be cool, once upon a time—scatterbrained and artistic. She was into pottery, these weird abstract sculptures, and would sometimes be so deep in a project that she'd lose all track of time. We'd wind up eating PB&J sandwiches for dinner and wearing pajamas around the house on laundry days.

It was awesome.

But then Dad left us to go play saxophone on tour with his jam band, and overnight it seemed she turned into this stranger—guzzling self-help books and going on motivational weekends designed to strip her of all spontaneity and turn her into a goddess of achievement and positive thinking. It worked out for her, I guess. She qualified as a life coach, and now she has a ton of clients, paying her ridiculous amounts of money to brainwash, I mean, *teach,* them, too.

But not me.

As far as Garrett and I are concerned, organization and structure are the mortal enemies of creativity. I mean, did Emily Dickinson plan her goals in a color-coded workbook? Did Shakespeare use an inspirational daily quote calendar?

I think not.

Mom turns to go, and I flop down on my—crisply made—bed. "Wait," I say, stopping her. "Did the mail come? Is there anything from camp?"

"Why don't you check your in-box?" Mom winks. I leap up.

There it is: a single white envelope. "Why didn't you say something?" I cry, tearing it open in such a rush that I rip part of the letter itself.

"Slow down!" Mom laughs, but I'm already eagerly scanning the printed letter, my eyes racing over the small type.

Dear Ms. Allen:

Thank you for your application to our summer program. However, we regret to inform you that due to the high number of eligible candidates this year, we have decided to limit intake to those who have completed at least their junior year of high school. . . .

I stop. That can't be right. But no, there it is, spelled out in hateful Times New Roman.

We regret to inform you . . .

I lower the letter, numb. "I didn't get in."

"What?" Mom snatches it and reads it through. "Oh, honey, I'm sorry. But see here: 'Your application was strong, so we welcome you to resubmit for next summer's session.' See? It was just the age criterion."

"Not age," I tell her through gritted teeth. "Grade."

She doesn't even have the decency to look guilty. "Maybe it's for the best. You wouldn't want to go and be the youngest there, behind everyone."

I don't even bother trying to explain that I wouldn't be behind everyone, that I'm *ahead* pretty much most of the time. Instead, I stand there, rereading the letter, feeling my last sliver of hope fall to the floor and shatter into a million tiny pieces.

No lit camp. No summer quoting poetry under the stars with Garrett. Nothing.

I'm on my own.

CHAPTER THREE

Garrett got in, of course. He's been published (twice!) in obscure New England literary journals, and he won a statewide contest for the best poem inspired by the work of Walt Whitman. I wouldn't have been surprised if they gave him a special TA position or invited him to run some of the workshops. I can see him now, strolling on the lakeshore, deep in meaningful discussion with the beautiful literary wunderkind professor (because of course there'll be a beautiful literary wunderkind professor, some charming twenty-four-year-old with published short-story collections and a taste for eager high-school seniors).

I torture myself for the rest of the week, trying not to wince every time Garrett slips up and shares some other enthusiastic news about his dorm assignment or lecture schedule. He thinks I'm devastated over the loss of my summer of intellectual and creative discovery, and sure, I am, but mainly I'm devastated over the loss of my summer with Garrett.

"Hey, it'll be OK," Garrett assures me yet again. I've escaped Shabbat dinner early for a party one of the outgoing seniors is throwing, out by the woods. He checks that the Vespa is securely locked and then turns back to me. "I'll e-mail all my notes—you can do all the classes right along with me. It'll be like an independent study program."

"Right." I try to act like the writing is what matters in all of this. "I'll have finished the Great American Novel by the time you get back."

"Not so fast," he says with a laugh. "Try aiming for the Fairly Good American Novel first."

We walk slowly up the driveway. "So . . ." I pause, doing the math on the few, precious days we have left together. "This is our last night hanging out?"

Garrett grins. "You make it sound like it's forever, not just six weeks." He puts his arm around me, hugging me close. "We'll just have to make it unforgettable, OK?"

I nod, not trusting my voice, and follow him up to the door, past the parade of shiny status cars. It figures. Paul lives a couple of blocks over from Garrett. The house isn't gated, as such, but the dead-end road makes it pretty clear there's no point coming out here unless you've got an invitation.

"Hey, Garrett, you made it!" A bunch of seniors absorb him into the crowd the minute we step through the column-flanked door. Garrett has never been the highest on the Sherman High popularity rankings—though he's swooned over in certain drama/lit-magazine circles, he's not one of the undisputed clique kings. But tonight, there's backslapping and general bro fist-bumps, as if they're all actually lifelong friends and not separated by class or status. It's a weird thing I've noticed about seniors the summer after school finishes: enthusiasm and camaraderie sweep through the graduating class, washing away all grudges and cafeteria hierarchies in their path, until girls who've spent four years bitching about each other suddenly start hugging, tearful, the best of friends, while the guys who spent their free periods stuffing geeks into bathroom stalls laugh with their former victims about how it was all just high school—no hard feelings, right?

The force is so strong, even a lowly sophomore like me gets caught up in it for a moment. Julie Powers traps me in a fierce bear hug as I loiter, waiting for Garrett.

"I can't believe it's over!" she cries, clutching me. Her mascara is flaking in a flutter of black freckles across her flushed cheeks; I'm clearly not the first victim of her nostalgia tonight.

"Mm-hmm," I murmur, waiting for her to release me.

"It's like, what do we do now? Who *are* we?"

"The ultimate existential question."

She pulls back and frowns. "What?"

"Nothing." I smile. "Have a great summer!"

I detach myself and move deeper into the party. Our high school is on the smaller side, so I know pretty much everyone by sight. There's the usual crowd of varsity kids over by the keg, and the skater crowd is sprawled out in the living room, playing Xbox on the wide-screen TV, while a group of girls dance at the other end of the room, sloshing brightly colored punch from plastic cups.

I take up residence in the kitchen, surveying the spread: chips and dip as far as the eye can see, pizza, a mountain of cookies—

"Boo," Garrett whispers, inches from my ear.

I yelp. "Oh, it's you." I smack him. "You scared me. Why do you always do that?"

"Because you always make that funny sound." He laughs and hands me one of the bright-red cups. I pause. "Diet Coke," he reassures me. "I wouldn't lead you astray, not when you're so young and impressionable."

"Ha." I take a sip. "Just try."

Garrett looks around at the scene. "So, I see tables, yet you're not up there dancing on them."

"I'm saving the floor show for later," I tell him. "After my opening acts are done." I nod toward the grinding girls, their moves getting more X-rated by the minute.

"Um, sure." Garrett blinks, dazzled by the sight of Jaycee Carter's gyrations. "Because you've got to bring your A game to follow that."

We watch in amusement for a moment, then I let out a warning murmur. "Uh-oh. Crazy ex-girlfriend at three o'clock. No, don't look!" I drag him back around. "You're done with the drama, remember?"

"Relax." Garrett carefully glances over at Beth, who's talking with a couple of her friends. She's wearing her red hair loose in waves, and even I have to admit she looks pretty tonight. For a jealous drama queen.

"It's not like I'm going to go beg her to take me back or anything."

I fix him with a dubious look.

"That was one time!" he protests. "And I admit, taking over the lit mag with a love poem wasn't the greatest idea, but are you ever going to give me a break?"

"I didn't say a word." That particular stunt was for Julie Sanders, a track star who dated Garrett for two whole weeks last year before breaking his heart. The public declaration of love held no sway with her; last I heard, she was at Bard, minoring in ambisexuality and drum circles.

Garrett looks back over at Beth.

"Garrett . . ." I warn. It's all about focus with him — leave him gazing too long at a pretty ex-girlfriend and suddenly he's got half a stanza already composed.

"No, it's OK — I promise." He turns his back on her, giving me his undivided attention. "And thanks."

"What for?"

"Just . . . being you." He smiles. "You always know what to do after these breakups."

I shrug. "You'd do the same for me." If, you know, I ever dated anyone.

"I know, but I appreciate it. So, how about we get out of range of her hotness force field before I'm brainwashed and reciting poetry in front of everyone?"

"Dear Lord, yes."

· · ·

We load up with snacks and find a quiet corner, away from the madness. Garrett sprawls out on the corner couch, I curl up beside him, and then we do what we usually do at parties like these: watch, gossip, talk about everyone and everything. Our own private club, just the two of us. "You know, I'm going to miss you," Garrett says. He gives me a rueful smile. "It's going to be weird not having you around at camp."

"And they say codependence always ends in tears," I joke, trying to make light of the impending tragedy. "You'll survive," I tell him, my tone still light. "You'll meet a girl named Cadie in the coffee shop on your first day and forget all about me."

"Never. We'll have to come up with a system: Skype, or IM, or something. Make sure to stay in touch."

"Speak for yourself," I tease. "I'll be off with all my new friends, having crazy parties every night."

"Now you decide to be the social butterfly!" Garrett pushes me playfully. "Admit it, you're counting the days until I graduate next year, so you can reinvent yourself into the Queen Bee of Sherman High."

"Darn it." I sigh. "My evil plan is foiled. And I was going to take the homecoming crown and everything." We laugh, even if mine is tinted with panic. Never mind six weeks of summer camp. What happens next summer, after graduation, when he's really gone?

"College will be fine," Garrett says, as if reading my terrified thoughts. He slings an arm casually around my shoulders. "You'll come visit. It'll give me mad status when all the guys see my hot high-school friend."

"Sure." I laugh, but then I catch his eye. He's looking at me with a kind of warmth—a new intensity behind that playful smile.

At least, I think he is.

"You'll be the one to forget about me," I say, hurriedly glancing away. I've fallen into this trap before: imagining things I only long for. "You'll reinvent yourself and never look back."

"Never," he says quietly. "You and me, we're set for life."

I catch my breath. "Really?"

"Guaranteed." He squeezes my shoulder, but not in his usual casual way. No, this is softer. Gentler.

My heart beats faster.

"You're getting sentimental," I say, forcing myself to sound casual. "All these seniors are rubbing off on you. You're not graduating just yet."

He shrugs. "Maybe so, but . . . I don't know. I guess it makes you think about stuff—what you want from life, what's really important." He pauses, then gives me that half grin. "Who is important."

"Glad I register somewhere in the top one hundred," I quip, clinging to our old casual banter in the face of this new, uncertain terrain.

Garrett shakes his head. We're close together now, me nestled in the crook of his arm, and I can feel the warmth of his body through his rumpled blue shirt. "Don't talk like that." He looks at me again. "You know how important you are to me."

"Oh." I feel myself blush. "You too. I mean, well, you know what I mean."

"Only because I'm an expert in Sadie speak." His fingers move against my bare arm, in what could almost be called a stroke.

"An expert, huh?" I try to stay calm. "Maybe you don't know me as well as you think you do."

"Nope." He smiles again, so warm and familiar. "I know everything about you."

We're silent for a moment, our eyes locked. There's a heat now, an intensity that's sending my pulse haywire. This is new territory. This is . . .

Too much.

"Then you know I need more soda!" I blurt suddenly. "How about a refill?"

I thrust my cup at him. He takes it, unfolding those long limbs as he gets slowly to his feet. "Your wish is my command. Don't go anywhere." He gives me a wink and then walks away, leaving me almost giddy with panic and delight.

Breathe, Sadie.

That was flirting going on right there. I'm not reading too much into something innocuous, stretching the realm of logic and reason like I've done a thousand times in the past. No, Garrett was flirting with me just then—that's a fact.

Breathe.

I clutch a cushion, trying not to soar away on this new, sweet wind of hope. So he just broke up with Beth and is vulnerable and confused, and maybe looking for some kind of rebound girl to make himself feel better. But as soon as the argument comes, I have to dismiss it. Because it's not a rebound if I've been his soul mate all along.

What if he's finally realized that his perfect girl has been right in front of him all this time? The end of the school year, the prospect of a summer without me . . . It's all made him realize what we have together, what we *could* have together!

I feel a thrill. I've stayed quiet all this time because I didn't know for sure how he felt. I mean, who wants to be the one jeopardizing an amazing friendship over mixed signals and wishful thinking? And what if I declared my love and got nothing but a blank look in return—or worse still, awkward embarrassment? No way. I wasn't going to risk everything on my own, but if Garrett has realized that he's in love with me . . . I can let him know I feel the same way!

This is it, everything I've been waiting for! I, Sadie Elisabeth Allen, am going to confess my love.

CHAPTER FOUR

The fateful day has dawned! Well, set, I guess, since it's after sundown now. But either way, tonight will go down in history: the beginning of a whole new chapter in my life. Garrett and me. Me and Garrett . . .

I check the time quickly, then sneak away for a quick touch-up. Obviously, he's in love with my shining inner self, but that doesn't mean I want lip gloss smeared on my cheek when he leans in for that perfect first kiss.

Miraculously, there's no one in line for the bathroom. I close the door against the party noise and sink back against it, just imagining how it'll feel to finally have Garrett's lips on mine. I've spent countless nights—and days, and third-period chem labs—lost in daydreams about this very moment. The look of wonder and appreciation in his eyes . . . The soft touch of his fingers against my cheek as he reaches to push back a stray lock of my hair . . .

Wait. I turn to the mirror and quickly muss up my ponytail, so that a few tendrils hang down. There. Perfect.

My stomach is still fluttering, so I run some cold water over my wrists, wondering if Garrett is as nervous and excited as me right now. I brighten at that thought, suddenly realizing how funny this whole situation is. I'm panicked here; he's probably freaking out over on the other side of the house. . . . We'll laugh about it one day, living in our cool loft apartment in the city, hosting elegant soirees for all our sophisticated friends. "We wasted so much time," Garrett will tell them, looking at me lovingly across the dinner table. "But it all worked out in the end. "

I give my hair a final check for "kiss me, darling" style and perfect my "I never knew, but of course I feel the same!" look, then swing open the bathroom door.

"Watch it!"

I barrel straight into a girl just outside the door.

"Sorry!" I look up to find Beth Chambers lounging with a group of her little drama club minions, looking irritatingly effortless in her simple white T-shirt and jeans. "Um, hi, Beth."

"Sadie." The word couldn't be less welcoming if she tried. Her gaze drifts over my head, which is a pretty impressive feat considering I'm two inches taller than her. But then Beth always has icy detachment nailed.

"What's up?" I try, aiming for upbeat. Just because

Beth always sneers at me doesn't mean I can't be the bigger person here. "I heard you got into UCLA. Congratulations."

She smirks. "Let me guess, you're happy I'll be all the way on the other side of the country, far away from Garrett?"

"Actually—"

She doesn't let me finish, leaning in close. "You think I didn't know what you were up to, trying to get between us all along?"

"Beth." I blink and take a step back. "I swear, I never did anything."

She snorts. "Of course not, and you never will. You'll just keep making puppy-dog eyes at him, hoping he'll notice you. It's pathetic, the way you've been trailing after him for years."

I flush. "That's not true."

Beth looks smug. "It's never going to happen, you know. He likes having you around because it makes him feel, I don't know, important or something. Like you're his own personal groupie. But you're deluded if you think you'll ever be anything more."

On that parting shot, she flounces into the bathroom. For some reason, her minions follow. I guess real stars never pee solo.

I stand there a moment, shaken. She's wrong, of course—there's nothing groupie-like about our friendship. Beth is just jealous that Garrett sees me as an equal, a partner. But still, the fact that my crush was so transparent to her, that she's been laughing about it all this time . . .

It doesn't matter now. Garrett is practically broadcasting "I want to be more than friends!" on a neon display board, and nothing Beth can say will ruin this momentous night.

I pull myself together and head back into the party. It's louder now, at that point where even the cooler-than-thou popular kids are cutting loose because they can pretend they're drunk, and the knot of grinding girls has expanded so the whole living room is filled with dancing bodies.

"Hey." Garrett is back on our couch, waiting for me. He holds out a cup. "As ordered."

"I think it was more a friendly request," I reply, heart racing.

He laughs. "Sure, next thing you'll have me fanning you with a palm frond and feeding you grapes."

"Palms are kind of hard to come by in Massachusetts." I sit back beside him on the couch, painfully aware of his body next to mine. "I'd settle for pine boughs."

There's a pause in our conversation, though the party is still loud around us, but suddenly, just the simple act of looking over at him feels like an epic challenge. I brace myself and slowly slide my eyes up to his face. Garrett is staring back at me, with that same new look in his eyes. Softer, more intimate. I've seen flashes of it before, in the way he looked at Beth, or Julie, or any one of his serial crushes, but it's never been directed at me.

My heart races faster.

"Listen, Sadie, there's something I wanted to talk to

you about. . . ." Garrett pauses, then gives an awkward cough.

"Yes?" I lean closer. The seconds stretch. He takes a breath, opens his mouth, and then—

"You know what?" He suddenly gives another rueful grin and sits back. "This probably isn't the right time."

"No!" I yelp. "I mean, this is the perfect time. To say anything!" I nod eagerly.

"You sure?" Garrett looks around at the dirty dancing and beer chugging. "I mean, this isn't exactly the place for a private conversation."

"So, let's go somewhere else!" I suggest. "The garden, maybe, or back to my place."

I can't take this any longer; I have to hear it now!

Garrett thinks for a moment, then nods. "Maybe some fresh air would be good. We could get away from all this for a minute."

I practically leap up and elbow my way through the crowd to the back porch. I never saw the appeal of the stuffy, fake English rose gardens in this part of town, but now, with the green hedges walling us in and moonlight softly dancing on the pond, it's the perfect secluded spot. The music from inside is muted; Garrett loiters on the far corner of the porch, hands in his pockets.

I take a few nervous steps toward him. "You were saying?" I prompt hopefully, striking a casual pose against the wall. The security lights cast shadows across us; Garrett's eyes seem even cloudier in the dim light. I gaze up into them, just waiting for the magic words—

"Coming through!"

I'm sent reeling as some jock pushes past me. He barrels to the edge of the porch and vomits loudly over the railings.

No!

I watch, helpless, as he groans, then vomits some more.

"Hey, man." Garrett moves closer. "Are you OK?"

"Jus' fine!" The guy spins around, looking at us with unfocused eyes. He lurches, then slings an arm over Garrett's shoulder. "How's it goin'?"

"Whoa, Dax, that's . . . an interesting look you've got going on." Garrett laughs, patting Dax's back. Dax just nods, oblivious to both the trail of vomit down the front of his shirt and the perfect moment he's interrupting here.

"Itsa party." He grins inanely. "Itssummmer."

"Yes, yes, it is." Garrett gently steers him back toward the house. "Why don't you get another drink? Water this time."

Dax stumbles back inside, nearly falling through the screen door. Garrett turns back to me, grimacing. "Wow. He's going to have a killer hangover tomorrow."

"Uh-huh," I say, impatient. "So, there was something you wanted to tell me?"

Garrett pauses. "Right, sorry. The thing is . . ."

I catch my breath again. The world shrinks to just us two, alone out here in the —

"Garrett! Whaddup!"

Argh!

A group of guys thunders up onto the porch. They're draped with toilet paper and glow-stick necklaces, shoving and hollering. "Xbox warriors! No surrender!" one of them cries, while another beats his chest and lets out a yowl.

I want to grab the nearest porch post and beat them all to death.

"Garrett." I take hold of his arm, desperately trying to keep his focus on me as the guys jostle around us. "You want to get out of here? We could go back to my place, and—"

"It's OK." Garrett sighs in defeat. "I said this probably wasn't the place."

"But this is our last night. . . ." I trail off uselessly as a couple of the guys playfully punch him in the stomach. Garrett laughs and punches them back.

"We'll talk later!" he calls as they hustle him away from me, and I'm left on the porch, alone.

Later. Does that mean "give me ten minute to lose these clowns" later? Or "after the party when I'm driving you home" later? I wait on the porch another twenty minutes just to be sure, then drift aimlessly back into the house.

"Hey, Kris, have you seen Garrett?" I stop one of Garrett's classmates by the dance area, but he, too, is entranced by the sight of Jaycee's gyrations—now into the table dancing portion of the night. "Kris!"

"What? Oh, yeah, I don't know. A bunch of guys went to get pizza." He shrugs and turns back to the show. "Maybe he went with them."

"Thanks." I sigh. Thanks for nothing, that is. Garrett wouldn't just ditch me like that, but after a half hour, three unanswered texts, and another three loops of the house, I have to wonder if Kris could have been right. Garrett is nowhere to be found.

I settle on the front steps out front and send my fourth *where r u?* text. This time, Garrett replies.

Sorry, went for food w/ the guys. Back soon!

I slump lower on the steps, my excitement vaporizing in an instant. It's eleven p.m. already; my curfew is eleven thirty. There's no way Garrett could get back, escape the marauding senior guys, seduce me under the moonlight, *and* have me back home in time to keep my mom from grounding me. Sure, I would happily risk never leaving the house for the rest of the summer if it meant a few sweet moments in his arms, but I can tell the moment has passed.

Boy, has it passed.

I stay sitting there, idly tossing handfuls of gravel farther up the driveway as I ponder the painful "almost" of tonight. I was so close! To having him for my own, to finally bridging that hateful space between girl and friend for good. To—

"*Ow!*"

A body jumps back, out of gravel-hurling range. I look up. It's Kayla, pulling on her jacket.

"Sorry!" I say quickly. "I didn't see you there."

"No problem." She gives me this bland smile, but my inner pain must show on my face, because she draws closer. "Are you OK?"

I quickly pull myself together. "Sure! I'm fine. Great!"

"Right." She doesn't look convinced, but doesn't ask

again, either. "We're just heading out." There's a pause, then she offers, "Do you need a ride?"

"Um, would you mind?" I haven't had a real conversation with Kayla in a long while, but right now she's offering the very thing I need most.

"Not at all." She shrugs. "There's a ton of room in Blake's truck. Once, he fit half the basketball team in there, like something out of one of those French mime movies."

"The clowns in the car," I say, smiling slightly. Garrett has a whole bunch of those movies, black-and-white scratchy things from the '40s.

Garrett.

I let out a wistful sigh.

"Ready, babe?" Blake saunters out. He's wearing low-slung jeans and a faded gray athletic shirt, his hair gelled into a mussed peak, the way all the jocks seem to be doing this year.

"Sure." Kayla beams and slips her hand into his. "OK if we drop off Sadie, too?"

"No probs." Blake gives me a nod. "What's up?"

"Nothing much," I reply, following them to where Blake's shiny blue pickup truck is parked askew, crushing half a bed of flowers. "You?"

"Same old." Blake shrugs.

"Cool."

I gaze absently out of the back window for all of the short ride home, pressing my forehead against the cool glass while Blake and Kayla murmur their *babe*s and *honey*s up front. They seem so easy together, as in sync as Garrett and I have always been—except for all the making out, of course.

And all that could have changed, tonight, if only—

"Here you go." Blake drums his fingers on the steering wheel, snapping me back to reality. We're home.

"Thanks for the ride," I tell him, and quickly climb out. Kayla kisses him for a long moment before hopping down. She waves happily as he drives away, and then we're left alone on the dark street.

"So . . ." I say. "Any fun summer plans?"

Kayla makes a face. "Find a job, I guess. I don't know where yet."

"I spent last summer working at the Dough Hole," I tell her.

"That donut place on Third?"

"Yup. Never again." I shudder at the memory. "My hair smelled like fryer grease way into October."

"Ouch." She laughs. "I'll stay away from there—thanks. What about you? Any summer plans?"

"I have no idea." I sigh. "I was planning on going to this literary camp thing. But that fell through."

"Shame. Well, I better get back." She sighs. "Curfew. You remember what my mom's like."

"Right. Me too."

Kayla gives me a little wave and heads back across the street to her house, a rambling brick place with ivy and wisteria crawling up the front. We used to play for hours in her attic, me bringing my My Little Ponies to trade for the contraband Barbies her mom had no qualms about buying her (mine banned them on the grounds that they'd damage my body image and crush my unique spirit). We never knew it at the time, how easy those days were — before love came crashing into our lives and everything else ceased to have meaning or purpose.

I let myself in. Mom is curled up in the living room with another of her motivational videos — some deep-voiced man talking about "the spark of change."

"Did you have fun, honey?" She pauses the DVD, beaming over at me expectantly. What can I tell her? No, my evening was ruined by a jealous ex-girlfriend, a future frat boy with a seemingly limitless amount of vomit, and a midnight pizza run?

"Sure," I tell her, mustering a smile. "But I'm tired now. I'm just going to head to bed."

"OK, sweetie, see you in the morning."

I close my bedroom door tight behind me and settle at my computer. Sure, I'm tired, but there's one thing I have to do first, the only thing that will lift my spirits in these desperate times. With a few quick clicks, I access the database and pick my search parameters.

Search: long-distance love.

I hit ENTER, and just like that, the results start scrolling. John and Abigail Adams, Virginia Woolf and Vita Sackville-West . . . A reassuring litany of couples who bridged the great geographical divide.

See? All is not lost.

I look at the list and feel my disappointment ease. It always does. The database is my own personal testament to Great Love, a secret catalog of romantic success. It was after I met Garrett that I realized that those Top Ten lists I'd made were wholly inadequate; Great Love couldn't be contained to a mere ten couples. It shouldn't! If my soul mate could stroll into the coffeehouse one unremarkable August afternoon, then there were hundreds, thousands, of other such matches out there to be recorded. No, I needed a better system for tracking my romantic heroes and heroines, one that spanned the breadth and depth of devotion.

And thus the website was born. Love affairs from history, literature, theater; every culture, any gender; cross-referenced by genre, type, lasting historical impact . . . What started as a small tribute has swelled to a mammoth database, and now I spend more time uploading everyone else's suggestions than posting new ideas of my own. I click through to my e-mail and skim the new messages. Three more quotes to add to the Elizabeth and Darcy page, a plea to allow noncanonical fan-fiction couplings. I have a user in the Philippines obsessed with chronicling every couple on *Days of Our Lives,* and a women's studies professor at Oxford intent on expanding the nonheterosexual listings with pages for Gertrude Stein and Alice B. Toklas.

Garrett doesn't know about the website; nobody I know does. It's my own private corner of the world, filled with hope and promise for my own glorious future. And on a night like this, with Garrett so close but already so far away, I'll take all the hope I can get.

CHAPTER FIVE

After the party, Garrett's parents sweep him into a whirl of camp prep–related activities, so he doesn't have more than five minutes to spare before leaving—barely long enough to hug me good-bye, let alone pledge his eternal and undying devotion. And just like that, he's gone.

He might have had second thoughts about confessing his feelings, I decide, or wanted to wait until we could actually be together—not just kiss and run. Either way, I'm still left in limbo. The hours pass without so much as a call or text, and I sink into a listless haze of longing with nothing to do except watch *An Affair to Remember* and *Casablanca* and every other tearjerker black-and-white movie that features doomed love. In other words, all of them. At least I'm in good company for my spiral of dejection; all I need is some perfect matte red lipstick and a gray fitted suit, and I, too, could be the tragic heroine on that steam-billowed train platform, watching the center of my universe be carried off to war and certain death. . . .

OK, so Garrett took the Greyhound up to a summer camp in the woods, but still—I'm left here alone. Even his promise for frequent text and phone updates has thus far failed to materialize: I haven't heard a single word since he left. Two whole days ago! Is it any wonder I don't want to get out of bed? But despite my perfectly reasonable grounds for despair, Mom bursts into my room first thing Monday morning and yanks my curtains back.

"Mm-hm," I mutter from underneath the covers. "Go away!"

"It's ten thirty," she tells me, pulling my comforter aside. "Time to get up!"

"Mom!" I bury my head under my pillow. "It's summer vacation!"

"Which means there are tons of exciting things for you to do." She bustles around the room, straightening things up. "I've let you mope around long enough. It's time for you to get that A into G."

"I'm not moping. I'm mourning."

"Looks the same from where I'm standing."

"Moping is self-indulgent teen angst," I inform her icily. "Mourning is the totally justified grief that comes from being separated from the love of your life!" I roll away.

"Come on, sweetie," Mom says, her voice hatefully

perky. "I've made lists of possible jobs and activities. I thought today would be a great day to work on your ambition chart!"

I yawn. "Of course you did."

"Sadie Elisabeth Allen. Out of bed. Now!"

"Five more minutes," I tell her, closing my eyes again. Before I was so rudely interrupted, I'd been drifting in a delicious daydream involving me and Garrett, strolling the cobbled backstreets of Paris, hand in—

Splash!

I leap up. "What the—?" I cry, cold water dripping down my face. Mom stands over me, wearing a smug look and holding an empty water glass in her hand. "You didn't!" I gasp.

"I did." The water-spiller has no shame. "Now, I'm heading into town in twenty minutes, and you're coming, too."

"But—"

"No buts. You're going to get out of those gross sweatpants, put real clothes on, and go and find a job." She sighs, softening. "I don't like seeing you like this, sweetie. You need some direction."

"I have direction."

"Toward your cell phone, to see if Garrett has texted you." She rolls her eyes. "It's like I always tell my clients: you'll feel better with some activity. And we can even go to the library," she adds brightly, as if it's some kind of bribe. Which, to be honest, it kind of is. I'm completely out of new reading material, and everything on my shelves just reminds me of Garrett: the books he's given me, the books we've read together, the books I got because he recommended them. . . .

"Fine," I tell her. "But for the last time: I am not making, nor will I ever make, an ambition chart."

"But I got—"

"Not even with the gold stars!"

Mom drops me at the library with strict instructions to canvas the town for babysitting and other such high-profile, fun-filled summer jobs.

"And snap out of this!" she orders through the car window. "Cheer up!"

I browse the fiction shelves, still suffused in my cloud of suffering. Why should I cheer up? Melancholy is a perfectly legitimate state of mind—artists have thrived on it for centuries. *War and Peace*—there, that wasn't exactly written in a fit of bright, purposeful energy, was it, now? And *Anna Karenina*. Tolstoy wasn't leaping around with happiness every hour of the day, and he still managed to achieve something.

Maybe I should move to Russia; they clearly appreciate inner torment there.

"Sadie? Your library card?"

I look up to find Ms. Billings, the librarian, waiting patiently behind the circulation desk. In the grand tradition of librarian clichés, she's wearing wire-rimmed glasses and a preppy little blouse with a tweed skirt, but she actually looks pretty stylish—kind of that British schoolteacher look. She seems stern enough to hush a crowd with a single glance, but she's a softy really—she's the one who slipped me a copy of *Forever* by Judy Blume when I'd read every pony, babysitting, and boarding-school book in the middle-school section.

That's public service, right there.

"Sorry," I apologize quickly, handing my card over. She scans the stack of novels, raising her eyebrows slightly as she notices the theme: long, bleak, Russian. "I'm embracing my inner pain," I tell her.

She smiles sympathetically. "Bad day?"

"More like bad year." I sigh. "Do you ever feel like fate is playing a cruel joke on you?"

Ms. Billings pauses a moment. "In that case . . ." She looks around, then takes a book from the recently returned stack and shows it to me surreptitiously as if we're covert spies or something. "*Miss Pettigrew Lives for a Day.* Never fails to cheer me up. You look as though you could use it."

I turn the slim volume over in my hands. "Thanks," I tell her, and add it to the stack. "I'll take everything I can get. Wait," I add, suddenly hopeful. "You don't need anyone working here this summer, do you?" A job at the library would be the least painful of all possible options.

She shakes her head. "Sorry. There used to be a part-time gig, but with the funding cuts . . . Volunteer positions only these days."

"Oh, OK." I sigh. Volunteering might keep my mom quiet, and look good on college applications, but it won't get me any closer to that distant dream of my own car. "Thanks, anyway."

All over town, I hear the same story again and again: the summer jobs were snapped up weeks ago by enterprising students who didn't have their hearts set on literary camp. Even the HELP WANTED sign at the Dough Hole is out of date—there apparently being no end of willing candidates ready to risk death-by-deep-fat-fryer on a daily basis for the sake of minimum wage.

I slink into Totally Wired and look over at our usual table with a sigh. Without Garrett around, it's not ours anymore; it's just mine.

"What can I get you?" LuAnn asks at the counter. Today's vintage dress is a blue gingham print, open low enough at the neck to show a scrolling tattoo across her collarbone, with text I can't quite read. It's a *Wizard of Oz*–meets–prison-yard look.

"Coffee. Please. Black." *Like my heart,* I add silently.

"Sure thing." She grins and pushes sweaty strands of red hair back from her forehead. "And a double espresso, right? For your boyfriend?"

I blink.

"Tall, cute, joined to you at the hip?"

"Oh. No." I blush. "He's not . . . I mean, he's not my boyfriend, and he's not coming. So, just the one coffee."

"Whoops." LuAnn grimaces, already reaching for the machine. "Bad breakup? Sorry. I have foot-in-mouth disease—can't help it."

She bustles off to make my order, leaving me with a fresh pang of loneliness. See? Even complete strangers think that Garrett and I belong together.

I linger at the back table all afternoon, watching the buzz of activity as morning Mommy & Me groups shift to a stream of junior-high gigglers in search of ice-blended sugar hits. I start and then discard half a dozen letters to Garrett—from the simple *What's up at camp?* to *I love you I love you I love you,* but none of them seems right. What am I supposed to do now? Sure, he said he'd call when he's settled in, but how long does it take to throw five T-shirts in a drawer and line up his volumes of Proust?

I slump lower in my seat. He's probably off having the most fun of his life, while I'm stuck exactly where I have been for years. Not moving at all.

"You have got to be kidding me!"

I—and everyone in the place—look up. One of the waitresses, an angular blonde in a plaid shirt and skinny jeans, is staring outside, where a skeezy hipster dude is smoking a cigarette—and flirting with a couple of sophomore girls. They twist their hair and giggle while he leans in close, playing it up.

The waitress turns an interesting shade of pink and dumps the tray of dirty dishes on the nearest table—right next to some poor businessman's half-eaten BLT.

"Hey!" he cries, but she ignores him, already stalking toward the doors. The sophomores see her and flee.

I watch, fascinated. Through the window, their yells

are muffled, but she's gesturing angrily, and he's shrugging, sullen. It's a knock-down, drag-out fight, right in the middle of Main Street for everyone to see—the most excitement this town has seen since Becca Larsen had an "accidental" wardrobe malfunction in the middle of the Founders' Day parade (which earned her the few dozen extra votes necessary to clinch the homecoming crown. Coincidence?)

"How about some muffin samples?" LuAnn calls brightly, but everyone stays riveted to the drama unfolding outside. With a final yell, Crazy Blonde Waitress turns away, then Skeezy Hipster grabs her arm, and just like that, they leap on each other, kissing furiously. Well, not so much kissing as swallowing each other whole. Her back is pressed up against the window so hard, it rattles with every new wave of passion.

As LuAnn strides outside to try and break up the amorous couple, for the sake of onlooking children (or, more to the point, public decency laws), I can't help but let out a wistful sigh. OK, so I don't want a boyfriend with nicotine stains, commitment issues, and a high risk of communicable diseases, but something about the way they're pressed up against each other, oblivious to the entire world . . . Even when LuAnn taps them on the shoulder, they keep necking until she's practically yanking Crazy Blonde Waitress away from him.

Oh, to be young and in (requited) love!

Crazy Blonde Waitress clearly thinks it's the most important thing in her life, because without even a moment's pause, she strips off her green apron and shoves it at LuAnn's chest. Then she takes Skeezy Dude's hand, and off they saunter to their blissful world of skinny black denim and graphic PDAs.

"Can you believe her?" LuAnn fumes, banging mugs into a tray as she returns to bus the forgotten tables. "Three days on the job and she just waltzes off. And now I'm stuck on shift alone, and Josh still isn't back from his lunch, and the espresso machine is this close to crapping out on me. Again!"

"Sorry," I offer quietly.

She takes a breath. "Thanks, kid. I didn't mean to rant." She looks at my long-since-empty cup. "You need a refill? Least we can do after scarring your impressionable young mind with that floor show."

"No, I'm fine."

She's halfway back to the counter before I realize what a shining, golden opportunity has presented itself to me. Salvation, in the form of Crazy Blonde Waitress and Skeezy Hipster Dude!

I leap up and dash after her.

"I can do it!" I say quickly. "I mean, the job. Waitressing. I can replace her." I put on my best responsible employee face, but LuAnn doesn't look convinced.

"I don't know, kid—it can get kind of hectic in here. And we don't usually hire high-school kids. . . ."

"But I'm seventeen! Practically graduated. And I've worked in food service before." I thank the Gods of Work Experience for those long, dough-filled months manning the sprinkle station. "I could help you out this afternoon, as, like, probation," I suggest desperately. "You said it yourself, you're on your own."

Suddenly, I want this job more than anything in the world. It's my only chance for a summer of non-suckiness—I just know it. Never mind what my mom will dream up if I don't manage to find honest employment; this gig would change everything for me. I wouldn't be Sad Sack Sadie, stuck pining for her true love during the long, empty days of summer. No, I'd be Badass Barista Sadie, casually dishing out pastries and eavesdropping on conversations to use in that novel Garrett is always saying I should write.

I want to be that girl. The world wants me to be that girl! And I could, if LuAnn would just give me a chance.

"Please? Pretty please?" I beg, crossing my fingers behind my back for luck.

She looks around. And at that moment—like messengers from the Gods of Excellent Timing—the door swings open and a stream of elderly customers enters the café. Ten or twelve of them maybe: wrinkled and blue-rinsed and wearing matching yellow Doolittle Falls Walking Club sweatshirts. They bustle around the space, prodding at the notice board, peering at the cake stands, deliberating whether to get a pot of tea to share or individual cups.

Ding! goes the bell as more of them arrive. *Ding, ding, ding!*

I've never heard a sweeter sound.

"Fine!" LuAnn relents, in the face of divine intervention—and a host of fussy customers. She plucks CBW's apron from the counter and tosses it to me. "You take register and bus tables. But no promises. This is just for today, OK?"

"Yes!" I cry, bouncing on the spot. "I won't let you down—I promise!"

I've never been so thrilled to clear dirty dishes in my life.

CHAPTER SIX

And there I was thinking that flair, wit, and diligence would be my tickets to greatness. Sure, that's what they tell us in school, but in the end, it's my ability to bus tables without running off with the nearest dirty hipster dude that seals my fate. After an afternoon's probation, in which I demonstrate my superior table-wiping skills (not to mention that all-important "Do you want that muffin warmed?" delivery), LuAnn agrees to make me a real live member of the Totally Wired team.

And then, as if things weren't working out well enough, bright and early the very next day, I get a message from Garrett that sends sunshine streaming through the dark clouds of my loneliness.

Camp is amazing. So busy w/ classes. But I miss you!

I pause outside the café on my way to my first-day orientation, rereading those few, precious words.

I miss you.

I miss you.

I miss you.

Were sweeter words ever texted?

I hug the phone to my chest with glee, and right away, I can see that I've been thinking about this all wrong. This summer apart isn't a hurdle in our destiny to be together; it *is* destiny! After all, what better way to make Garrett realize what I mean to him than for us to be split apart? Absence makes the heart grow fonder—that's what everyone says—and sure enough, after only a few days apart, Garrett is missing me. Whatever second thoughts he had about confessing his feelings will soon be swept away—I'm sure of it. At this rate, he'll be declaring his love by the end of summer. I just have to make it through without him until then.

Easy!

I bounce into the coffee shop full of new hope and determination. It's before official opening hours, but the rest of the staff is already gathered around the tables at the back, slumped over coffee and pastries. LuAnn waves me over, a nail-polish wand in her hand.

"Am I late?" I whisper, slipping into a free seat beside her. I recognize some of the other staff from the café, but nobody seems too concerned to have a newcomer in their midst, they just mumble among themselves, yawning and scratching as if seven a.m. is way too early to drag their scruffy, hipster asses out of bed.

"Don't worry," she says at normal volume, applying

purple sparkles to the nails on her right hand. "Carlos isn't awake yet."

She nods toward a guy who's practically comatose at the far table. He's in his thirties, maybe—unshaven, in wrinkled denim and a black T-shirt that has definitely seen better days.

"Who's Carlos?" I ask, curious.

"The boss man," LuAnn replies. She sticks her tongue out with concentration as she finishes up the nail-polish job. When her last nail is sufficiently sparkled, she continues, "He was in a minorly successful indie band ten years ago. They split, but one of his songs got used on a car commercial. Big money. Hence, he opened this place."

"Wow," I whisper. "At the donut shop, my boss was this balding guy named Kenny. He'd scream at us if we ever switched the radio from Top Forty."

"Carlos is OK." She shrugs. "As long as you don't talk too loud when he's hungover. Or ever call him in for something before noon."

"People, can we get this done already?" Carlos finally pulls himself out of his chair and pushes a stack of printed sheets at the nearest person, a petite girl with blue streaks in her hair and rubber-band bracelets on both arms. "New time sheets, yada, yada, I don't care if you switch shifts—just fight among yourselves." He yawns. "Anything you guys want to share? No? Good."

"I do!" LuAnn waves her hand in the air. "Katy quit on me yesterday."

Carlos swears. "Another one? What are you doing to them?"

"It's not me!" she protests.

"Sure, but I'm the one who has to find a replacement." Carlos doesn't seem happy at the prospect, which is when LuAnn pushes me out of my seat.

"I know. See? That's why I already hired her! Everyone, this is the new kid."

"Sadie," I say, waving awkwardly. A dozen faces stare back at me. "Um, hi."

Carlos gives me the once-over, frowning. "Wait, who are you?"

"She's a total lifesaver!" LuAnn interrupts. She pats me on the head and beams at Carlos. "New waitress, no fuss. Everyone wins!"

"I'm sorry," I add quickly, feeling everyone's eyes on me. "I thought it was OK. I can fill out an application if you need me to. And I have references! Or if you want to interview me for the position . . . ?"

"Interview?" Behind me, someone laughs.

Carlos stares at me sternly for a second. "You got experience?"

I nod eagerly.

"Criminal record? Drug problem?"

I shake my head. "I . . . I'm seventeen," I tell him, suddenly panicked. I knew it! I'm not old enough to work here for real. And I'm clearly not anywhere near cool enough. I may as well just resign myself to a summer with my mom's Positivity Now! road show, handing out name tags and pamphlets until—

Carlos suddenly laughs. He takes a gulp of coffee and wipes his mouth with the back of his hand. "Relax, kid—it's cool. You're hired."

"OK!" I collapse back into my seat with relief.

"Not OK!" someone says, her voice ringing with disapproval—and a French accent. Which is kind of the same thing, I think. I look over to find a polished, preppy girl glaring at me. She's wearing a crisp button-down shirt and tortoiseshell glasses, her Afro shaped in a small perfect sphere. "Does this mean I have to swap shifts? Because I'm not swapping. Not for anyone."

"That's Dominique," LuAnn whispers. "A total team player."

Carlos rolls his eyes. "You'll swap if I ask you to."

"I have classes!" Dominique's voice rises. "And don't forget, I'm in law school, not some third-rate technical college where they don't care if you ever show up!"

"Hey!" the tiny, blue-haired girl cries in protest. Dominique just gives her a withering stare.

"Like I said, some of us go to real schools."

Carlos puts his hands on his hips. "And like I said, you'll take whatever shifts I give you or go find another job!"

"Maybe I will!" Dominique shoots out of her seat. "Maybe I'll leave you to try to do the accounts on your own. You wouldn't last a week without me, *idiot*."

I feel a tug on my arm. "Come on," LuAnn says through a mouthful of muffin. "I'll show you the ropes."

"But . . ." I glance back at Carlos and Dominique,

now yelling about opening hours and labor rights. "Shouldn't we . . . ?"

"Leave them." She sighs. "She'll storm out, and he'll apologize. Or maybe he won't, and you'll get more shifts. Win!"

The rest of the staff is dispersing around the fight as if it doesn't exist, heading out front for a cigarette break or starting to barter over shifts with the time sheets and markers.

"Um, sure," I say, edging out of my seat before Dominique starts hurling things. "I love ropes. Show them to me!"

LuAnn breezes through my introduction to the register, baked goods, and fearsome coffee machine in ten seconds flat. "It's easy, kid. You'll be fine," she tells me with another reassuring yet condescending pat on the head.

"But where are you going?" I blink as she rounds the counter.

"I'm not on until this afternoon."

"Then who . . . ?" I trail off as LuAnn points to Dominique. "Oh."

"Don't worry," LuAnn tells me carelessly, armed as she is with her awesome vintage style and unshakable confidence and—oh, yes—age. "Just ignore the attitude. She's a marshmallow, really."

But if she is, it's a stale, hardened marshmallow, because nothing I do or say during that first shift makes any impact.

"Two lattes—one soy, one decaf—and one iced chamomile!" Dominique yells over at me later that afternoon.

"Sure thing!" I reply, quickly dispensing with the easy tea option before facing my new foe: the dreaded espresso machine. Having spent the morning busing tables and working from the relative safety of the register, she's finally pushed me to the back of the counter and set the Beast loose on me. Sure, you think I jest, but you haven't seen the thing—a looming silver monstrosity of dials and switches and funnels, all which (if caressed in just the right way) supposedly work to produce Totally Wired's famed coffee, "the best in New England."

"Sometime this week would be nice!" Dominique adds, raising an eyebrow at me in disgust.

Yay, team unity.

"What are you doing, trying to fly that thing?" Our resident chef, Josh, appears in the hatch window, brown hair sticking out in unruly tufts over blue eyes. He watches with amusement as I gingerly prod and press the machine.

"I'd settle for a latte." I try not to look like such an idiot, still painfully aware that I'm the new kid. *Kid* being the operative word. LuAnn was right to assign me that nickname—all the other staff is clearly way older than me. Carlos is thirty or something ancient like that, Dominique is maybe in her twenties, and that blue-haired waitress, Aiko, may look young, with her petite frame and steampunk T-shirt, but it turns out she's a junior graphic-arts student at college nearby. The next-youngest person around is actually Josh—Aiko told me that he's nineteen, a year out of high school—but he's kept mostly to himself, hanging out in the kitchen, pressing panini all day.

And, of course, popping his head out to watch me flail around in utter confusion.

"Try hitting the thing," Josh suggests. I prod a shiny silver button. "No, next to that other thing."

I follow his directions, still half-convinced that the Beast is going to reach out and skewer me with one of its levers. There's a hiss, a groan; the machine gives an almighty shudder, and then . . . success! Two cups of espresso stand before me.

"Lifesaver!" I beam. "Now, um, if I can only remember how to do that again. Another hundred times . . ."

Josh laughs. "Hold that thought." He ducks back into the kitchen and reappears a moment later with a pack of Post-it notes. "These should help you keep track," he says, scribbling *1, 2, 3* with a black marker and slapping the notes on each of the knobs and dials in turn.

"Thanks," I tell him, grateful. "I can't believe I didn't think of that."

He grins. "That's why you're a serving wench, and I have a whole kingdom of my own!" He gestures grandly at the tiny kitchen. "Behold, my domain."

I laugh. "Wow, impressive. You've got running water and everything."

"Well, most days."

"Sadie!" Dominique doesn't even turn as she yells.

"I better get back to serving. And wenching," I tell him. "But thanks!"

I deliver the drinks—probably lukewarm now—to

Dominique. "That's just wonderful," she drawls. "Maybe next time you can wait until we all drop dead from old age."

"Sorry, I—"

"Look, just go clear the tables out front." Dominique lets out a weary sigh, as if my incompetence is just too exhausting. *"Tout de suite."*

I stare blankly. "I took Spanish."

"Now!" she translates.

I grab the cloth and duck out from behind the counter. I take my time cleaning each table—not so much out of my faultless work ethic as in the hope of eavesdropping on some juicy plotlines for that novel I'm going to write one day. But, as usual, Sherman fails me.

"You know, I told him to paint the fence. It's bringing the whole tone of the street down."

"And they're having a sale on paint right now at Mike's Hardware."

"Exactly! Some people have no sense of community."

See? If I wanted to write about the minutiae of existence, I'd be in heaven right now. Or maybe that's the point: I could write about a waitress in a small-town coffee shop, doomed to spend her days listening to conversations about DIY home repair while her love is far away. . . .

A flash of red outside the window catches my eye, and I look up to see a trail of grade-school kids in summer-camp T-shirts, winding down the street in an unruly snake formation. Kayla walks alongside, outfitted in her very own red shirt and weighed down with water bottles and sunscreen. She beams, perky as ever, adjusting one kid's falling baseball cap, then nudging another back in line. The very picture of summer enthusiasm. I should have guessed that she'd wind up working with kids—or the elderly, or cute fluffy animals.

She sees me watching, and raises her arm in a wave. I manage a vague gesture, balancing dirty dishes.

By the time I'm done clearing, my stomach is rumbling at an alarming volume. I was so busy picking out my first-day outfit that I skipped breakfast; I haven't had time to eat all day.

I approach Dominique apprehensively. "I was thinking maybe I could take my break . . ."

"Whenever we hit a lull," Dominique finishes for me, her expression stony. "Does this look like a lull to you?"

"If *lull* is French for 'Sure. It's slow—go take your break,'" LuAnn interrupts, breezing past us from the back entrance. She dumps her purse on the counter, spilling makeup and quarters from the fringed, beaded, bedazzling bag. "Go ahead. I can cover for ten."

"Thanks," I say, already pulling off my apron. "I won't be long. I just need to grab some lunch."

"Lunch?" LuAnn blinks. "Honey, it's, like, three p.m." She turns to Dominique. "What have you been doing to her?"

Dominique gives a lazy shrug. "She's here to work."

"You are a cold, heartless woman," LuAnn tells her

sternly. Dominique just shrugs again and turns back to the fashion magazine she has stashed behind the coffee grounds.

I watch them bicker, curious. When I was on the other side of the counter, just a lowly customer, I figured that the staff here were all the best of friends. It sure seemed that way from my vantage point at the back table, watching them laugh together across the room. But after listening to LuAnn talk about Carlos, and Dominique talk about . . . well, just about everyone else, I can see they're really more like family — the big, dysfunctional kind that fights over everything and doesn't care what each other thinks.

"Josh!" LuAnn yells, pulling her hair back into a twisty bun that she secures with a couple of pencils.

He pops his head out and affects a low southern drawl. "Yes, ma'am?"

"Get this girl some sustenance before she passes out."

"Really, I'm fine," I say, embarrassed, but LuAnn is in full flow.

"Fetch a chair! Find some water!" she cries, dancing around the small space. "We don't want the child-labor people beating down our door for exploitation again!"

I cringe, but Josh just laughs along.

"Look, she's pale with malnutrition." LuAnn squeezes one of my cheeks. "Make her one of those fantastic BLTs."

"Um, actually, I don't eat bacon," I pipe up awkwardly. "Or ham. Or, you know, any pork products, really. . . ." I trail off.

"I am," I agree. I hesitate, then say casually, "I wish you could meet them all. You'd get a kick out of LuAnn, she's the one with red hair. She's great."

"I keep thinking the same with people here," he says. "My bunkmates are probably sick of hearing about you. It's 'my friend Sadie' all the time."

Delight dances in my chest. See, he's thinking about me. He's *talking* about me! But before I can find out exactly what he's been saying, Garrett sighs.

"Look, I've got to get to a workshop." He sounds regretful. "Will you be around later? I've got a ton of stuff to tell you."

"Yes!" I cry. "I mean, sure, just call anytime."

"Great, later then."

He hangs up, and although I'm tempted to just mooch around the house for the rest of the day until he calls back, my poor, coffee-stained wardrobe is calling out for reinforcements, so I grab the keys to Mom's car and drive out of town thirty minutes to the looming concrete vista of the Hadley mall. I usually try to stay away from this place—Garrett calls it a soulless temple to modern capitalism—but my budget limits my options.

I'm browsing the department store bargain basement when a familiar face appears from around the next aisle.

"Sadie? Hey!"

"Kayla." I pause, embarrassed. She's looking cute and shiny as always, in jeans and a snap-front plaid shirt. "Um, hi."

"Hey!" She beams, her blond hair falling in effortless waves. Effortless for her, anyway—she was born without the dreaded frizz gene. "What's up? Are you—ooh!" she exclaims, suddenly reaching for the rack behind me. "This is perfect!"

"It is?" I blink. Kayla's holding up a pair of hideous shorts: khaki, with a red flower print, they reach at least to her knees when she holds them up against her body.

She catches my expression and laughs. "No, I mean, they're disgusting, but that's perfect. Those kids destroy everything I own." She plucks a lurid chartreuse T-shirt and adds it to her basket.

"I know what you mean," I say. "About the destruction, anyway. You have no idea how hard it is to get melted chocolate-chip smears off your jeans."

"Oh, I do," Kayla says, "if it's anything like finger paints. I swear they do it on purpose." She adds, "This one kid, Jaden? He slapped bright-blue handprints all over my favorite shirt. Ruined!"

"How is it?" I ask as we stroll toward the dressing rooms. "Working at the playgroup. That must be fun."

"Sure, they're just adorable," she says. "For the first five minutes. And then I want to wring their adorable little necks."

I stop, shocked. "I always figured you loved kids."

"Yeah, no." Kayla shakes her head emphatically. "One kid, I can do, even two—just stick them in front of a Disney movie, let them play Xbox all night. But a herd of them?" She shudders.

I laugh. "Come on, they're just kids."

"Have you been stuck with a group of ankle biters

before?" Kayla stares at me, wide eyed. "Sure, they toddle around quietly, but if they turn on you . . . it's like in the movies. The ones that seem sweet and innocent are always, like, possessed. Or zombie spawn."

"The kids are demons?"

"It would explain a lot. But hey, I get to use it on college applications. I want to major in psychology," she explains. "And it's fun watching the parents, trying to figure out how traumatized and messed up their kid is going to be." She beams happily at the thought of all the future therapy the kids will require.

"Um . . . great." Clearly, I've been underestimating Kayla.

She looks around at the fluorescent-lit room full of limp sale signs and people dejectedly picking through the remainder bin of underwear. "Oh, my God, this place is so depressing. I should go buy these before I change my mind. Or kill myself."

"You're not going to try them on?"

"And see just how bad they look?" Kayla backs away. "You're way braver than me. See you!"

As I watch her walk away, I feel a strange pang. This conversation must be the longest one we've had in years, and right now, I can't even think of the reason why.

"Kayla, wait!" I call suddenly. Then I stop, embarrassed, but she's already turned. "Do you have plans?" I ask. "I mean, we could maybe get a soda or something. Exchange stain-removal tips," I add, my face heating up.

Kayla pauses for a minute, then shrugs. "Sure, I don't have to be anywhere."

"Great!" I realize how eager I sound and dial it back a couple of notches. "I mean, OK. That's cool."

"Meet me out front when you're done." Kayla smiles. "I swear, I'm breaking out in an allergic reaction to all this polyester."

"OK!" I feel a weird sense of achievement. "See you outside."

"So, Totally Wired," Kayla starts as we claim our monster neon Slushies from the food-court stall. The mall is busy with gaggles of preteen girls camped out on every bench and weekend shoppers drifting aimlessly down the fluorescent-lit fake streets. "Want to switch? You take tiny demons and I'll serve coffee. That place has the cutest guys on staff."

"It does?" I slurp at my drink, feeling a strange sense of nostalgia. Or is it déjà vu? Either way, this is a scene I must have played out with Kayla a hundred times when we were younger, back when a day at the mall and icy treats were pretty much heaven to us. "Like who?"

"Where do I start?" Kayla asks, flipping her sheet of blond hair over her shoulder. "The chef guy, with the messy hair? And that tall one who's always in black."

"That's Denton." I nod. He's joined at the hip with Aiko, or rather, joined hip to thigh, since he towers about eighteen inches over her. "I don't really know him—our shifts never overlap. He's dating Aiko—they're really cute together. But Josh, the chef guy, he's nice. Kind of a goof."

"Oh?" Kayla gives me a look.

"What?" Just then, I feel my phone buzz. Garrett! I sneak a glance at the screen. Nope, phantom buzz.

Beside me, Kayla keeps talking. "You know, he's cute, and you're working all those long shifts together. . . ." I look back in time to catch her giving me a meaningful wink.

I suddenly realize what she means. "Josh? No way. He's like, old."

Kayla smirks. "And?"

"And he's always goofing around," I tell her, and tuck my phone away. "Yesterday, he wore bunny ears the whole day. Not my type."

She lets out a disappointed sigh. "I forgot, you don't date."

"Um, can you blame me?" I say, self-conscious. Is that my reputation—the nondater? "You know what Sherman boys are like."

"Come on, there are some good ones!" she protests. Suddenly, her eyes brighten. "Ooh, maybe I could set you up with one of Blake's friends—"

"Don't!" I yelp. She looks startled. "I mean, that's sweet," I add quickly, "but I'm OK for now. Being single."

"Suit yourself." She shrugs. "But those guys are a ton of fun. Trust me." She winks again, and I'm reminded of what different high-school lives we lead. Me with Garrett, her with her table of peppy friends and weekends partying up at the lake.

"So what's Blake up to this summer?" I ask, steering the subject away from me and my long dateless nights of solitude.

Kayla makes a face. "Mainly college prep. He's heading to NYU in the fall."

"Oh." I pause. "Are you guys going to try and stay together, or . . . ?" I trail off, not wanting to bring up any potential angst. But instead, Kayla just slurps her mammoth raspberry Slushie, unconcerned.

"Oh, it's going to be fine. We'll do long distance, and vacations and holidays, and then in two years I'll be at Columbia." She says it casually, as if it's a plan for the weekend, and not the next few years of her life.

"Wow, that's . . . great," I venture. "That you've got it all figured out, I mean."

She shrugs. "We're meant to be together. So we'll make it work."

"Oh."

I can't help but wonder about her resolve. I mean, sure, I'm certain that things will work out with Garrett, too, but we're *destined* to be together. Kayla and Blake are cute, but can a high-school crush really last? "Good luck with that," I offer. "It's not easy to keep things together when you're both off doing different things."

"Oh, that's right," she says. "Garrett's gone for the summer." She pauses. "I've always wondered, did you two ever . . . ? You know."

"Nope," I say. At least, not yet.

"Really?" She crinkles her forehead in a frown. "Not even a 'friends with benefits' thing?"

"No!" I reply, horrified. "We would never risk our friendship for something like that."

"Oh, sorry," Kayla looks as if she's mentally reassessing something. And that's when my back pocket buzzes. For real this time.

It's a text. *Tried calling, got your voice mail. Can you talk?*

Garrett. How did I miss his call?

". . . don't you think?"

My head snaps back up. "Um, what was that last part?"

Kayla sighs. "Do you need to call someone? You've been checking that thing, like, every two minutes."

I can tell from her face that "Yes, I have to go, now!" wouldn't be the right answer. "It's fine," I lie, snapping the phone shut and stowing it in my back pocket. "It can wait."

"OK. Hey, can you hold these? My lips are crying out for ChapStick." She passes me her shopping bags and Slushie until I'm laden with handles and cups in both hands. "Man, where is that thing? I'm sure I saw it in here somewhere. . . ." Kayla digs through her purse while I juggle our collected junk.

"Um," I murmur, trying to keep hold of everything. "I don't think I can keep . . ."

"I swear, this thing is like a portal to some other dimension." Kayla grins, still rummaging in the cavernous confines of her pale-blue shoulder bag. "It swallows everything whole."

And then I feel the buzz of my phone again.

"Kayla?"

But she's upended her bag and is dumping makeup and spare change and tampons out onto the floor. I edge over. "Could you . . . ?"

"Sure, just a sec!" '

My phone buzzes again, this time with Garrett's ringtone, an obscure Belle & Sebastian song he loves. He's calling!

That second drags into an eternity as I watch Kayla hunt for the mythical missing ChapStick. Garrett's ringtone sounds again. And again. This is torture. I can't focus on Kayla, the mall, anything! Not when Garrett is waiting on me, somewhere out there. . . .

What if he can't deny it anymore? What if he *has* to tell me how he feels?

Enough! Carefully, I move one of the Slushies over into the crook of my right arm, so I'm clutching it to my chest. Then I set about transferring shopping bags out of my left hand, hooking two onto my pinkie and trapping the handle of another between my teeth. There: my phone hand is free! Now, if I can just stay very still, I might be able to reach around. . . .

I grope across my body for my left back pocket and reach my ringing phone with the very tips of my fingers. Gently, gently, I nudge it closer, until I can almost—

"Found it!"

Kayla suddenly bounces to her feet, proudly clutching the pink tube of ChapStick.

"No!"

But it's too late. She knocks into me; I teeter, losing balance, and then—as if the world has slowed—I realize in a split second that I have a terrible choice to make: answer Garrett or keep my load stable.

Phone or Slushies. Phone or Slushies.

So I choose.

CHAPTER EIGHT

I'm not proud of what happens next: the horrifying arc of lurid red liquid spilling through the air, Kayla's squeal of disbelief. But what was I supposed to do? Destiny doesn't wait for a convenient moment to call, and if you're too slow, then you risk letting it pass you by forever. No, you've got to cling on to fate—or your cell phone—tight with both hands, and to hell with the consequences. Which in this case are a ruined outfit, and Kayla fleeing from me as fast as her cute blue sneakers will take her.

Even the next morning, I still feel bad, and after all that, Garrett only wanted to know the name of the guy who wrote that book about all the sad young literary men. At least, that's what he *says* he was calling about, but who knows what emotional truth was lingering on the tip of his tongue, had I only picked up the call sooner?

I'm saving all the notes and handouts for you. Garrett's IM bubbles to life on my screen. Early mornings are the best time for him to chat, before classes get started. *I'll mail them this weekend—I promise.*

No problem, I type back, wistful. For the first time in years, I don't know exactly what he's doing; the stories he tells me are all at a distance, secondhand narrations of what he's been seeing, and doing, and thinking. *Are the classes fun?*

More work than fun. His reply comes a moment later. *But worth it. I'm learning so much.*

"Honey, I'm leaving in two minutes!" Mom calls upstairs.

"OK!" I yell back, typing a quick good-bye. *Text if you want to talk!* I even allow myself a casual *x* sign-off before I log out, grab my bag and my comfiest pair of sneakers, and hurtle downstairs.

"You look nice." Mom smiles as I burst into the kitchen, but she can't stop herself from reaching out to rearrange my hair. I bat her hand away. "I'm glad you're finally growing those bangs out."

"Nope, I just forgot to trim them," I tell her, taking a slice of leftover apple strudel from the fridge and then—at her expression—adding a real apple.

"But they'll be so cute longer."

"Cute is for six-year-olds," I tell her as I nibble at my cold, delicious breakfast. "Cute is only one step away from *adorable.*"

"And what's wrong with that?"

I sigh. If she had it her way, my mom would still be

braiding my hair and tying satin bows on the ends, but there comes a time in a girl's life when she has to take other things into consideration when it comes to her hairstyle choices. Male things. And so when I sat down to watch *Amélie* with Garrett back after we first met and he commented on how stylish she looked, I figured, why not? The blunt-cut bob works for me, kind of. It balances out this nose of mine, and on good days, I even look foreign and interesting.

"We should get going," I tell Mom before she can segue from my bangs to my clothing, demeanor, and general life choices. "I don't want to be late for work."

No such luck. My mom can segue with the best of them. "Are you sure you want to serve coffee all summer?" She follows me out to the car. "It's not too late to quit, and I still need an assistant for the Positivity Now! seminars next week."

"No, thanks," I tell her carefully, rather than explaining why handing out name tags to a flock of lost souls in search of purpose via seven-step plans is pretty much my idea of hell. I'd rather wrestle with the Beast than hear how a simple organizational chart can save the world. "Anyway, there's a whole literary tradition I'm following. Garrett says even Trotsky wrote in the coffeehouses of Vienna."

Mom doesn't look convinced. "I can pay ten dollars an hour. And you'll have free entry into all kinds of motivational talks."

Motivation enough to turn her down. "Thanks, but I'm having fun."

Lie.

"And the people are great."

Well, some of the people. Now that I'm a vaguely competent employee, Dominique has exchanged disdain for icy detachment and doesn't say a word to me aside from orders and occasional demands to go clean something. Josh is friendlier than her, thank God, but he's still so goofy; it's hard to get him to stop messing around long enough to have a straight conversation.

I'm just starting to set up for the morning when he barrels through the door, carrying a fishing rod and a toolbox dangling with hooks. His nose is sunburned and peeling, and his brown hair is sticking up in wayward tufts.

"You fish?" I ask, resisting the urge to pick pecans from the tops of the muffins as I lay out the day's pastries. Oh, caramelized deliciousness! I turn to Josh before I break, like, five different health and safety laws. "I didn't know you were the huntin', shootin' type."

"Sure." He grins and unloads his gear with a loud clatter. "Birds, beasts, mammals, I'll kill 'em all. There's actually a couple of rodents out back if you're feeling hungry. . . ."

"Eww!"

"What?" He laughs. "Nah, the fishing's more my dad's thing. He likes to drag me along sometimes. His idea of bonding, I guess."

"You're lucky." I sigh. "My mom's idea of bonding is for us to sit down and fill out goal charts together. Or go for manicures. But, well . . ." I hold up my bitten nails as evidence of just how futile that cause is. "It's cute, though, that your dad wants to bond." Finished with the morning setup, I hoist myself onto the countertop. We haven't officially opened yet, and the coffee shop is a quiet sea of neat tables and full sugar dispensers. The calm before the storm. "My dad and I kind of have the same thing. He's always traveling," I explain. "But whenever he's in town, we always go to a show together, some band I want to see. It's dorky, I know, but . . ." I trail off, embarrassed. "I don't know, it's kind of nice, to have a thing like that. Just us."

But Josh doesn't seem to think I'm being childish. He nods, drumming absently against the counter with a couple of spoons. "Right. I have three older sisters, so my dad has a lifetime of it stored up. You know, football, baseball . . . Pretty much anything involving guns and balls—and don't even think about cracking a joke right now." He laughs and points a warning spoon at me. "Because believe me, I've made them all."

"Lips, sealed." I mime, trying to keep a straight face. "But didn't your sisters like sports? Us girls can like balls, too." I stop, realizing what I just said. Josh cracks up. I blush. "Stop it! You know what I mean!"

He coughs. "Too easy."

I roll my eyes. That's the thing about talking with Josh; I never know when he's going to take what I've said and twist it into something funny or gross.

"No," he explains, recovering. "He tried to get them

into hunting and sports, but they were just into other stuff. Dance, swimming, books."

"Heaven forbid." I press the back of my hand to my forehead. "Us girls, with our fancy book learning."

"Right, you're a reader, too," he says, as if it's a bad thing. He snags one of the forbidden muffins, breaks it in two, and offers half to me. I pause only a second before taking it. "You know, it's not good for you," he says through a mouthful of muffin. "All that sitting around, reading. What are you going to do when the zombies come? You'll be too out of shape to run."

"I thought zombies just kind of shuffled."

"The regular kind, sure." He grins. "I'm talking about the genetically modified ones."

"Right, silly me." I laugh. "Well, when they show up, I guess I'll just throw my big, heavy books at them and hope for the best."

"Good luck with that." He stuffs the rest of the muffin in his mouth and hops up on the back counter next to me.

"So are you starting college in the fall?" I ask, curious.

He shakes his head. "No, I'm done with school—the sitting in class, writing papers kind, anyway. It's just not my thing."

"So what is?"

Josh gives me a crooked kind of grin. "That, I haven't figured out just yet. But I will. Believe me, my parents are making sure of that."

The door dings with our first customer of the day:

a bleary-eyed man in a suit who trudges toward us in a familiar sleepy gait.

"Hey, Mr. Hartley," I call, hopping down from the counter. "The usual?"

"Mmgmmhm," he murmurs, yawning.

"One triple espresso and a cheese danish, coming right up!" I set to work on the Beast, hitting the combination levers. It shudders and splutters in protest, but I don't even pause. I just give its side a smack, and it quickly gurgles out the drink.

"No Post-its," Josh notes. He holds his hand up for a high five as he passes.

I grin and slap his palm. "It knows who's boss!"

My mastery of the Beast comes just in time, as we're soon deluged with a morning caffeine frenzy that doesn't let up for hours. I find myself shifting into a zen-like state of order/froth/pour, letting my mind wander to more important things—like Garrett. I've always had, ahem, an active imagination when it comes to the two of us, but now that he's out of reach, my wistful daydreams have taken on a vivid new fervency. I've played out the scene at the party a hundred times: if that drunk guy hadn't wrecked the mood, if Garrett had been able to say what was on his mind. Then there are the "rushing back home" scenarios, where—in the middle of a lecture—Garrett looks at the epic love poem and is struck with the realization it's about *us*. He flees the classroom, hitchhikes back to Sherman, and bursts through the café doors to sweep me into a passionate embrace—

"Hey." An exhausted voice interrupts my daydream. I look up and see Kayla on the other side of the counter, clutching three of her camp kids.

"Kaylieeee, I needa peepee!" one of the boys bleats.

"I'm thirsty!" a girl with pigtails demands.

"In a minute," Kayla says. Her eyes meet mine. "The things we do for summer wages."

I'm already flushing with embarrassment. "Listen," I start, shamefaced, "I want to apologize for the other day. . . ."

But instead of seeming mad, Kayla just shakes her head. "No, it's my fault! I was the one who loaded you down with all my stuff."

"But still . . . I feel bad about what happened. Did you get cleaned up OK?"

"Sure." Now it's Kayla's turn to look awkward. "I'm really sorry I bailed on you, but that wasn't really the color to have splashed all over my jeans. . . ."

"Oh, man," I say as the implication of red Slushie stains down her pants becomes clear. "I didn't even think of that."

"Me neither," she says, "until a group of guys started pointing and laughing. I just had to get out of there."

A large man behind Kayla clears his throat loudly. "Right," I say quickly. "What can I get you? On the house," I add in a whisper.

"Oh, awesome." She grins. "Just give me something with ice and syrup."

"You sure?" Her bratlets are now terrorizing an

unfortunate Seeing Eye dog in the corner. "They don't look like they need any more sugar."

"Not them—me," Kayla says. "I've got another two hours until their parents come!"

"Sugar rush, coming right up," I say, marking down an extra-large order.

My Zen-like work state lasts through the end of the week—if you can call it Zen when I'm obsessively checking my phone every break for word from Garrett. His ambitious course load is taking its toll, and our morning chats have been getting briefer and briefer: barely time for a "How are you?" let alone time for a confession of love, before he's off to breakfast, or class, or whatever else he's doing out there in the woods. Without me.

"Any hot weekend plans?" LuAnn asks as we sweep the floors on Friday night. The café is empty except for a lone woman in the corner determined to leech our wireless Internet until the lights go off and we forcibly throw her out.

I shrug. "Nothing much. Just hanging out. I can cover a shift, if you need me to."

"No wild parties and illicit hookups?" She sighs wistfully. "Man, what I wouldn't give to be seventeen again."

I want to laugh. Where do I start? With the fact that I have no access to those wild parties without Garrett or that the closest I've been to an illicit hookup is when Kenny Mendolson accidentally touched my chest while reaching for a pipette in chem lab last year?

"Sure," I murmur, remembering Kenny's horror. The least he could have done is looked pleased. "It's a blast."

"I remember when I was your age," LuAnn begins, sounding as if she's a jaded fifty-year-old rather than barely into her twenties. "I snuck out past curfew so many times my mom just gave up on me. I had a thing for guys on motorcycles," she adds with a wink.

"I know what you mean," I agree. Well, a Vespa is *almost* a motorcycle.

We finish clearing the debris of empty plates and coffee mugs, then take a break by the counter to share the last of the day's pastries. LuAnn nibbles daintily on a scone.

"So, are you in school?" I ask her, curious. Most of the staff here juggle their shifts around study of some kind, but I've never heard LuAnn talk about her life outside of Totally Wired.

"Not right now." LuAnn shrugs. A faint shadow flits across her face. "I tried fashion school," she says after a moment's pause.

"That sounds great. What happened?"

"It *was* great, until I dropped out." She puts down the scone and begins twirling hair around her index finger. "After that, I went to college for a while. English. Then drama. I switched to art history, then dropped that as well. I'm great at starting things," she tells me, her voice suddenly bright and metallic. "And excellent at dropping out. I do it all the time." She's wound her hair so tight that blood begins to pool in her fingertip.

"So what brought you to Sherman?" I ask, changing the subject. LuAnn may seem offhand about it, but I can tell that she isn't as blasé about her checkered history as she would like me to think. I circle around the counter and begin to wipe it down. LuAnn reaches for another pastry.

"The usual." She gives an expressive shrug. "Love. Hope. Delusions of happiness."

I keep cleaning, not wanting to push her anymore.

"It was a guy," she finally explains with a self-deprecating look. "He got into grad school around here, so I quit and followed him."

"Oh." I pause. "Are you still . . . ?"

"Together? Nope." LuAnn still sounds flippant, but her eyes aren't quite so light anymore. "He managed to last about a month before sleeping with his TA. His T and A, I like to call her."

"I'm sorry."

"Whatever. That'll teach me not to build my life around a man whose favorite book is *Atlas Shrugged*. Listen, kid." She waggles her finger, as if scolding me. "Nothing good comes from Ayn Rand. Trust me on this."

"Garrett loves that book," I protest.

She hoots with laughter. "I'll bet he does."

By the time we finish cleanup, and finally get our Wi-Fi leech to leave, it's dark and clouded over outside, another summer storm on the way. "You want a ride?" LuAnn offers, locking up behind us.

"Are you sure it's not out of your way?" I ask, pulling my sweater down over my hands against the chill.

"It's no problem." LuAnn leads me toward an old red Civic, parked just down the street. "You'll have to overlook the mess. And the smell."

But just as she pulls the door open for me, I feel a buzz in my pocket. I wait a second, sure it's just another phantom ring, but no: there it is again.

I check caller ID, my heart already racing.

Garrett.

CHAPTER NINE

"You know what? I can take the bus," I tell LuAnn, already backing away.

"Private caller, huh?" LuAnn winks. "I get it. Have a good weekend!"

I hurry down the street, eagerly pressing the phone to my cheek. "Garrett? Hey!"

And there he is, loud and clear and perfect down the line. "Sadie, what's up? How's life toiling down in the mines?"

"Oh, you know." I take a seat on a bench by the bus stop, his voice slipping over me like a relaxing balm. No more tired muscles or pain in my back from hoisting dirty plates all day; no, right now there's nothing in the world but me and him. "Same old. How's camp? Did you get that poetry paper back yet?"

"No, the professor's taking his time with it, but I have this short story I'm working on, for the end-of-summer magazine." He pauses, and then there's a cough. "So . . . there was actually something I want to talk about."

"Yes?" I take a breath, leaning forward in anticipation.

It couldn't be, could it?

Garrett gives a nervous-sounding laugh, completely unlike him. "This is so weird, not being able to see your face," he says. "I mean, there's Skype, but it's not the same, either."

It is! This is it, the moment I've been waiting for. Maybe those guys with *The Secret* are onto something after all. The hours—no, days—I spent imagining this moment weren't in vain. Just the opposite! Picturing this moment sent something into the universe and made it happen. I manifested my romantic destiny!

"Uh-huh," I say, the evening chill and overcast street fading into nothing around me. Nothing exists except the sound of Garrett's voice and my own quickly beating heart.

"We've been friends forever, and I know I can talk to you about anything—"

"Anything!" I interrupt quickly, then catch myself. What am I doing? Cutting him off before he has a chance to even say it! "Sorry, you go ahead."

"Uh, well . . . The thing is . . ."

Garrett pauses again, and I can almost hear the drums rolling, the trumpets sounding. My life is about to change forever as I sit here on this nondescript bench across from the Laundromat. Everything is about to change!

And finally, Garrett takes a breath and says them, the precious words I've been waiting so long to hear.

"The thing is, I . . . I'm in love."

Adrenaline floods through my body, a sweet rush of joy. "I love you, too," I breathe, dizzy, but Garrett doesn't hear me. He's still talking.

"Her name's Rhiannon," he says. "Rhiannon," he repeats reverently. "We met the first night, and I knew right away she was the one, but I thought she had a boyfriend, so I didn't even hope. But—"

"Wait," I stop him. "Rhiannon?" I gasp for air. "I . . . You never said . . ."

"She's only the most incredible girl I've ever met," he breathes. "And I know I've said this before, with Julie, and Beth, but she's the one. They were just silly crushes. This is the real thing. I love her," he says again, so sincerely that I know he really believes it.

Garrett is in love. With somebody else.

My heart breaks.

"She's here on a special scholarship," Garrett babbles on, while I stay frozen in shock and horror. The adrenaline in my veins has turned to lead. "She's already written her first novel, and she just signed with a literary agent. Isn't that amazing?"

I have no words.

"You'd love her, too. You guys are so much alike. It's

why I noticed her to begin with," Garrett continues, twisting the knife that's embedded deep in my heart. "She's got your crazy hair, and our same exact taste in music and movies. She even has that shirt of yours, the one with the maple tree on it? Only hers is in blue. It's her favorite color."

I stifle a whimper.

"I can't even describe it, Sadie, what it's like to connect with someone like this. And for us to wind up here, at camp together . . . It's fate. It has to be. She's my soul mate."

Garrett, who always laughed at the idea, so I made sure never to breathe a word of my own faith in the Gods of Destiny, is telling me about fate? About soul mates?

Tears sting the back of my throat. "I'm sorry—I have to go," I say abruptly, trying to keep the anguish from my voice.

"Oh, OK," Garrett says, clearly thrown. "But you'll call me back later, right? I want to tell you everything!"

"Uh-huh." I manage a strangled response before snapping my phone shut.

Rhiannon.

I slump on the bench in disbelief. I can't even form a coherent thought. I just stare at my battered sneakers in a daze. Some part of me registers that it's raining now, a cold drizzle falling on my thin sweater, but I don't move. I can't. Everything I have is focused on the news he just delivered with such obvious joy.

Another girl. Garrett is in love with another girl. It doesn't make sense. It *can't*.

I feel a sob rise in my chest, tears now hot on my cheeks. How could I have been so stupid? All this time, I've been certain he feels the same way about me. I was so sure that my feelings were requited that I'd convinced myself he was just getting up the courage to confess. But I was wrong. Garrett's feelings for me are nothing but friendship—plain, simple, and overwhelmingly platonic. I built his love out of thin air, I realize in horror—crafted it from e-mails and late-night conversations as if my sheer will would make it so.

It was all in my head. *Again!*

But why? Why does this keep happening? What's wrong with me? I don't understand why Garrett doesn't see what's right in front of him, and this time, it's even worse. I could always take comfort in the fact that maybe I just wasn't his type—not one of those high-strung redheads, drama queens, or tiny blondes—but this? Rhiannon? He said it himself: she's just like me.

But she's not. Because she actually gets to be with him, and I get to hear about how madly in love he is. Again.

The rain keeps falling. A cold drizzle drips slowly from my hair and settles on my face. I want it to pour, to storm and rage and distract me from what I'm thinking, what I'm feeling, but instead, I just get this damp inconvenience, a halfhearted summer shower, as if even the weather is underestimating my feelings.

The bus finally arrives, rolling to a stop with a screech. I haul myself on board and slink to a free seat, water squelching in my sneakers with every step. But the discomfort is nothing compared with the sharp ache in my chest, the fierce pain of rejection and sorrow. I slump in my seat, broken. Because he doesn't love me. Not like that, not how I desperately want. He never has.

I'd thought maybe if I just kept waiting . . . that this was our fate. Maybe the Gods of True Love were testing me or this was just the path our story had to take. Wanting him for so long, well, that would just make it sweeter when we could finally be together.

The old excuses tumble through my mind as the bus jerks slowly through town: month after month of trying to rationalize and explain away the simple fact that . . . he doesn't love me.

He never will.

Worn out, I rest my head against the cold, smudged glass. Sherman passes me by as we drive the familiar route, lush trees damp and dripping, streets washed in rain. My breath fogs the window, and suddenly, I see it with painful clarity—my whole friendship with Garrett, laid out. Because this isn't just about Rhiannon, or Beth, or any one of the parade of girls Garrett falls for with heartbreaking regularity. This is about me. And how I will never get to be one of those girls, no matter how much I hope and pray and want it.

He'll never compose whole odes to my beauty and grace. He'll never show up with a boom box to reenact *Say Anything* outside my window. He'll never drive over at three a.m. because I'm sick and can't sleep and just want to feel his arms around me. I can pine away for him for the rest of my life and turn into some Miss

Havisham—old and embittered and wondering *What if?* forevermore—but it won't make a difference.

Two whole years I've waited for him. Two years with him as the center of my whole world—the only number on my speed dial, the first thought I have every morning, and the last thought I have at night. And now . . . ?

Now I know for sure. This can't go on.

I can't keep doing this to myself, getting my hopes up so high, only to have them come crashing down. I can't keep waiting for him to come to his senses, having my whole emotional state rest on what *he* decides. What if he never wakes up to how perfect we'd be together? What if I spend another year pining for him—or longer even? In a terrible flash, I see my future stretching out before me: waiting for his calls, rearranging my life around college visits, and decoding texts and instant messages like they could be something real, something true.

This isn't love; this is pure torment.

And suddenly I know what I have to do, with more certainty than I've ever known anything in my life before. I have to be done with this. I have to cast off this wretched unrequited love, any way I can.

I need to get over him for good.

CHAPTER TEN

By the time I get home, I know for sure I have no other option. Either I spend the rest of my life uselessly pining after a boy who will never be mine, or I find some way to break free from this hold he has on me.

But how?

I take a long, hot shower. But all the Peach Bliss Bubble Buff in the world won't scrub away my misery. I towel off and wrap myself in my softest pajamas, as if the well-worn flannel could cocoon my poor, broken heart. But not even my favorite knitted bootie slippers provide me with the magical answer of how, exactly, I'm supposed to get over a boy who has been the center of my entire world for two entire years. Where do I even begin? Am I supposed to cut him out of my life completely? Hypnotize myself into believing I'm not in love with him anymore? Stage an exorcism to get him out of my heart forever?

I wish it were that easy.

Mom finds me on a stool in the kitchen, tearing into a plate of leftover chicken potpie.

"Did you make it back OK?" she asks, filling the teakettle and setting out mugs. She's back in her favorite around-the-house sweats—purple velour this time. "I called to see if you wanted a ride, but your cell went to voicemail."

I nod slowly. "Garrett called."

"How's he getting along?" Mom asks, oblivious to my plight. "Is that camp turning out to be fun?"

I nod again, the gravy and vegetables suddenly tasting like cardboard in my mouth. "Yup." I push my plate away. "He's having all kinds of fun."

"That's nice." Mom bustles away with the hot water and herbal tea bags. "I know you were disappointed not to get in, but maybe it's for the best. You can spend the summer making friends here in town and then try for it next year."

"Uh-huh." I sigh, and finally she notices my dejection.

"Are you OK, honey?" She pauses by the sink.

"Sure." I muster a halfhearted shrug. "Just . . . tired. It's been a long day."

She smiles warmly. "I remember. I worked a summer job at the diner when I was in high school. I was run off my feet every night. I had to wear this red-and-white-checked dress," she adds, turning back to the tea, "with snaps all down the front. I'm sure I have the photos somewhere. . . ."

"Sounds cute."

I wish for a moment that I could tell her everything, but Mom and I don't really go too deep when it comes to our feelings. We never have. Every time I forget and talk about feeling stressed from school, say, or upset about something, she always leaps in with action plans and life-coach psychobabble about transforming my reality, when really all I ever need is for her to say that yes, life sucks sometimes, and that's OK. I never really minded before—after all, I had Garrett for the deep emotional wrangling, and I could always rely on him to bring out an insightful quote from some classic novel or a story about some famous writer and how she used her inner pain to fuel works of greatness.

But I don't have him anymore. At least, not for this. And all the wallowing in the world isn't getting me closer to that mythical goal of getting over Garrett.

"Mom . . ." I start, reluctant. "Suppose you wanted to do something . . . like, a project," I say vaguely. "But you didn't know how to do it. Where would you start?"

She brightens. This might well be the first time in history that I've asked her advice, let alone on something so near and dear to her heart.

"Well . . ." Mom brings her tea over, sitting across from me at the big wooden kitchen table. "I always like to start with a plan."

"A plan. Right. I should have guessed." I exhale, disappointed. Somehow I don't think one of her cute blue workbooks is going to cut it when we're talking about the vast, aching depths of my heart here.

She laughs at my dubious expression. "I know you

think plans are the enemy of all creativity—or whatever Garrett said that time—but they really do work. There's nothing you can't do if you break it down into simple steps."

"Nothing?" I repeat, still unconvinced. "But that's not true! I mean, I get the appeal when it's for something practical—assembling some IKEA shelves or making spaghetti carbonara—but what about emotional things?"

"What do you mean?" She pours two cups of herbal tea, a smile tugging on the corners of her lips. She's enjoying this.

"Well, what if you had a client who wanted to stop feeling stressed, or angry, or being in love with someone?" I say, ultracasual. "You couldn't just tell them to make a plan not to feel that way."

"Sure, I could."

"Mom!" I protest, frustrated.

She laughs. "I'm not teasing you, Sadie—I promise. I know you think feelings are something we have no control over, but we do. We can control our actions, and eventually, we feel different. Take your example of someone feeling stressed," she suggests. "He could make a plan with things to do that relax him and ways to avoid things that cause tension. He could take up yoga, consider a career move, even—"

"OK, OK, I get it!" I interrupt her logical list of solutions. "But what about falling out of love?"

"Love?" She gives me a knowing smile that makes me wonder if she can see right through all of this.

"Hypothetically," I say quickly.

"Of course," she agrees, before taking a thoughtful sip of tea. "Well, you're right—that would be harder. But not impossible."

"No?" I ask, feeling a tiny glint of hope.

"Nothing's impossible if you set your mind to it. Hypothetically speaking." She grins.

"So . . . you can plan to fall out of love with someone?" I ask, still not quite believing her, but surprised to realize just how much I want it to be true. What's my alternative? Sitting around, aching with this broken heart, hoping that one day I'll just magically wake up and find I'm not in love with Garrett anymore?

"I think so." Mom nods. "You might not be able to choose how you feel, but you can choose how you act. Decide to focus on something else, and stay busy, and soon you won't feel so tied to the person anymore. I mean, that's what I'd tell my client," she adds.

I nod slowly. I can't believe it, but it kind of makes sense to me. "Thanks," I say quietly.

"Anytime." She pats my hand. "Let me know if there's anything else you need."

She's halfway to the door when I call out. "There is one thing."

"Yes?"

I cough, embarrassed, but if I'm going to do this, I need to go all in. "Can I borrow some of those self-help books?"

Upstairs, I settle in front of my computer, already turning over ideas for this new plan of mine. But staring at my e-mail in-box, and the database icon sitting there at the bottom of my screen, I'm gripped with sudden frustration. I know what's wrong with my Great Love project—the one thing I've so conveniently overlooked all this time.

Enter new profile field: The End.

I feel a surge of new energy as I click through the pages, updating every relationship with their dismal demise. Shakespeare is easy. Desdemona: murdered by her husband. Ophelia: drowned. Cordelia: hanged. Uplifting. Then there are the Russians; with them, it was all a painful end in a gutter somewhere. The French were big on tragic consumption; the Greeks loved nothing more than a good sacrificial slaughter or mistaken identity. Banishment, divorce, retreat to a nunnery, inconvenient icebergs—my fingertips fly across the keyboard as I fill in the missing details. There are myriad ways Great Love is torn asunder; I've just been too lovestruck to see it until now.

And even the supposedly happy endings . . . well, we don't know for sure what happens after the final credits roll. Elizabeth probably dies in childbirth while Darcy sits stoically outside the bedroom door. Nurse Hathaway might get bored of Doug Ross and his cable-knit sweaters and run off to a tropical island. Even Bella might discover that Edward always hogs the remote and has an annoying laugh and decide to call it quits—no hard feelings.

The hours slip past me in a blur of Google and database updates, until three a.m. rolls around and I finally drag myself away from the desk and collapse into bed. I've barely scraped the surface of the couples on the site, but instead of being bereft over the long catalog of death and dejection I've added to my shining tribute to True Love, I feel strangely inspired.

Just because they were soul mates doesn't mean they had to last forever. Just because they felt true love doesn't mean they couldn't have a new life after that love was over.

I yawn, snuggling deeper under my covers. Martha Gellhorn had a passionate marriage to Hemingway but decided she didn't want to be a footnote in somebody else's life. She divorced him and traveled the world as a trail-blazing reporter, having all kinds of adventures long after her supposed Great Love was over. I could be Martha! I decide in my sleepy haze. Sure, reporting from war zones can be kind of hazardous for the health, but that life—that moving on—that's what I'm after here.

And with my new plan, I'm going to make it happen.

Total Detox

People go on crazy juice fasts or flush water through their insides to get rid of the toxins in their systems. And that's what **he** is: a toxin. A chemical. An addictive substance wrapped up in magnificent cheekbones and a devastating smile. So if you're going to get over him, you need to start by getting *away* from him: no calls, no texts, no e-mails. Nothing. Not until you can get through the day without him being the first—and only—thing on your mind.

CHAPTER ELEVEN

I wake the next morning with sunlight spilling through my open window and the spark of determination in my veins. I bounce out of bed, full of energy. This is it: the first day of the rest of my life. I never really bought into that kind of thinking before, but now the simplicity is irresistible. Things are going to be different now. I'm writing my own rules. Well, steps. No waiting around for Garrett to call, no hanging on his every message . . . Maybe it won't even be as hard as I think, I decide, flossing enthusiastically. Sure, it feels like being in love with him is the only state of being I've ever known, but that will pass, it has to, and soon—

Bing!

The familiar sound of my IM alert bubbles to life.

I freeze.

Bing! it goes again. I look over at my computer

screen; there's a new chat box up, the text scrolling as the sender adds to the message.

There's only one person that could be.

I stay stranded in the middle of the room with my tank top pulled halfway over my head. I shouldn't be so surprised. We always chat in the mornings—it's become our new summer routine. But despite the breezy promises that were just running through my mind, I find that every instinct I have says, "Go! Read it! *Reply!*"

I pause, considering. I mean, it's one teeny, tiny IM. And it's not like I'm going out of my way to talk to him—it's only four steps away! *Besides,* a little voice whispers, *what harm would it do?* I could start the detox after. And shouldn't I warn him somehow—mention I'm going to be busy and not around to talk, so he doesn't get worried when I ignore him?

But then one message will turn into five, and then he'll call, and I'll be powerless to resist.

No!

I lunge across to my keyboard and click the *X* at the top of the chat box, keeping my eyes fixed on a spot on my wall above the screen so I'm not tempted to read the message. Then I quickly pull on the rest of my clothes, grab my book, and thunder down the stairs.

It's eight a.m., and already I feel the pull. Something tells me this is going to be a long day.

You know that thing where somebody says "Don't think of an elephant," and suddenly, the only thing on your mind is just that: a whole parade of elephants stomping through your thoughts? All it takes is for me to try and not think of Garrett, and suddenly, he's consuming my every idle musing. Picking a radio station? Garrett only listened to NPR. Browsing the refrigerator for orange juice? Garrett likes the pulp style best. I stare for ten minutes at breakfast options, remembering the many times Garrett has dropped by in the morning to mooch my scrambled eggs and drink coffee before giving me a ride to school, until finally I have to pass on eating anything at all.

How am I going to deal with this? What single thing can I think about that doesn't have some Garrett-related story attached? In the end, I fold myself into lotus position on the back porch and try to just think about nothing at all. Meditation. Clearing my mind. Focusing on calm breathing and the delicate slant of light through the railings rather than other, less important things. Like, say, the message I left unread upstairs, and whether my Internet service has it saved in an emergency file somewhere. . . .

"Do you want some pancakes, honey?" Mom calls from inside.

"No, I'm fine!" I yell back. *Think calming thoughts, Sadie. Calming, non-Garrett thoughts . . .*

"Are you sure?" She comes outside, lingering in the doorway. "Have you eaten anything yet? Because coffee has zero nutritional value, and you know that breakfast is—"

"The most important meal of the day," I finish, sighing. So much for an uninterrupted calm. "Yes, I know."

"Maybe something else then," she tries again, giving

me that head-to-toe look that I just know means she's assessing my height-to-weight ratio and comparing it with whatever charts she has pinned up in the Sadie's Developmental Progress corner. "I could do some French toast. You always like—"

"I told you, I'm not hungry!" I snap.

She blinks.

I catch my breath. "Sorry," I add, "I'm just . . . cranky this morning."

"Clearly."

"It's nothing." I wave away her concern. "And yes, I'll have some pancakes. Thank you."

"OK, batter's in the fridge. I'll be at the conference until five, but you can use the car. Oh, and your father called." She tries to keep her voice even, but I can hear the usual disapproving tone slip through the moment she mentions Dad.

"What about?" I ask.

She shrugs. "I don't know, nothing urgent. He said you weren't picking up your cell."

"Oh, yeah, I'm keeping it on silent at the moment. Too much distraction," I quickly explain. "I read an article about teens and ADD."

"Is that what you were talking about last night?" She looks impressed. "Technology detox. What an excellent thought. I might add that to my course." She kisses me on the forehead, then goes back inside, already whipping out her cell phone to record a note to herself, completely unaware of the irony.

I wait until she's inside before retrieving my own phone. I've kept it on silent as a defense against Garrett, but I guess I need a tactic that doesn't cut off everyone else from my life, too.

"Hey, Dad."

"Pumpkin!"

Yes, I'm seventeen years old. No, he won't stop calling me that.

"What's up?" I ask. "Everything OK?"

"Hold on a sec, will you?"

I wait. There's music in the background, the familiar jagged edges of a jam session, but it recedes as Dad leaves the room. There's a click, and then he comes on again, clearer this time.

"So how are you doing? How's summer shaping up? You written that magnum opus yet?"

"Not yet." I laugh. "Summer's . . . OK, I guess. I got a job at the café, which is fun."

"I used to make a mean cup of joe myself, back in the day."

Dad lives in D.C.—when he's in one place for long, that is. He plays the saxophone—not just for kicks or like those guys playing for money on the subway but as an actual career. He does session music for singers, his band gets booked all over, and they even have a CD that was nominated for a Grammy way back when. Sure, it was for Best Zydeco/Cajun Album, and they didn't get invited to the big main ceremony with Beyoncé and everybody, but it still counts.

"Did you get my e-mail?" he asks. "I sent you this great link to a dog playing piano."

"No, I'm just . . . trying to stay off-line." I sigh. "Not so much e-mail and Internet, that kind of thing. But it's hard. I keep wanting to check my phone, it's like a compulsion or something."

"Too right. It's the habit that gets you. Remember when I was trying to quit smoking? I nearly went crazy at first, but it turns out the key was just to keep busy, give my hands something to do instead of holding a cigarette."

"Busy," I repeat. "I can do busy."

"Sure, you can. Listen, I'm sorry I didn't get back for your birthday, but I'm going to be in Boston soon for a show. Do you want to come up? We can hang out, make a weekend of it."

"That sounds great!" I brighten. "Can we go see this singer, Jonny Pardue? He's playing in the city for the next few weeks, I think."

"Absolutely. Look, I've got to get back to practice, but I'll figure out the details with your mom, OK?"

"OK, see you soon."

I hang up, thoughtful. Dad's battle against cigarettes was epic—won and lost on many occasions. While Garrett's messages aren't rotting my lungs, they're definitely corroding my soul. Doing less clearly isn't working out, but maybe I should be doing more instead. Sure, there's the usual list of errands and odd jobs tacked to the fridge, but how am I supposed to focus on anything with my computer so tantalizingly close?

Check mail! it calls to me. *Check mail!*
I've never been one of those technology-dependent
kids—the ones who go into meltdown if they're dragged
away from their computers for all of five minutes—but
now my hand is reaching for my cell phone as if it's
possessed. Garrett has texted twice already (at least I
assume it's him, since I've stoically ignored the tantalizing
buzz), and that's not even thinking about whatever could
be lurking upstairs in my e-mail in-box. . . .
It's clear that the house is way too dangerous in my
current state of Garrett OCD. Here, peril and temptation
lurk at every turn, so I do what any smart warrior would:
I grab my keys and bag, and I flee.
It's time for some distraction.

I never figured Totally Wired as a sanctuary, but it turns
out there's nowhere safer from my cruel addiction than
the noisy, bustling café. Three days of Garrett detox later
and I have my coffee serving down to a graceful ballet.

"Order up for table five!" Josh hits the bell and
deposits two plates on the hatch ledge.

"I need two lattes and a soy tea!" Dominique calls
from behind the register.

"Excuse me? Can someone come clear this table?" A
customer lingers by a trash- and mug-littered table, trying
to catch my attention.

"Coming, right away, absolutely!" I call back to each
in turn. Flicking some switches on the Beast, I start the
lattes, then grab the full plates and swoop through the

café, depositing them at table five with a cheerful "Enjoy!" and a handful of utensils before pivoting, sweeping up the debris on the next table, and stacking my arms high with dirty plates. By the time I get back to the counter, fresh espresso is dripping obediently into the mugs, herbal tea is steaming, and even Dominique is looking at me with what could be admiration—if admiration can be masked beneath a scowl, that is.

"You're learning fast," she tells me grudgingly.

I beam. With my cell phone stowed safely in the staff locker and my idle hands put to good use, I can almost, *almost* forget the texts I'm deleting unread (because having them there in my in-box is a temptation too far) and the e-mails that must be piling up back at home. I unplugged my computer that first night and haven't touched it since, instead, filling my evenings with gritty cop shows on TV (the least romantic thing I can find) and reading my way through Mom's extensive library of self-help books. By the time I collapse, exhausted, into bed, it feels like I've run a marathon of self-control.

But it's working. I've struggled through seventy-two hours of a Garrett-free existence, and it almost, *almost* feels like that itch is lessening. To, say, a fiery burn, rather than a full-on red-ant attack. Soon, it might even fade to a mild irritation.

I can but dream.

But just when I feel like maybe, just maybe, I can make it through another day triumphant, the door dings open and an icy chill blasts through the café. OK, so maybe not a literal one, but the sight of Beth Chambers sauntering in is enough to freeze me in my tracks.

"Hi," I gulp. "I mean, welcome to Totally Wired. What can I get you?"

"You work here?" Beth asks, looking slowly around. Oversize sunglasses are propped just-so on top of her hair, and she's wearing another of her fabulously stylish outfits—skinny black pants and a striped shirt that just scream Audrey Hepburn.

Right then I decide, she's not going to get to me. Nothing is going to ruin my sunny mood, not even Little Miss Drama Queen and her chic monochrome wardrobe.

"Yup, I do." I brace myself for a scathing retort, but instead she just smiles at me.

"That's cool. It's a great place," she says, then orders a frothy chocolate concoction. "Is that OK?" she asks. "I can get something simpler, if you don't want to . . ."

"No, it's fine." I blink at her, thrown. What happened to the über-bitch of old—the Beth who would send Garrett out for a bottle of water during lunch, and woe betide him if he came back with Poland Spring instead of her precious Evian? "Do you, um, want whipped cream with that?"

"Sure—if it's not too much trouble," she adds quickly.

There it is again: trouble. As if she cares about my time and energy. For what would be the first time in the history of the universe.

I assemble the drink, wondering what has prompted

this personality makeover into a new, humble, conscientious Beth Chambers. Did finally graduating the confines of Sherman High make her realize that treating people as if they're nothing more than inconvenient gnats might not, you know, endear her to people, out in the real world? Or is this all an elaborate ploy, to set me up for another confidence-shaking smackdown?

"Here you go." I put her drink on the counter, still staring at her suspiciously.

"Thanks so much," Beth gushes. She passes me the money for her drink and stuffs a couple of dollars in the tip jar, then meets my eyes, looking awkward. "I, um, want to let you know, I'm sorry for saying that stuff to you at the party."

I blink, truly amazed now. "Oh," I manage. "That's OK."

"No, I mean . . . I was such a bitch, it's not even funny." She gives me this shrug, seeming to be genuinely uncomfortable. "I was just so mad at you. I mean, you guys were always so close. I guess I was just jealous, that's all."

"Jealous? Of me?"

Beth stares at me. "Of course. You're, like, his favorite person. I could never compete with that." She exhales. "Even now . . . I mean, we were so close, and suddenly, I can't even talk to him anymore. You're so lucky," she tells me. "You're still friends with him, but I don't get him in my life at all anymore."

Her words sit between us on the counter. I know I

should say something nice back, something reassuring, but I'm wordless with sudden horror.

She gives another rueful shrug and then takes her drink. "Thanks. Good luck with . . . well, next year. Maybe I'll see you around, during breaks, you know?" And with that, she sashays away.

CHAPTER TWELVE

What am I doing?

I stare after Beth, a rush of absolute, unfettered panic speeding through me. She's right, I *am* lucky. Garrett has been the best friend a girl could want, so how could I be so stupid as to think about shutting him out for good? I've been so busy thinking about my unrequited love, I haven't even stopped to consider the other, more important part of our relationship.

Friendship.

Ignoring him now would make him think I don't care, that I don't want to be friends. I want to get over him, not lose him for good! How must he feel, with me not replying to his texts and e-mails like this? What kind of friend am I?

"Sadie!" Dominique snaps me out of my panicked reverie. She dumps an armful of dishes on the counter, then strips off her apron. "I have to go," she informs me.

"Are you off already?" I stare at her, still fixed on my Garrett dilemma. "I didn't see LuAnn come in."

"She hasn't." Dominique shrugs, with typical insouciance. "But you can handle it."

"Um, sure, I guess." I look around. The café is half full, and everything seems quiet enough. "But can you . . . ?"

My words fall into empty space; she's already gone. But then I realize, I'm unsupervised, with no one to bark disapproving orders in French if I check my phone, say, or make a quick call. . . .

I snatch my phone out from my locker and dial with shaking hands. It's pure instinct—I don't even think about the hours of struggle I'm rendering useless here; I only want to make things right.

Voice mail.

"Hi, Garrett," I say, trying to keep the panic from my voice. "How are you doing? I just wanted to say I hope you're OK, and call anytime." I pause. "I, um, know I've been busy, and not returning some of your messages, but I'm here for you—I promise. Just call. Anytime!"

I hang up, still feeling a lurch of guilt. It's not Garrett's fault I've been in love with him all this time, and it's not his fault I've had to pull away for the sake of my mental health and general sanity. No, he's the innocent party in all of this. And here I am, abandoning him as if our friendship doesn't mean a thing. I think of the messages I didn't return, the IMs I didn't respond to, the e-mails languishing unread in my in-box. He must think I'm ditching him, that I couldn't care less. I want to get over him to save our friendship, not destroy it!

"Excuse me? Hello, can I get some service?"

"Sure! Just a sec," I call, quickly typing out a text in case he's stuck in a lecture or class and can't check his voice mail.

"Like, now?"

Some people have no patience. *Call me!* I finish, then tuck the phone under the counter and turn back to work. The itch is back to a full-on burn, but there's nothing I can do but wait now.

Wait, consumed by the panic that I've ruined everything.

Half an hour later, it's clear that my friendship with Garrett isn't the only thing I've destroyed; my new skills as Super-Barista have fallen apart as well.

"I ordered a latte, like, ten minutes ago!"

"And I'm still waiting on the mocha whip."

"The tables are all dirty!"

CRASH!

A tray of dirty plates tumbles to the floor, but I ignore it, yanking down hard on the Beast. It splutters but doesn't deliver me the caffeinated elixir I need. I try again. Nothing. It's as if the universe can sense my Zen barista focus has been broken; the peaceful, placid café has degenerated into sheer chaos, dirty dishes are piled on the tables, the orders are stacked overdue, and I'm left to dash around, desperately trying to satisfy the ever-growing line.

"Hello! We're waiting here!"

"Uh-huh!" I call, my voice tinged with panic now. "Be right with you!"

Aren't there laws against this—leaving a teenager in charge of, well, anything? I'm not even allowed to vote, yet suddenly I'm the sole being standing in the way of a full-on coffee riot!

"Two cappuccinos!" I cry, trying to swirl the foam into our trademark heart. It comes out a confused blotch, deformed and broken—a metaphor for my current psyche, if ever there was one. Garrett still hasn't replied to my messages, despite my checking every five minutes—make that every three.

Josh peers out of the hatch at the mess. "Sadie?" he says, his voice edged with concern as he takes in the loud, angry, near-rioting scene. "Maybe we should close the kitchen to new orders, and I could come help you out."

"But it's the lunch rush. They want lunch!" I tell him, wiping sweaty bangs from my forehead, and smearing hot chocolate mix across my face in the process. "You can't leave the kitchen."

"OK, if you're sure. . . ." He makes a reluctant face and then goes back to work.

"I wanted low-fat milk." A scowling blond woman thrusts her drink back at me. "And there's cinnamon on top. I hate cinnamon."

"If you could just wait a moment . . ." I beseech her as I throw three pastries on a plate and push them toward the nearest person. Why must people be so picky? It's a three-dollar coffee, not the center of their existence!

"But I told you specifically when I ordered, no cinnamon."

With a sigh, I take back the drink, scoop off the offending foam, dump it all in a fresh cup, and hand it back. "Better?" I scowl.

"Well!" She opens her mouth in shock. "I'll be filling in a feedback form about this."

"You do that!" I call after her. "They're right by the register!"

I snap back into action. The Beast is shaking so hard that the row of coffee cups stacked on top of it begins to vibrate. I snatch the jug of frothed milk away from the steamer, spilling half of it over my arm.

"Ow!" I reel back as the scalding hot liquid hits my skin.

"Hey, Sadie?" Kayla appears by the counter exit, making me jump back in the other direction and drop the jug. "Do you have those workbooks?"

I stare at her blankly.

"I left you, like, three voice mails about it," she tries again, looking completely exhausted. "You know, the dream ambition book things?" She's got two camp kids by the hands. There are suspicious brown stains all over her Sunny Dayze Camp T-shirt, her hair is splattered with blue paint, and her trademark perky ponytail is hanging limp.

"I'm sorry," I tell her, still trying to stem the flow of coffee from the Beast. "I, um, didn't get your messages."

Truth is, I've been skipping past anything that isn't immediately Garrett related. I have my priorities, especially with the café in meltdown!

"Oh." Kayla deflates. "I have the whole Lion Cub group waiting for them. They riot after snack time. And you know how it is—there's never enough tranquilizing cough syrup to go around." She manages a grin.

"I'm sorry!" I turn to quickly jam three new filters under the unceasing *drip-drip-drip*. "It's crazy here."

"But Sadie—"

"Hey, miss? I'm waiting here—"

"Order up!"

"So, like, I have an allergy to sugar, and—"

The buzz of demands kicks up to a roar—moving beyond chaos to an utter disaster zone. Hurricane warning, Category 5. And then, through it all, I suddenly hear a faint but unmistakable sound.

My cell phone is ringing.

And it's not just any ringtone. It's Garrett's, the familiar melody of Belle & Sebastian, aka his favorite band in the known universe.

"Sadie? What's going on?" LuAnn pushes through the crowd, out of breath. "I saw the crowd from down the street. Where's Dominique?"

But I barely hear her. I don't hear any of them anymore. Everything fades away to that one sound, taunting me, begging me, *commanding* me to go answer my phone.

He's calling.

My heart leaps. Like a girl possessed, I abandon the espresso machine and leap for my purse. My cell phone tumbles out and skitters across the floor. I lunge after it on all fours behind the counter.

"Hello?" I press my hand to my free ear to hear better. "Garrett?"

"Hey, Sadie." His voice is distant and blocked by static.

"I can't hear you. Are you there?" I duck lower to the ground to block them all out. On some level, I hear a clatter and a high-pitched yelp, but it doesn't matter, not when Garrett actually picked up the phone and called me. He's not mad! I haven't ruined things! "What's going on?"

"Nothing much, I just figured I'd check in. Are you OK?" he asks. "Your voice mail sounded kind of weird."

"No, I'm fine. Good!" I yelp, still crouched behind the counter. "I just didn't want you to worry. You know, that I haven't been in touch."

Garrett laughs. "You know, I didn't even notice. Things have been so busy here. . . . You didn't . . . and with the . . . tomorrow."

"Garrett? You're breaking up!" I hear static and bursts of noise.

"Look, I've got to run. . . ."

"Garrett?"

But he's already gone.

I hang up.

"Sadie?"

I stay on the floor, clutching my phone. He didn't notice? I've been killing myself for three days now, fighting my epic battle not to pick up the phone—aching with missing him—and he barely even noticed I wasn't around?

"Sadie!"

Nothing's changed, I realize, feeling completely lost. Sure, I made my big detox plan and thought it would make a difference, but here I am, still orbiting around him as if he's my gravity, still filled with thoughts of him— even if they're thoughts about how *not* to think of him.

"Sadie!"

I finally look up. LuAnn is standing two feet away from me. "You're here," I say, flooded with relief. "Great."

"Great?" she splutters, and only now do I realize she's turned a strange shade of pink. No, make that raspberry—clashing with her crazy punk red hair and the fluorescent pink of her retro blouse. "Does this really look great to you?!"

I look.

The espresso machine is going into meltdown, gushing scalding black liquid in a tide of deadly caffeine. Three of Kayla's brats have broken free and are splashing around in the mess, tracking gritty footsteps across the café floor, while the four-deep throng of angry customers jostles and yells. Plates are piled high, with overdue orders cooling next to stacks of dirty dishes.

I exhale in a whoosh, and just like that, the madness subsides. The real world slips back into focus, and suddenly it hits me: I'm sprawled facedown on the floor in a puddle of frothed milk, and preschoolers are staring at me in shock and disgust.

"I have a problem," I say slowly, pulling myself into an upright position. The truth is ugly, but nowhere near as ugly as the half-eaten eggplant panino that was just inches from my cheek. I can't keep this secret any longer, so I say it again, every word full of cringe-worthy, cheek-flushing shame.

"I have a serious problem, and his name is Garrett Delaney."

LuAnn swings into action and calls the whole crew in to save the place from complete chaos. Denton and Jules, another barista, take duty out front, while the rest of them sit me down in the back office for what they call a staff meeting but I know is more like an intervention. Even Kayla joins us after dropping the kids back at the community center; she lines up with LuAnn, Dominique, Aiko—all of them looking at me as if I'm teetering on the edge of a complete breakdown. And I guess I could be, if the scene out front is anything to go by.

"So this is all because of a guy?" LuAnn repeats slowly.

I nod, shameful.

"OK . . ." she says with a mixture of relief and confusion. "I thought it might be drugs or something."

"You've been acting kind of weird these last few days," Aiko agrees. "Really nervous and jittery."

"She could be lying," Dominique announces. She

lunges forward, takes my face in her hand, and turns it side to side to examine me. "See? Her eyes are all bloodshot."

"I'm not on anything!" I break away. "I promise. I can't even drink more than two cups of coffee a day!"

"Hmmm," Dominique sits back, stony-faced.

"But I still don't get it," Kayla says, speaking up for the first time. "Garrett's away at camp, and you said you guys have always just been friends."

"We were. I mean, we are." I pick at the skin around my thumbnail, avoiding their confused, judgy eyes. "But . . . I'm in love with him." The words sound strange and foreign; it might just be the first time I've ever admitted it out loud.

"And?" LuAnn prompts.

"And I'm trying not to be." I bite my lip and plunge on. "I had this plan to get over him, a whole detox program to get him out of my life, with rules and steps, and little gold stars. But I don't want him out!" I find myself carried away with frustration. "I miss him so much, it hurts. I just want us to be friends again. Just friends."

I look up, hoping they understand what I'm trying to do. But instead of sympathetic gazes, I find a line of blank stares.

"A detox program? That's so . . . cute." LuAnn tries not to smile, but I can see the twitch at the corner of her lips.

"Who is this guy, anyway?" Aiko asks. "A movie star? A sparkly vampire?"

"Just this guy from school," Kayla answers before I

can. She shrugs. "Some girls think he's cute, but . . ." She trails off, the implication clear: Garrett is nothing special, and I've lost my mind.

"So, you were never dating, and now he's in another state? Why not just get over him already?" Dominique looks disapproving, as if her heart has never done a thing her brain hasn't vetted and sanctioned.

"Haven't you ever adored someone, even though you knew it couldn't work?" I ask desperately, trying to make them see. I'm not crazy—this is something real I'm feeling here! "So you try, and try, to move past it and forget about them, but it's like they're stuck in your head—you can't just flip a switch and stop loving them! So you hate yourself for it, because you know it's no use, but nothing you do seems to ever make a difference."

Silence.

LuAnn and Aiko exchange an amused look. Dominique just smirks at me, as if I'm the main exhibit in the Museum of the Hopeless and Lovelorn. Only Kayla looks sympathetic, but she's probably thinking how lucky she is not to be stuck here working with a psycho.

I feel a rush of humiliation, hot on my cheeks. "Forget it," I mumble, pushing my chair back. "I'm . . . um, sorry about the mess."

"Sadie, wait—" Kayla starts, but I just turn and flee, hurrying out the back exit and through the narrow alleyway to the main street so I don't have to revisit the site of my meltdown. I choke back a sob, furious with myself for rambling like that. I don't even blame them for thinking I have serious psychological issues. I mean, this is not normal—it's not anywhere close to normal—to be so dependent on a guy. I get that! But it's not just a guy. This is Garrett we're talking about here, and even if it seems crazy when you just lay it out in black and white, it's real to me.

I have a quote from Anaïs Nin up on my wall: *"Each friend represents a world in us, a world possibly not born until they arrive, and it is only by this meeting that a new world is born."* And that's how it was with Garrett. Because he understood me, the me I wanted so desperately to be. Think about your best friend—how you tell them everything, how they're the person who knows you best, all your deepest fears and insecurities. They're the one you call when something amazing happens or when everything falls apart and you need someone to come over and watch movies and tell you that everything's going to be OK. It's not like family, who are obligated to love you and even then sometimes fail to be everything they're supposed to be. Your true friend has chosen you, and you them, and that's a different kind of bond.

That's Garrett to me. I'm used to talking to him all the time, about the most meaningless stuff. To have him gone feels like a loss, an absence haunting me every day. Without him, there's just the empty space that used to be filled with laughter and friendship and comfort.

Can you really blame me for finding it so hard to let go?

Find the Flaws

It's hard to grasp now, but **he** isn't a shining god among teen boys. He's just a guy. A guy with radiant eyes, a chiseled jaw, and the ability to quote Sartre—in the original French—sure, but a guy nonetheless. Which means he has faults. Flaws. Aka glorious little gifts from the Gods of Regular Guy Behavior, there to help you get over him.

List them. Count them. Make a collage of all the irritating things he's ever done, the stupid things he's ever said. Meditate on those flaws night and day, until that pedestal you've had him on comes crashing down, and maybe you can see him clearly for the boy he really is, not the romantic hero you've built in your mind.

CHAPTER THIRTEEN

Now that I've managed to humiliate myself in front of the entire Totally Wired crew, I slump back into pitiful despair, my shiny new "How to Get Over Garrett" guide languishing under a pile of dirty laundry, crumpled and used up, like my dignity. So much for the power of a good plan; I couldn't even make it past the very first hurdle! I may as well just quit now: the getting over him and my coffee-shop job. Not that I can show my face in there ever again. They probably have me up on a poster by now. *Warning: this girl is emotionally unstable. Do not allow near hot beverages.*

But when I go to fetch the newspaper Sunday morning, I find Kayla waiting on my doorstep, looking annoyingly perky in tiny denim cutoffs and a candy-pink tank.

"You can't quit," she says.

I blink at the bright sunlight—closed curtains being an integral part of wallowing. "What are you talking about?"

"Garrett." Kayla beams at me. "You can't quit your detox program thing now. You've just had a tiny setback—that's all."

"You call yesterday tiny?"

She wavers. "OK, maybe not so small. But it's a good idea! You just need backup. Like all those support groups for people with sex addictions and drug problems."

"Garrett Anonymous?" I say, dubious.

She laughs. "Exactly!"

I let out a long, weary breath. It's sweet of her, but just the sight of Kayla so perky and full of optimism makes me want to turn around and burrow under my comforter for, well, the rest of my life. "You don't have to humor me," I tell her. "I know you think I've lost my mind. You made that pretty clear yesterday."

Kayla makes a face. "I'm sorry about that. We should have been more supportive. But I was thinking about it, and it's a good idea—it really is. You just need help, to keep you on track."

"It's too late." I mope, sagging against the doorframe. "It was stupid to think I could just cut him off. I'm going to be a slave to this forever."

She rolls her eyes. "OK, enough of the drama-queen act. Go get your swimsuit."

"What?"

"Your beach stuff. Now. Come on." She claps briskly,

as if I'm one of her Sunny Dayze camp brats. "I'm heading to the lake with some friends, and you're coming."

"Kayla—" I protest weakly.

"Nope, I'm not taking no for an answer." She talks over me. "It'll be fun. And distracting. You can tell me about this plan of yours, and we'll figure out how to make it work."

"I forgot how bossy you are," I grumble.

She grins. "Hell, yes. Blake's picking me up in fifteen minutes. If you're not out front, I'll come drag you out myself."

"OK, OK!" I put my hands up in surrender. "And . . . thanks," I add shyly. "I could use the break."

"Anytime. And make that fourteen minutes!" Kayla calls, heading back across the street.

I take the world's quickest shower, grab my things, and make it outside just as Blake's truck rolls down our block, blasting some dirty rap song and overflowing with varsity jocks.

Suddenly I have second thoughts about this whole socializing thing.

"Ready to go?" Kayla catches my look of apprehension as I take in the various inflatable pool toys and amount of hair product on show. "They're harmless, promise." She grins, reaching for my beach bag. "And the plus side is they'll carry all our stuff!"

She's right. I suffer the journey squeezed in back next to three guys introduced to me in a blur. TJ, or KJ maybe, and Darren or Darnell (who I swear I've never laid eyes on before in school) argue over the finer points of the big weekend game, but when we pull up to a free parking spot over the ridge from the water, they hoist the coolers and deck chairs and assorted supplies like they weigh nothing at all.

"See?" Kayla links her arm through mine, leaving Blake to jostle and race with the other guys. "I tell them I can handle my own stuff, but it's like a mark of pride or something. I'm surprised Blake doesn't just hoist me over his shoulder and try to carry me, too!"

I laugh, starting to relax. "Is it bad I can actually picture that?"

We follow the well-worn path past the parking lot and down through a dense section of trees to the lake. On hot summer days like this, it's our town's main respite: sitting lazily at the base of Turner's Hill, the lake clear and blue and edged with the thick green of grass and more trees. On one side, a pebble beach curves, with a couple of wooden piers set up, and on the far end, the water winds away into the Sherman River, stretching out past town. When I was a kid, we'd come here almost every day in summer, Kayla and me splashing in the shallows, chasing dragonflies while our moms sipped iced tea from the shade of a big umbrella. But since high school, I haven't really been back. This is a place for the more popular kids to hang—girls stretched on the dock in tiny bikinis while the guys toss a football around or cannonball into the lake. Garrett and I prefer to go farther up the river, to quiet spots where the trees overhang the water and you can lie for hours under the leaves, trailing one hand in the cool water.

"Awesome, they got the best spot," Kayla exclaims, waving happily to a group lounging on the far dock—prime popular-kid real estate. "Come on, I'll introduce you to everyone."

I brace myself and follow her. This is where Kayla and I most definitely diverge; I've spent the last two years hanging out with Garrett, while she's been happily bouncing between rallies and sleepovers like, well, a normal teenage girl.

"Hey, everyone, this is Sadie! Sadie, you know Trish, right? And that's Suzie, Yolanda, Lexie, Lauren M., and Lauren B."

The girls roll over to look at me from behind an array of oversize shades.

"Hi." I give a hopefully-not-too-awkward wave. "What's up?"

"Nothing much." Lauren M. (or is that B.?) assesses me with a long stare. I must pass whatever test she gives me, because she finally cracks a smile. "We're trying to decide if it's too early to break out the snacks."

"It's never too early for snacks," Kayla declares, retrieving our bags from the pile of stuff left by the guys. They've already splashed into the water and are whooping and hollering as they try to drown each other. "I vote chips."

The girls chorus their agreement and delve into the junk-food bags, while Kayla begins laying her towel out in a space on the end of the dock. After a moment's hesitation, I follow, claiming a strip next to her and cautiously shucking off my shorts and T-shirt to reveal my basic black bikini. "Cute suit," Kayla tells me, her own a powder-blue halter affair. "Here, turn around and I'll do your back."

"Thanks." I pass her my industrial-size bottle of superstrength sunscreen. "You know how easy I burn."

"Oh, my God, yes!" She snorts, smearing a liberal helping over my shoulders. "I remember you were walking around like a lobster forever. What was that, like, fifth grade?"

"I think so." I take the bottle back and carefully cover myself with a layer of white goop, still feeling like something of an interloper.

One of the other girls, Yolanda, pauses her attack on a jar of salsa to look at me thoughtfully. "You were in my lit class, right?"

I nod.

"And she's friends with that senior guy, Garrett," the other Lauren adds, talking to Yolanda like I'm not even there. She hasn't moved from her prone, sunbathing state since I arrived, but I detect a vaguely hostile tone in her voice.

"The football guy?"

"No, the serious-looking one," Lexie corrects her. "He's kind of cute."

"You think?" Suzie wrinkles her nose. "Not my type."

"Yeah, well, we know how picky you are."

"Better picky than, umm, indiscriminate!" Suzie says. Lexie makes a squeal of protest and tosses a chip at her.

"Eww, now I've got salsa all over me!"

Yolanda looks mischievous. "Maybe we should get TJ over here to lick it off."

Suzie doesn't dignify that with a reply. Instead she gets to her feet, steps over the tangle of tote bags and bronzing limbs, and cannonballs off the end of the dock. A great splash goes up; the girls shriek some more.

"Suzie!" Yolanda wails. "I got this weave put in, like, yesterday!"

"Sorry!" Suzie's reply is faint as she swims away, out toward the boys.

I stretch out in the hot sun, listening to them bicker and laugh around me as the day slips past in that hazy summer way. It's weird, but once the initial shock is over, I don't feel so out of place anymore. In fact, the difference is good, like a comfort. It's a world away from my dynamic with Garrett, so much more effervescent. The girls flick through magazines, gossiping over celebrities and fashion. It's a foreign tableau of bright bikinis and purses spilling sunscreen and makeup and sweatshirts, while cotton-candy clouds drift slowly across the blue sky.

It's like a vacation for my soul.

I sit up to take a drink of water and see that Kayla has moved apart from the other girls. She's sitting on the end of the dock, her legs dangling in the water, peeling red licorice strands one by one as she looks out across the water.

I walk over and take a seat on the damp wood beside her. "Thanks for inviting me. I really needed to get out."

She looks up, startled, as if she was lost in thought. "Oh, no problem."

I ease my feet into the water. "It's cold!" I yelp, surprised.

She grins. "Wimp. You get used to it. Or, you know, your skin just goes numb."

I laugh. "Anyway, thanks for thinking of me. This is fun."

"Sure." Kayla pauses. "I've thought about asking you to do stuff before, but I wasn't sure. . . . I mean, you're always off somewhere with Garrett." She turns to me with an awkward smile. "I didn't know if you would even want to hang."

"Oh." Thrown, I splash the water with my toes. "I never thought . . . I mean, you're always with Blake."

"Not always." She rolls her eyes. "Not like you and Garrett. I swear, you guys are glued together."

"Were," I correct her quietly.

"Right." She's quiet for a moment. "So what changed? Did something happen with you guys, to make you want to move on?"

I shrug, tracing the rough wooden planks of the dock. "I guess I just woke up to something that was true all along. He doesn't feel the same way about me, and no matter how much I hope, and wait . . . well, it's not going to happen."

Saying it out loud, to someone else, makes it truer somehow. Real. Done.

"That must have been tough." Kayla's voice is soft,

and when I look over, there's genuine sympathy on her face.

"Not nearly as tough as trying to do something about it," I reply, rueful. "As you probably figured from my performance yesterday."

"It'll get easier," Kayla reassures me, and suddenly I want so desperately for her to be right. Out here, in the bright sunshine, it seems like a new world: shiny and fresh, where maybe getting over him isn't the insurmountable obstacle I've been thinking it is.

I return her smile. "I hope so."

We're silent for a moment, listening to the distant yells of kids playing and the murmurs of the Laurens deliberating about some star's new hairstyle. I breathe slowly, feeling the sun seep all the way to my soul and the tension ease right out. This is what I needed, to be out, away from everything.

Kayla splashes the water some more. "So, this plan of yours . . . You start with avoiding him?"

"Yup. Detox. And then I have to start focusing on his flaws—to think about him as a regular person, and not Garrett," I explain.

She smirks. "That should be easy. Don't get me wrong," she adds quickly, "I'm sorry you're hurting, but, well . . . to be honest, I always thought he was kind of a jerk."

My mouth drops open, and she hurries to explain. "I mean, he always acts like he's so much better than everyone."

"He does not!" I protest.

"Seriously?" She laughs, peeling off another strand of licorice. "Come on. I know he totally looks down on me, just because I don't read all those stuffy books or watch boring foreign films."

"That's not true."

Kayla fixes me with a look.

"Well . . ." I trail off. The truth is, Garrett is kind of dismissive about Kayla—with her blond ponytail and perpetual cheer and the way she always wears school colors on game days. "Suburban" he called her, as if that was the worst kind of insult—doomed to marry by twenty, pop out three kids, and never live more than ten blocks away from her parents.

And I laughed right along with him.

"Don't worry about it." Kayla must have seen my expression, because she smiles, seemingly unconcerned by his-slash-my judgment. "Besides, it can go on the list, right? 'Stuffy and judgmental.'"

"I guess. . . ." Even though it's part of the plan, it still feels disloyal to be talking like this.

"Come on," she encourages me. "Your turn."

"Um . . ." I shift, uncomfortable—and not just because of the splinters sticking into my thighs. "I guess he has this thing where he interrupts a lot. Only because he's so enthusiastic about stuff," I add quickly.

"'Talks over you'!" Kayla cries, then hands me a strip of licorice like a reward. "Next?"

I think. "That beat-up military coat he always wears," I offer, still hesitant.

"Yes!" Kayla agrees. "What's with that? Like he's some Russian general."

I giggle. "And, he shows up late. All the time. I mean, it's not a big deal, but—"

"Sure, it is," Kayla argues. "You can't settle for that stuff. Blake used to do it when we started dating, so I just stopped waiting. If he didn't send me a message or something, I'd leave after fifteen minutes."

I blink. "Wow, that's . . . brave. Weren't you worried he would just stop asking?"

She shrugs. "It would have been his loss. But it worked. He's always on time now, because he knows I won't wait around."

There's a whoop from the middle of the lake, and we look over to where Blake is wrestling TJ for control of an inflatable raft.

"Last one out to the buoy buys Popsicles!" Kayla cries, then suddenly pushes off the dock and slides into the water with a splash.

"No fair!" I cry, and jump in after her. I let out another shriek as the water hits me, sharp and icy cold. "You got a head start!"

We play around in the water, racing to the far side of the lake and then fighting the boys for control of the floats, until our fingertips begin to shrivel.

"We're only letting you win," Blake announces, finally ceding possession of a lurid green raft to Kayla.

"Aww." She leans over the side and kisses him lightly on the lips. "There's room for two!"

He hauls himself aboard, while I try to get comfortable on the inner tube without flashing anything compromising to the guys. But they've already lost interest and are racing back to shore, yelling threats and promises to the girls on the dock about just what—and who—they're going to throw in the lake.

"You good hanging out a while longer?" Kayla calls over, snuggled in the crook of Blake's arm.

"Sure." I nod. "I'm good leaving whenever."

"OK."

I watch them drift gently back toward shore with their hands intertwined. I still feel a flush of shame about what she said earlier. She was calling Garrett the jerk, but I deserved it just the same. Maybe even more, because I was the one who was friends with her, way back when. I can see me and Garrett now: huddled together on the edge of every party, pointing out all the ordinary kids who we were sure would go on to lead such ordinary lives. At the time, it always felt like an affirmation. I wouldn't settle for the easy path; I would be someone extraordinary, no matter how hard that made things right now. But now, looking back, I wonder if we weren't just as bad as the bitches and cliques we made fun of, thinking we were different, above them all.

I paddle aimlessly around the edge of the water for a while, watching dragonflies buzz in the reeds. It's cooler now, and the kids splashing with their water wings have made way for adult swimmers, and dog walkers are skirting the edge of the lake. But by the time I reach the dock again, the girls are packing up, shrugging on sweatshirts and jeans over their swimsuits. "Hey, good timing." Kayla hands me a towel as I pull myself out of the inner tube. "We were thinking about heading out for something to eat."

"My mom went to the store this morning," Suzie offers. "There's, like, a ton of meat we could grill."

"Grill! Grill! Grill!" The guys chant and beat their chests.

"Could you be any more Neanderthal?" Yolanda sighs, fixing her hair up in careful braid.

"I'll be your caveman," TJ says with a wink.

"Animal, more like." She rolls her eyes at me in solidarity. "Anyway, I vote the Burger Shack. Then we don't have to worry about cleaning up."

"Sounds good to me," Suzie says. There's a general chorus of approval.

"What about you, Sadie?" Kayla asks, packing up her stuff. "We can drop you, if you need to be anywhere."

I look around. These aren't my people, and I know I'm just tagging along, but right now, tagging along feels just fine to me. Better than sitting home alone, anyway — trying to ignore the messages from the only other friend in my life.

"I'm good," I decide, smiling at Kayla with genuine enthusiasm. "Count me in."

Don't Go It Alone

This task is way too big for one girl to handle on her own. No matter how humiliating it seems to admit that (a) you're madly in love with a boy who (b) doesn't love you back and (c) has broken your heart so thoroughly that (d) you have to work through a twelve-step program to get over him, be brave.

Why suffer alone when you could share the burden? Friends bring comfort, support, and snack foods for every occasion. And heartbreak goes so much better with cookies.

CHAPTER FOURTEEN

I creep into work Monday morning, unsure if I even have a job to creep to. I didn't get any "You're fired" voice mails over the weekend, so perhaps my prayers were answered, and the Gods of Short-Term Amnesia managed to wipe out all recollections of my last shift.

"Here she comes—guard the china!" LuAnn calls out, laughing, as I slink through the door.

No such luck.

"Um, hi." I look around, nervous. We haven't opened yet, so the place is still empty, aside from Aiko, who is curled up at a corner table, working in her sketchbook with her hood pulled up and the blue tips of her pigtails peeking out. "I wasn't sure if you wanted me to come in, or . . ."

"What are you talking about? Catch!" LuAnn tosses me my apron.

I fumble for it. "Are you sure? Because after Friday . . ."

"Ancient history," LuAnn declares. "Now, give me your phone."

"What?"

"Your phone," she repeats, holding out her hand. Her nails are painted a bright apricot, tipped with green. "Hand it over."

"Your buddy Kayla called," Aiko adds, looking up. "She explained your whole unrequited love thing. Said you needed support."

"So we're going to help," LuAnn finishes with a smile. "I'm on phone duty today, and Aiko will . . . what is it you're doing again?" She looks over.

"Providing artistic inspiration," Aiko says. She turns her sketchbook to show an elaborate sign: GARRETT-FREE ZONE! it says, with a big red X across his name.

I'm overcome with a rush of emotion. After everything I did? "You guys . . ." I feel myself start to tear up. They've only known me a matter of weeks here, and still they want to help out?

Then I'm struck with a sudden insecurity. Maybe Kayla guilt-tripped them into it. Or worse, they feel obligated, like I'm a charity case. "You know, you don't have to," I tell them quickly.

"Sure we do!" LuAnn exclaims, surprisingly enthusiastic. "I love a good project."

"She's right," Aiko agrees. "You'll be doing her a

favor. And us," she adds. "If nothing else, it'll get her off my case."

"Hey!" LuAnn lobs a sugar packet at her. "I've just *suggested,* a couple of times, *in passing,* that you should be selling your art on Etsy, that's all."

"Ha!" Aiko snorts. "Try 'incessantly nagged.'"

LuAnn pivots to face me again. "Anyway, I'm sorry that we didn't take you seriously before," she tells me sincerely. "It wasn't fair to tease you like that."

"Oh," I pause, awkward. "Well, thanks."

"Yay!" She smothers me in a quick hug, then steps back to show she's plucked my phone from my back pocket. "So, starting today, it's a clean slate. We're going to get you through this—for the sake of our jobs as well as your mental health. Friday's takings were . . . let's just say below average."

"I'm really sorry," I say again as she hustles me behind the counter. "I'll make it up to you—I swear."

"We're counting on it, kid."

I'm just tying on my apron when my cell phone begins buzzing loudly in LuAnn's grip. She checks the screen. "It's him!"

I freeze. Aiko bounces over. "What do we do now?" she asks, excited. They huddle over the phone, full of excitement, like . . . well, like *me.* For a moment I forget that they're supposed to be the calm, mature adults in this equation.

"I can decline the call," LuAnn suggests.

"No!" Aiko objects. "Remember, she's trying to be friends with him. Normal."

"Right." LuAnn nods, passing me the phone. "Answer it. But keep it quick!" she adds.

"Breezy," Aiko agrees.

"Like you don't have time to talk right now."

"I don't!" I tell them, rolling my eyes, but inside, I'm captive to a whole host of butterflies. "Hello?" I answer casually.

"Hey, Sadie, what's going on?" Garrett sounds calm—certainly not like he's just spent minutes debating picking up the phone.

"Nothing much," I reply, keeping my voice even. "Work, you know. . . ."

LuAnn and Aiko give me a thumbs-up. I angle away for some privacy, but they just scoot around the counter to stay in my face.

"Put it on speaker!" LuAnn whispers. I roll my eyes, but click SPEAKER so that they can hear everything, too.

"That's cool," Garrett is saying. "Listen, I need some advice. Can you help me out?"

"That depends," I say, trying to sound natural, and not like two overhyped women are hanging on our every word.

Garrett laughs. "It's for Rhiannon, actually. Our anniversary is coming up. This Saturday, it will be two weeks since we met."

LuAnn's mouth drops open. "Is he kidding?" she hisses, and I have to cover the mouthpiece to mask the sound. "Seriously?"

"Shhh!" I order her.

"So I want to do something to celebrate," Garrett continues, oblivious. "Maybe a special picnic or a gift or something, but I don't want to come on too strong. Do you have any ideas?"

I pause. This is when I usually tell him everything that *I* would want. The date of my dreams. But it's clear from Aiko's face that this isn't an option now, she shakes her head so fast her pigtails whip back and forth.

I take a deep breath. "I, um, I think that's something you need to figure out for yourself," I tell him, my voice quivering. "I mean, I don't know her. And . . . this is personal stuff. Between the two of you."

LuAnn holds up her hand and gives me a silent high five.

"Oh, OK." Garrett sounds thrown. "But can't you think of anything? I mean, usually you're so good at this stuff, and—"

"Sorry." I cut him off. "Look, I have to go. I have customers. We'll talk later. Good luck!"

And with that, I hang up.

"Way to go!" LuAnn cheers. Aiko whoops in agreement. I look back and forth between them, suddenly exhilarated.

"I did it!" I exclaim.

"Sure, you did." LuAnn laughs.

"No, you don't understand," I tell them. "I can never say no to him! I want to, but then he begs for help and does this thing with his eyes, and I crumble. I always wind up listening to him go on about his relationships and plans and how much in love he is." I catch my breath. "But this time, I did it. I said no."

Progress. Finally.

"You did great," LuAnn agrees. "That can even be one of your rules or steps or whatever: no relationship talk. He has to find someone else to talk to about girls." She grins. "Look at you, kid. Movin' and shakin'—soon you'll be all growed up. I'm so proud."

"That makes one of us." Dominique emerges from the back room, shooting us an icy look. "I thought she was done here."

"Hush, you," LuAnn scolds her. "One of our brethren needs help. It's our duty to assist!"

Dominique just rolls her eyes. "Don't you mean *sisterhood*?"

LuAnn gasps and presses a hand to her forehead in a mock swoon. "You mean . . . Glory be! You know the meaning of that word!"

"Ugh." Dominique gives us all withering stares and takes up her position behind the register. "Just keep her away from me. I don't want anything spilled on my shirt."

A busload of enthusiastic German tourists keeps us busy for the rest of the morning, leaving us with a sinkful of dirty dishes, zero tips, and a serious shortage of salami.

"I hate it when national stereotypes are true," LuAnn grumbles, clearing the tables with me. "See? Two quarters. Are they kidding me?"

"Maybe they don't realize they're supposed to tip," I argue. She's not impressed.

"Read a guidebook! Twenty percent, baby, all the way."

The door *dings!* and I look up to see Carlos sauntering in. He's wearing scruffy jeans and a Pixies tour shirt, with dark sunglasses and three-day stubble on his face. He doesn't look happy.

"Uh-oh," LuAnn breathes as he slouches over to the counter, takes off the shades, and squints at the bright light. "Don't take any of his crap," LuAnn tells me as she gathers her tray.

"What do you mean?" I feel a flash of panic, but she's already waltzed away, leaving me alone in the glare of Carlos's hungover gaze.

He points at me, then heads to the back office.

I gulp.

I knew it was too much to hope for, that clean slate LuAnn promised. Never mind needing money for that distant dream of a car. I'll never make it without Garrett if I don't have a job—and LuAnn and Aiko—to distract me through the long, lonely days of summer.

I hurry back and find Carlos slumped behind the desk, rubbing his temples.

"I've had some complaints, about Friday. . . ."

"I'm sorry!" I cry, "I really am. It won't happen again."

"I hate it when customers complain," Carlos continues as if he hasn't heard me. He pulls a bottle of aspirin out of the desk drawer and gulps back four of them in one go. At least, I think they're aspirin.

"They call me up, and whine away, and expect me to actually care that you messed up the lattes with the cappuccinos," he grumbles, "or put peanut butter on their PBJ when it gives them a fatal allergic reaction."

"I really am sorry," I apologize again. "Please, just give me a second chance. I promise, I'll be the best employee ever, and—"

"I'm sorry, kid. We're done," he cuts me off, still clutching his head. "I can't deal with the drama. This is why I don't hire teenagers. You're always having some crisis over something."

"Ha!" There's a snort of disapproval behind me, and we both look to see Dominique in the office doorway, arms folded. "Maybe there wouldn't have been a crisis if you hired more staff to cover the shifts."

"This is a private meeting, Dom," Carlos snaps back.

"I'm just saying." She gives a haughty glare. "And maybe if you hadn't forgotten the wholesaler order— again—I wouldn't have had to leave her alone to go get more supplies."

I blink. Dominique ditched out early on her shift that day. She wasn't on some mission for supplies, but I'm not about to argue, especially when Carlos is scowling so ferociously.

"Are you telling me how to run my business?"

Dominique shrugs. "Why not? You clearly need the guidance."

Carlos scrapes back his chair, enraged. "I've had

enough of you ordering me around. Don't forget: you're just a waitress!"

"*Just?*" Dominique's voice goes up a couple of decibels in outrage. "Who here does your taxes, and checks the books, and saves your derrière when your buddy Fitz decides to skim five thousand dollars off the operating budget?"

"He was borrowing it!" Carlos yells back.

I look between them, furiously raging at each other, and decide to make a tactical retreat. "I'll, um, get back to work," I murmur, quickly scurrying past Dominique as she launches into a tally of Carlos's many failings.

"Don't even think I've forgotten about the frozen yogurt incident. *Imbécile!*"

And so instead of being the most humiliating experience of my entire life (OK, as well as), my oh-so-public meltdown actually turns out to be a meager token from the Gods of Fresh Starts. Because suddenly, I'm not alone in this anymore. Instead of being scornful, they actually want to help. I can't believe it. Even Dominique comes around (when she's done laughing all over again at my plight), probably to spite Carlos, or at the prospect of pulling out her military dictator act in the guise of a good cause.

Dominique. Helping.

I know.

"Repeat after me: I don't need a guy to feel good about myself." LuAnn prods me with a pair of serving tongs. Barely a week has passed since I came clean to them all, but already she's settled in to her role as tutor-slash-slave-driver extraordinaire, determined to rid me of my love for good.

"LuAnn!" I protest. "I'm not out obsessing over every guy I meet. This is about Garrett."

"Repeat it!" she orders, prodding me harder. "I'm serious, kid. You need to say it until you believe it. Fake it till you make it."

I sigh. Arguing will only prolong the fight. "I don't need a guy to feel good about myself," I parrot obediently. "There, happy? Now, can I get my phone back?

"Ask Dom." LuAnn shrugs. "She's the communications keeper."

This strategy—holding my phone hostage, except for brief visitation rights on my breaks—is designed to keep me from another crawling-on-the-floor incident.

I scoot around the counter to where Dominique is sitting at a back table, freshening her manicure before her shift starts. "Phone?" I ask. "Pretty please?"

She doesn't look up. "You've still got another half hour."

"But I promised I'd call my dad," I say. "I'm taking the afternoon off to meet him in the city, remember?"

"You know the rules." Entirely unimpressed, she blows on a freshly painted nail. "And you're the one who asked me to keep it away from you."

I sigh. She's right—we picked Dominique for this because we knew she'd never let me slip. LuAnn is the voice of reason, Kayla my cheerleader, and Dominique?

She's the hard-ass, and thus perfect for minding my cell phone, letting me have it only for approved callers and rationed texts to Garrett. But right now, her hard-assedness is the last thing I need, when I have a legitimate reason for needing that phone.

"Come on, Dom."

She glares.

"Dominique," I correct myself quickly. "He needs to know which bus I'm taking." Right on cue, my cell begins to ring. She starts painting the other hand.

"Just look at the caller ID!" I tell her, "It's not Garrett, I swear."

With infinite slowness, Dominique plucks my phone from her purse and checks the screen. "Fine," she says, rolling her eyes. "You can take it. But no cheating!"

I take it eagerly. "Hey, Dad."

"Hey, pumpkin, what's going on?"

"Nothing much, just work." I drift toward the back hallway, away from the chatter at the front of the café. "I'm just leaving. I'll be on the eleven o'clock bus. We get in about two—"

"Here's the thing," he interrupts. "They canceled our shows here, so we're heading up to Montreal for a last-minute booking."

I stop. "Canada?"

"I know—it's crazy." He laughs. "I really wanted to see you, but we have to drive through the night to make it tomorrow. I'm sorry," he says, "but we'll do something when I get back—I promise."

"Oh." I recover. "Sure, that's fine."

"OK, I've got to run. They're loading up the van. I'll call you later, OK? Love you!"

"Love you," I repeat dully, hanging up.

I stay there in the narrow space, trying not to feel that familiar wave of disappointment. He does this too often, changing plans on a whim, and although I thought I was too old to feel let down by him again, I can't help the tightness in my throat and the flashbacks to being twelve, thirteen, fourteen: waiting on the couch at home for him to come pick me up, invariably an hour late.

"What's up?"

I blink. Josh has paused from salad assembly and is watching me through the open kitchen door, his hair looping out from under his baseball cap in lazy curls.

"It's nothing." I force a smile. "Just, I was going to go to Boston to see my dad. But he can't make it." I shrug, nonchalant. "I guess that means I can take my shift after all."

"What's this about Boston?" LuAnn bounces beside me, a riot of patterns in a floral tea dress and striped cardigan. "Are you going to meet Garrett? Sadie, you know that's forbidden. *Verboten! Prohibido!*"

"*Interdite,*" Dominique adds, coming up behind her.

"No!" I yelp, cornered. "It has nothing to do with Garrett. And I'm not even going. I was going to see Jonny Pardue with my dad, but he can't make it."

"Jonny's playing?" Josh asks, looking over with interest. "I saw him last year. He's pretty great live."

"I know." I sigh. "I guess I'll catch him on his next tour."

"No need!" LuAnn exclaims. "Let's."

"What?"

"Go see him." She grins. "I could use a break from this town. Ooh, road trip!" she sings out in glee. Dominique turns to make a hasty retreat. "Not so fast, missy." LuAnn grabs her arm. "You can come, too!"

"I think not," Dominique replies, looking mildly disturbed at the thought. "Besides, somebody has to cover if you all take off on some idiotic trip."

"True." LuAnn releases her. "Thanks for offering. You're the best!" She makes as if to hug her, but Dominique has learned from her mistakes and backs away, disappearing into the café in a flash of crisp cotton.

"Look, you don't have to." I try to calm LuAnn before she gets carried away on her usual tide of enthusiasm. "It's fine. I can go in another time . . . and if I'm not seeing dad . . . well, there's not much point."

"Sure there is: shopping!" She clasps her hands together. "My wardrobe is crying out for new stuff. This is perfect. Josh?" LuAnn turns to him, batting her eyes. "Wanna tag along?"

"Come on." He groans. "Shopping?"

LuAnn sighs. "And music, and food, and other manly things. You don't have to stick with us all day. Go look at the harbor or something while we do the girly stuff. Pretty please?"

He pauses, thinking. "I guess I could walk the Freedom Trail again or tour Fenway Park—"

"Perfect!" LuAnn leans through the window and gives him a loud kiss on the cheek. "Sadie, want to call what's-her-name? Kaylie?"

"Kayla," I say, still thrown. "Um, sure. But—"

"No buts!" she demands. "Well, except Josh's, and that's only because he's so cute." She blows him a kiss. He mimes catching it. "Come on." LuAnn shoos me out of the hallway. "I'll get music, you grab some snacks for the road. This is going to be the best!"

STEP 4:

Redraw the Line

Sure, you want to stay friends with **him,** but friends don't have to listen to every excruciating detail about his new True Love—not when it leaves you a broken, miserable mess on the floor. Set new boundaries for your friendship: nice, solid walls that keep out all news of romance and breakup angst. With a shark-infested moat. And guard dogs. Killer guard dogs.

You may feel guilty, as though you're being a bad friend. But this is your heart you're protecting here. It's worth feeling "unsupportive" to keep you off that miserable floor.

CHAPTER FIFTEEN

Kayla is working all day and can't make it, but Aiko jumps at the chance to get out of town for the day, and a couple of hours later, the four of us are packed into Aiko's car, winding our way through Boston's downtown traffic, gleaming office blocks towering above turn-of-the-century churches and old brownstone buildings. I look happily out the windows, absorbing the buzz and rush of life on the busy sidewalks. I always love this first swoop into the city, when you're hit by the rush of energy and confusion: a million people racing along in their own worlds, all in a few square miles. One day, I'm going to be a part of these crowds—here or someplace else—striding along with their certainty, living some extraordinary kind of life. . . .

"Julian Casablancas," Aiko muses from the front seat. She has cherry-red plastic sunglasses on and her hair braided into pigtails. "Several times. Then marry Jack White; kill Sufjan Stevens."

"Really?" LuAnn's voice is outraged, as if these are serious life choices Aiko is debating, instead of a fantasy FMK league. "I can't stand that whole New York hipster art thing. Kill Julian, have a wild night of passion with Jack, then spend the rest of my days baking and knitting things with Sufjan." She breaks off a chunk of scone from the snack bag and chews, happily contemplating her craft-filled future.

"What about you, Josh?"

"No comment."

"Come on!" LuAnn protests. "If you had to, if someone lined up your family with a gun to their heads and demanded you pick."

He sighs. "Fine. Kill Sufjan. I dated a girl once who kept playing his stuff—it drove me crazy. Then flip a coin for the other two. Happy now?"

"Ecstatic." She grins. "Ooh, turn left, just up ahead." LuAnn leans forward from the backseat. "There are some fun vintage shops on Newbury Street."

Aiko follows her directions, then pulls over to the side of the street. "Sure you don't want to come?" I ask Josh as we collect our purses and jackets and pile out.

He laughs. "Trail you guys around dressing rooms all day? No, thanks. I'll meet you later, for the show."

"OK!" LuAnn slams the car door. "Call us whenever you're done being such a history nerd."

"Geek," Josh corrects her. "Get it right. We take pride in our geekdom."

"Sure, you do." LuAnn laughs. "I bet you have T-shirts and everything!"

LuAnn and Aiko wave him off, jumping up and down and blowing kisses like they're sending him off to fight in a war, and not just visit old battle sites. "Right." LuAnn turns back to us, her whole face lit up in anticipation. "Let the wild rumpus start!"

"Somehow, I don't think this what Maurice Sendak had in mind," I say later that afternoon, watching LuAnn pull items from the display racks with a whirlwind mix of joy and efficiency. Aiko left us for the record store long ago, and now we're in yet another vintage place, this one a tiny cave of gleaming curios, velvet drapes, and racks packed with outlandish outfits.

"To each her own." LuAnn gives me a mischievous grin. "And my own is definitely this."

I laugh. "Why don't you try going back to fashion school or something? I mean, it seems like it's your true calling."

"What are you talking about?" she asks, a touch sarcastic. "I knew even as a little girl, I wanted to serve coffee for the rest of my life."

I remember what she told me about following some guy to Sherman. It seems weird, that someone so self-possessed and secure would mold herself around a guy like that.

She holds up a swingy red dress. "What do you think?"

"Cute." I browse idly, but there's nothing much in the

store for me. All this quirky vintage stuff, with its bright colors and patterns, is made for the other cool, artsy girls digging through bins of fedoras and trying on '50s-style circle skirts. I watch them, curious: a foreign tribe with their wing-tipped eyeliner and oceans of self-confidence.

"What size are you?" LuAnn eyeballs me, then checks the label in the dress. "This should fit. Here, try it. Ooh, and these too." She plucks a matador's blouse and pencil skirt from a heap nearby and holds them out to me.

I shake my head vigorously. "No, I'm good."

"But they'll look great on you!"

"No," I say again, shoving my hands in my pockets so she can't fill them. "Thanks, but it's just not my style."

"So, what is?" LuAnn pauses. "This *normal* thing you've got going on? No offense, kid, but it doesn't say anything about who you are."

"Maybe that's the point." I shrug, getting defensive. I know my style has always been pretty, well, understated, but it suits me just fine. "Maybe I don't want to play dress-up just to stand out in the crowd."

"Okaay," LuAnn backs off. "Have it your way. Be boring." She grins, as if to tell me she's only kidding. "But I still think you'd look fabulous with a whole prewar look going on, lashings of red lipstick and pin-curled hair."

"Right," I reply dryly. "Well, you'll just have to do it up for the both of us."

Arms laden with bags—all of them LuAnn's—we head to meet Aiko in the record store. It's full of older, bearded men and younger guys in Sonic Youth T-shirts and horn-rimmed glasses, but we find her in the back, flipping through old vinyl and humming along to The Smiths.

She takes in the sight of LuAnn's bounty and laughs. "Wow, you guys really went to town."

"It's all mine." LuAnn drops her load on the ground and I follow suit, creating a great heap of packages that still somehow came to less than a hundred bucks. "I did my best, but she wouldn't let me try a thing."

"Smart girl." Aiko applauds me. "I gave in once, and she had me dolled up like a mod girl from 1962."

"And she looked amazing," LuAnn adds before turning her attention to a bargain bin of battered old CDs.

"So, you like The Smiths?" I ask Aiko. The cases hit each other with a rhythmic clacking sound as I methodically flip through the stands.

"Hate them," she replies cheerfully. "Overwrought pretension for teenage boys who think that just because they're old and British, it makes up for all that emo self-indulgence."

"But this album is a classic!" I protest, shocked.

"And?" She shrugs, seemingly unconcerned by the musical sacrilege she's just committed. Aiko sees my expression and laughs. "Just because people say something's great, it doesn't mean you have to agree, not if you don't actually enjoy it."

"Well, it's not that I *enjoy* them," I admit, because seriously, those aren't the most uplifting songs in the world. "But still, there are some things you should listen to. You know, like reading great literature or watching classic films. You just should."

"Why?" LuAnn looks up.

"Because!" I splutter. The question of why has never come into it for me, but now I scramble for an answer. "Even if you don't like them, they're still important."

"Says who?"

"People!"

LuAnn laughs. "Easy there, kid. I'm not saying you can't be into that stuff if you genuinely like it. I just mean, your argument kind of dooms us to spend all this time on books and movies and music that we don't actually like."

"She's right," Aiko adds, her arms full of vinyl selections. "What was that book you were talking to me about the other day? That Russian one you've been reading forever."

"*Crime and Punishment.*" I gape at them. "You can't tell me that's not a great book."

"Great with a capital *G* great?" Aiko asks, head tilted to watch me. "Or great because you found it moving, and inspiring, and it made your life better somehow?"

I don't answer for a moment. Sure, Dostoyevsky is no picnic, but he's not supposed to be! And yes, I spent the better part of a year trying and failing and trying again to finish that lump of a book because it was so unbearably dense and depressing, but that's not the point.

"Isn't Garrett the one who introduced you to this stuff?" LuAnn asks meaningfully, before I can answer. "Maybe you just think it's great because he said it was?"

I tense. "So, you're saying I'm just some sheep, doing everything he says? Gee, thanks."

"Sadie," Aiko says, trying to placate me, "we're just trying to help."

"How is this helping, to say I'm some pathetic girl with no mind of my own?"

"You know that's not what we mean." LuAnn puts down her CDs. "But it sounds like this guy has been the center of your entire universe for way too long. Believe me, I've been there! That's why I just want you to think about it." She looks at me dead-on. "How much of your life do you choose because it's what *he* likes?"

I snap. The pity in her expression is too much to take. "I'm not one of those girls who gives up everything for a guy," I tell them, my voice rising. "I'm not! And just because you threw away your life on someone and it didn't work out, it doesn't mean I'm doing the same thing!"

Silence. LuAnn's face tightens, and right away I feel a wash of guilt—but not enough to take it back or apologize. Not after what she said.

For a moment, nobody moves. A boy in skinny jeans and a plaid shirt edges past us to reach the vinyl. Up at the front counter, a trio of tweens in brightly colored vests demands the latest album by Justin or Jason or Jared.

"OK," Aiko says, looking back and forth between us. "Time out. Let's go get some ice cream and calm down."

Neither of us replies.

"Gelato?" she tries. "Fro-yo?"

"No, thanks," I answer shortly. I hoist my bag onto

my shoulder. "Look, I'm just going to take a walk, get some air. I'll meet back with you guys later."

"Sadie—"

I hear Aiko call after me, but I'm already striding away. I push past the giggling tweens and out onto the street, not once looking back.

STEP 5:

Brand-New Old You

Admit it: you've been shopping for **him** all this time—hunting the sales racks in the secret hope that yes, *this* low-cut shirt is the one to make him see you in a whole new nonplatonic light, *those* skinny jeans will spur a blinding epiphany, and *this* raspberry lip gloss will finally make him fall hopelessly in love with you.

Forget raspberry gloss. You like plain lip-balm better. And forget low-cut shirts and skinny jeans, too. Forget everything you wouldn't choose without his opinion in the back of your mind. When you look in the mirror, what do you want to see: yet another reminder of your hopeless attempt to be the girl of his dreams, or you?

The answer should always be you.

CHAPTER SIXTEEN

How dare they?

My sneakers hit the ground with angry purpose as I cut through lazy shoppers and the crowds of tourists with their backpacks on and cameras looped around their necks. How could LuAnn say that stuff—look at me like I was just a pathetic girl, repeating everything a boy told me? She's the one who sacrificed everything to trail some guy across the country; my friendship with Garrett is nothing like that! He cares about me, we're on the same wavelength. That's why we even became friends in the first place!

I walk and walk, the city blocks disappearing behind me as that burn of indignation in my chest drives me on. I've always looked down on those girls in school. You know the ones: they start dating a skater guy, and suddenly they're scribbling skate-punk lyrics all over their notebooks. And then they break up, and they become someone else entirely—waiting on the sidelines during football practice or trailing the emo rock guys to every crappy show in someone's basement. I could never understand it, don't they have any self-esteem at all? Their entire identity revolves around some guy who probably never even considers changing anything about himself for her.

And now LuAnn is saying I'm just the same, as if I have no independent thoughts or opinions. Of course I do! So, yes, my tastes overlap with Garrett's, and I like most of the same things as him, but that's not the same at all. I like our music, and movies, and books because, well, I like them—not *just* because he's the one who introduced me to them.

I leave the busy stores and sidewalks behind, running out of steam as I reach a wide-open square, skyscrapers looming above neat areas of grass and trees. I stop by the edge of a fountain and sink onto the wide marble edge. Kids with their cuffs rolled up are playing in the shallow water. They look so carefree and happy that I kick my shoes off, swing my feet over the edge, and sink my toes into the clear, cold water.

There.

Now that my initial rage is dissolving, I remember the hurt look on LuAnn's face and feel a flush of shame, hot on my cheeks. She opened up, telling me about her past, and what do I do? Throw it right back in her face, when all she was even trying to do was make sure I didn't make the same mistakes. I splash my feet, watching the way the sun glints and glitters on the water. I was such a brat, to her and Aiko, too. And they've been so nice to me! Taking me under their wing, treating me like an actual friend with support and guidance, instead of just leaving me to battle my Garrett problem alone.

Garrett . . .

I let out a long, weary sigh. The truth is, he *is* the one who brought a lot of this stuff into my life. OK, most of it. The books I read, the movies I watch—even most of my music first found its way onto my iPod via Garrett's mix CDs and playlists. And I love it—that he opens this whole new world up to me, showing me all these new writers and artists and songs that I'd never stumble across on my own. It always makes me feel so special when he collapses into the seat next to me and starts telling me about this amazing new novel he's reading, and how he'll lend it to me when he's done. I read those dog-eared copies cover to cover, savoring the notes he's penciled in the margins, knowing he made them just for me.

But what about the stuff *I* like, without him?

The question niggles at me, but I try to block it out, pulling my sandals on over damp feet and heading back into the busy pedestrian throngs. I'm not those girls, I tell myself firmly, striding onwards. I'm not that weak.

I pause at a crosswalk, watching the street vendors set up on the corner, selling jewelry and handcrafted mobiles from tiny kiosks. And then I catch sight of my reflection in one of their mirrors, hanging lopsided from the side of a cart of Red Sox memorabilia.

Dyed black hair forced into a short, angled bob and ironed straight. Blunt-cut bangs. Regular jeans, a faded T-shirt. I'm carrying a beat-up leather satchel and wearing an arm of bangle bracelets.

I stare carefully, as if looking at a stranger.

And maybe I am one. I started wearing my hair this way because of Garrett, because I wanted to look like the exotic French movie stars he always seemed to rave about. I bought this satchel because Garrett has one just like it. The simple, nondescript clothes . . . Well, Garrett always seems to mock the girls who dress retro or outlandishly. He laughs about how they're trying to make up for their lack of personality: dressing up to pretend to be themselves. Real creative types don't care about their clothes, he would tell me. They have their minds on other, more important things. And so, I never looked beyond my standby jeans, shirts, and sweaters, not wanting him to think I was one of those desperate types.

I blink, the truth finally dawning. I *am* one of those girls. God, I'm practically the *queen* of those girls. Just look at me!

The light finally turns red, and the people around me hustle forward. I stumble on, still in a daze. *What about the music you loaned him, but he said wasn't his thing?* a voice whispers in the back of my mind. I stopped playing those bands when he came over, took them off my playlists in the end. *And why don't you read your mom's bodice-ripper romance novels like you used to? Is it because Garrett saw a stack of them in the living room once and laughed about the trash that passes as literature these days?*

I wanted so badly for him to think we were the same: cultured minds, people who know great art and appreciate the classics. I could drink espresso, read Franzen and Flaubert, and debate long into the night with him about the themes of obsession and sexuality in *Lolita*. But now when I think back to all that time we spent together, I only hear Aiko asking if I even liked any of it or if I just wanted to be the kind of person who did.

This whole recovery program thing started out as a survival tactic—for me to learn how to get by without him, to go about my regular life despite the massive Garrett-shaped hole in my existence. But now I wonder if that isn't far enough. What if I have no regular life apart from the one I constructed around him? What if the very fabric of me, Sadie Elisabeth Allen, has been molded and shaped so much by who *he* is that I'm like the plants Mom grows in tubs on the back porch: you plant them next to a taller, stronger structure and they adapt around it, snaking their whole body around the frame until they have no shape of their own, just the outline of something else?

I gulp. I want shape! I need an outline! And just like that, it becomes painfully clear that my simple steps for getting over Garrett don't go nearly far enough. It's one thing to survive once he's gone, but now I need to go further. Much further.

I need to find out who I am without him.

.   .   .

I walk the city streets in a daze a while longer, as those big questions roll around my mind. Finally, Aiko texts to let me know they're at a café nearby. I go to meet them, finding them tucked in a back booth in a dark dive of a place, LuAnn sipping a cream soda and Aiko attacking a mountain of pie.

"I'm sorry," I tell them quickly before either can speak. "I was a total brat, and mean, and cruel, and I didn't mean any of it."

Aiko smirks. "That's a pretty comprehensive apology."

"Well, I was a pretty comprehensive bitch." I offer up an apologetic smile, but LuAnn is still stony-faced. "I really am sorry," I tell her, desperate. "You were right, what you said, but I just didn't want to hear it. It's kind of hard to admit your entire life is based on a guy."

I stand there, anxiously awaiting my fate. I didn't realize it before—how much their friendship means to me—but now that I might have screwed it up for good, I see just how great they've been. How much fun I've been having, just hanging out. My voice catches in my throat as I think of losing them. "Forgive me?"

LuAnn just lets out a long breath, then nods.

"OK," she says quietly. She scoots over in the booth to make room for me.

"Come on," Aiko adds, her mouth full. "Help me out with this pie. I can't eat all of this alone."

"Sure, you can." LuAnn laughs at her. "Remember Thanksgiving?"

Aiko groans. "Don't! I dreamed about pumpkins for

weeks after that. And evil little yams, dancing all over my room."

I take a fork. "Did you buy any other stuff?"

"Some," LuAnn answers, managing a glimmer of a smile. "But I hit my spending limit an hour ago, so the city can breathe easy for a while."

"Maybe not," I say. She raises an eyebrow. I take a breath, as if preparing myself for battle. And, in a way, I am. "Could you offer your expertise for a good cause?"

She looks at me carefully. "Depends what for."

"Me," I tell her firmly. "I want to try that haircut. And some new clothes—and anything else we see. It's time I figure out who Sadie really is."

I try vintage dresses and modern hipster looks, preppy pullovers and '60s-style pencil skirts. Wedges and boots, scarves and bangles, lipstick in a dozen shades, and more types of denim than I even knew existed. Nothing is rejected; no style is judged too extreme. If I'm going to find out what I like outside my Garrett-shaped bubble of a world, then I have to try everything for myself. And I mean, *everything*. I feel like Columbus setting out for the New World, braving new territories with nothing but a compass and a collapsible telescope. Only instead of discovering foreign lands, I'm navigating a treacherous sea of mirrors and shiny hair appliances, thanks to the tiny salon LuAnn swears is the best in the city.

"And maybe then some soft waves, just around here. What do you say?" Derek, my stylist, asks but before I can even open my mouth, LuAnn jumps in.

"Yes, absolutely. And maybe some color?"

"Streaks. Pink!" Aiko demands, swiveling in a chair to my right.

"No pink," I tell them, panicked. My reflection stares back at me: wet haired and swathed in blue towels. I begin to have second thoughts. "And are we sure about this?" I venture. "Maybe a haircut is going too far right now. I don't know if—"

"Trust me, kid," LuAnn interrupts with a reassuring smile, but for a terrible moment I wonder if this is all just elaborate revenge for our fight earlier. Lull me into a false sense of security with the wardrobe, then scar me for life—well, a few months—with a disaster of a haircut.

I gulp.

"Think about it," Aiko says, pausing to blow a bubble with her gum. She waits for it to pop before continuing. "A whole fresh start. You'll look in the mirror every morning and know you did this for you, not him."

"But that isn't exactly true." I try one last excuse. "I mean, I am here because of Garrett, kind of, even if it's in reverse. So really—"

"Enough!" LuAnn spins my chair back around. "No more excuses. And honestly, kid? This Amélie look is so two thousand and five."

"She's right." Derek meets my eyes in the mirror and gives me a reassuring wink. Well, it *would* be reassuring if his own hair wasn't styled in a towering purple Mohawk. "You'll be fine—I promise."

.   .   .

Two hours (and a headful of goopy paste that stung so hard I cried a little) later, I emerge from the salon: new, and — I hope — improved.

"Love it!" LuAnn declares, clapping.

"Really?" I reach up and touch it gently, still not used to the soft waves and general bounce of the whole thing. I'm used to battling it for half an hour with a blow-dryer and a straightening iron, but with some magical serum from Derek's cupboard of wonders, the frizz is miraculously tamed. Throw in the lighter brown dye that caused me such pain, and I feel . . .

Different.

"Different bad or different good?" Aiko asks as we walk to meet Josh at the gig venue.

"I don't know. . . ." I bite my lip. They insisted I change into that red vintage dress, too, and now every time I catch my reflection in a store window, I have to do a double take. "It's just . . . so not like me. The me I've been, I mean."

"You'll get used to it," LuAnn tells me breezily. But then again, she would be breezy; she's the one who wears denim farm-girl overalls on regular workdays and manages to look cute and quirky in them, instead of deranged. "There's a whole world of fashion possibilities out there! You're just getting started."

"Uh-huh," I murmur. Now that I've gone ahead with this whole makeover idea, I'm beginning to have second thoughts. Old Sadie may have been predictable and understated and, sure, kind of on the conservative side of things, but I knew her! I knew I could roll out of bed in the morning, grab my jeans and a shirt, and be done. Dressing: achieved! And now to just cast that off and set myself loose in the dangerous jungle of original style, where fashion faux pas lurk at every turn?

"Calm down. You look like you're having a panic attack." Aiko giggles. "This isn't like you're trying to be someone else. It's about finding out what fits you. You!"

Me.

I take a short breath. They're right—I was comfortable with my old look, but the reminder of how much I molded myself around Garrett snaps me back to reality. Enough with the exploration metaphors; it's time to just relax and see how I feel in this new skin.

Besides, if I don't like this look, I can always try a new one.

"There he is, the nerd himself!" LuAnn calls ahead. Josh is just up the street, feeding quarters into the meter. "Sorry," she adds cheerily, greeting him with a kiss on the cheek. "I meant geek."

"How'd it go?" He takes a look at our armfuls of bags and then laughs. "Wait, don't answer that."

"This? Ha. It was a slow day." LuAnn starts piling things onto the backseat.

"You kept up with them? I'm impressed," Josh tells me as I pass over my own bags. I shrug, suddenly self-conscious.

"How was the harbor, or wherever you went?" I ask, too aware of his eyes flicking over me. But despite the fact that I started the day a gawky girl with overgrown bangs and came back looking completely different, he doesn't seemed surprised, just . . . curious.

"Fun." Josh breaks into a smile, waiting until all of our bags are unloaded before locking up again. "I walked the whole city."

"Great." We start to head up the street to the venue, where a line is already snaking back from the doors. "Well, great for you," I correct myself. "I think I was better with the shopping."

He laughs. "To each his own."

"Josh!" Aiko suddenly elbows him. "You haven't said anything about Sadie's new look!"

"Ooh, yes. Tell us what you think," LuAnn insists. "Gorgeous or what?"

"Guys!" I protest, flushing. "Stop it." I turn to him quickly. "You really don't have to answer that."

"Yes, he does!" LuAnn nudges him from the other side, joining Aiko in an elbow onslaught until Josh is bent double, laughing.

"OK, OK." He pulls away from them. "It's, uh, nice."

Nice? I blink. Is that a good thing?

"Nice? *Nice?*" LuAnn screeches. "Boy, you need help. Sadie is a work of art. A vision. A dream!"

"LuAnn." I blush, pained. "Please . . . ?"

She must see the embarrassment on my face, because she stops her theatrics. "Oh, fine." She sighs. "He's a boy, 'nice' is like a soliloquy from them. We're lucky he didn't just grunt."

The doors finally open, and the line begins to inch forward. "You ready?" Aiko asks me, rolling up her sleeve in preparation for the underage wristband. I pause. If I was with my dad, we would already be inside by now: me camped out on a prime stool at the bar with a lemonade while he trades touring war stories with roadies and bouncers he knows from way back when. But even though I'll probably spend the gig crushed up with everyone else on the main floor, getting my toes trampled by some overenthusiastic frat boys from Vermont, I'm actually more excited than ever. I'm in the city for a show with my new friends, and if that sounds simple to you, then you clearly have a way more exciting high-school life than I do.

I grin, giving my head a tiny shake to feel the curls flutter against my face. Suddenly the dress doesn't feel so foreign; the armful of cool carved bangles I picked out feels just perfect. It's different, sure, but as I'm finally starting to see, different can be good.

"Ready!"

STEP 6:

The Clear-Out

It's time to get ruthless. Living in a shrine to your failed non-relationship isn't helping with this whole moving on thing, so something's got to give. And that something is every photo, every gift he gave you, and every crappy mix CD he made full of depressing British indie bands from the 1980s.

Get thee gone.

Keep a couple of mementos, sure, for when you're way older and wiser—like, in college—and can laugh about the time you wasted on him. But for now, that crap needs to be stuffed in a shoe box on the very back shelf of your closet—out of sight and even further out of mind.

CHAPTER SEVENTEEN

"One copy of The Smiths' *Meat Is Murder*?"

"Donate."

"A program from the Sherman Amateur Dramatic Society production of *Brigadoon*?"

"Trash."

"The collected poems of Rainer Maria Rilke?"

"Keep!"

Kayla pauses rifling through the great piles of my possessions littering my bedroom floor. Like me, her hair is tied back and she's wearing her oldest jeans; unlike me, she's armed with a garbage bag and a look of steely determination. "Sadie . . ." she warns, her tone exasperated.

"I like Rilke!" I protest. " 'Live the questions now,' " I quote. "See? It has nothing to do with Garrett."

Kayla flips the book open and reads the inscription. "'Sadie, Happy Hanukkah. Love, Garrett.'"

I snatch it away from her. "So he likes Rilke, too. I am allowed to keep *some* stuff!"

"You said you needed my help," Kayla cries. "Total Garrett detoxification. But we're not even halfway through your library, and you keep wanting to save things."

"But look at everything I'm donating." I point to the not-at-all-insubstantial stack of books, movies, and CDs that I've decided to purge from my life. Sure, my mom reorganized the place just six weeks ago, but that was merely a surface job. This? This is an archaeological excavation we're on here; delving through the sands of time and/or my hoarding habit to find every Garrett-related artifact and purge it from my life. Everything I have only because of Garrett goes, that's the rule. No exceptions, no excuses. It's time I figure out what *I* like for myself.

At least, that's the theory. But watching Kayla toss aside my precious memories with such casual disregard is too much for my sentimental heart to take. "Not that!" I yelp as she grabs a handful of faded old flyers from my dresser.

"This?" Kayla holds up a crumpled blue sheet of paper. "'Library sale, Wednesday, 2 p.m.' Wow." She laughs, "I can see why you want the reminder . . . from two years ago."

"It was the first time Garrett and I hung out." I take it from her and smooth out the paper, remembering how nervous and excited I'd been. Meeting him by accident was one thing, but the first real, live plans we made? That was momentous. "It stays."

Kayla sighs. "OK, let me see it." I pass it back to her, but she doesn't pause for a split second before announcing "Nope!" and ripping the flyer in two.

I let out another yelp. She rips the pieces again. I whimper.

"Sadie!" She laughs. "Get a grip. These are just things, remember?"

"They're memories." I look around, feeling a pang. "And once he's gone, they're all I'll have left of him. Don't you keep things from Blake, to remember all the time you've spent together?"

Kayla shakes her head. "Not like this. Photos are memories. Special gifts are memories. A room full of junk is just a creepy stalker shrine."

"I'm not creepy!" I object. She doesn't reply, just holds up an old shirt of Garrett's I "borrowed" six months ago and conveniently forgot to return.

"When was the last time you washed this?"

"Um, never?" I reply in a small voice. "I didn't want to lose the scent of him!"

"Just listen to yourself." Kayla shakes her head in despair. "Personal hygiene isn't negotiable!"

I blink.

"You're right," I say in shock. "What have I become?"

And just like that, I see the clutter for what it really is: sad, pathetic hoarding, a testament to my powers of denial and self-delusion. But no more.

"Trash it!" I say, a new surge of energy coursing through my veins. "Trash everything!"

"Yes, ma'am!" Kayla grins as I tear into the stack of stuff anew. All those dreary indie bands that Garrett loves so? Gone! The endless parade of books about twenty-something men having identity crises in Brooklyn? Out of here! My shelf of snooty foreign films about existentialism and the constant betrayal of death? *¡Adiós, amigos!*

Soon, the garbage bags are filled to overflowing and everything useful is packed up and ready to take to Goodwill. "Somewhere, a pretentious teenage boy is about to get very lucky," I joke, hauling the last box to the doorway.

"Wow." Kayla exhales, sinking onto the bed. "It's like a blank canvas. You can be whoever you want now."

I sit next to her, taking in the spaces on my shelves and the white gaps on my walls where my set of Criterion Collection movie posters used to hang. She's right—it is kind of . . . freeing, to be rid of it all. I'm liberated from reminders of that pining, angst-ridden past: no signs of Garrett hanging around, waiting to fill me with indecision and second thoughts. Now I just have a few boxes of photos and gifts stored away, safely out of sight in the top of my wardrobe.

But how empty the room looks is heartbreaking in a whole different way.

"Was I really this pathetic?" I ask quietly.

Kayla turns to me in surprise. "What do you mean?"

"Beth said once that it was obvious how much I loved

him, that I trailed around like some kind of puppy." I gulp, anxious. "Is that what everyone thought?"

"No!" Kayla gives me a hug. "I mean, we knew you were superclose. It just seemed like . . . you were in your own world together—that's all."

"Really? Because I want to know if it was a running joke or something."

"I swear." Kayla squeezes my shoulder. "To tell the truth, some girls were kind of jealous of you. Garrett's up there on the school hot list."

"He is?"

"No idea why." She laughs.

"Yeah, yeah, pretentious jerk, I know." I manage a smile. "But he wasn't, not to me. He still isn't," I add. "But I just can't believe I ended up like this."

"Like what?"

"Like my entire world revolved around him. I didn't even realize—that's the crazy thing," I tell her. "All this time, I've been walking around thinking I'm some strong, independent girl who would never lose her head over a boy. And it turns out, I'm nothing but a Garrett clone."

"You're not!" Kayla protests, grinning. "You have way better hair."

I laugh, despite myself.

"It's OK," she tells me. "We all go crazy for a guy sometimes. And then we date him, figure out he's not this perfect mythical god, and get over it. Maybe that was your thing," she suggests. "You never got together with him, so he stayed up on the Perfect Boyfriend pedestal."

"Maybe." I look around. "Anyway, come on. Let's get this stuff into the garage."

Kayla pulls me to my feet. "You know what the best thing is about this clear-out?" she asks, hoisting two bags of trash down the hall.

I struggle under the weight of the boxes. "I don't have to go to sleep with Vladimir Nabokov staring down at me?"

"Sure, that, but also you'll be able to bring guys back here now."

"Guys?" I laugh, following her downstairs. "What guys? Aside from Garrett, the only man ever to step foot in my room was there to fix the heat."

Kayla grins. "Exactly! But that's all going to change. And when you do bring a guy up to, ahem, *pretend* to watch a movie, he won't take one look around and run."

"OK, now you're just exaggerating."

"Trust me on this, Sadie. Obsession is not cute in a date, especially if they're obsessed with someone else." Kayla dumps her bags in the garage. "It's like those girls who collect dolls or have a wall full of kitten posters. *You* might want to look up at adorable bundles of fluff every night, but just think how it looks to someone else. You know Lizzie Jordan, right?"

I shake my head.

"Junior, blondish, student council?'

I shake my head again.

"Sadie!" Kayla sighs as we head back into the kitchen. "You're oblivious. Anyway, she was dating Chris

Leeds last year. They'd hung out a little, nothing serious. He goes over there to "study," walks into her room, and finds pictures of her ex everywhere. Like, everywhere! He dumped her like that." She snaps her fingers. "Now everyone thinks she's a psycho bunny boiler." She goes to the fridge and pulls out a jug of lemonade.

"Charming."

"But true." Kayla shrugs. "Anyway, don't worry, we've saved you from that fate."

"For which I'll always be grateful." I laugh. "No, seriously, thanks for helping out with this. I know it's not the ideal way to spend your Saturday."

"No problem." She shrugs again. "These days, if it doesn't include an army of evil brats, I'm in."

"Didn't you have plans with Blake?"

She shakes her head, following me out into the backyard with the drinks. "He's with his family on some trip to Philadelphia this weekend."

"Oh, that sucks." I head for our usual spot under the far tree—sunny enough to get some tan on our legs, shady enough for those epic games of Connect Four we used to play or, today, to cool down after all that manual labor. "Every minute probably counts, before he goes away, I mean." I settle on the grass.

Kayla nods slowly. "I'm not thinking about it." She gives me a weak smile. "Otherwise, I'll just get sad and mopey for the rest of summer."

"Denial: the ultimate coping tactic." I grin and clink my glass to hers in a toast.

We stretch out, relaxing beneath the sun-dappled canopy. It's one of those perfect cloudless summer days: cool breeze rustling the leaves above us, the distant comforting hum of a lawn mower somewhere down the block. I slowly relax, feeling a strange sense of belonging to be back here with Kayla after so many years.

"Can I ask you something?" I prop myself up on one elbow to look at her.

"Sure."

"Don't take offense or anything, but I'm curious. . . ." I bite my lip, trying to find the right way to ask. "What is it you see in Blake? I mean, I don't know him all that well," I add quickly. "I'm just wondering. Most people our age don't make those kind of plans."

Before, I always figured Kayla was being naive and predictable, thinking she could make the high-school golden couple thing last in the real world, like those prom king and queen couples who get hitched after graduation and start having kids right away. But now that I've spent time with her, I just can't make those pictures gel. Kayla is smart and sensible—not the kind of girl to buy into that happily-ever-after vision of romantic perfection.

Kayla stares into the canopy, as if organizing her thoughts. "I don't know how to describe it, but we just fit. He's my best friend, and I . . . I can't imagine us not being together."

"But tons of people date in high school and then split up," I point out. "I'm not saying you will. It's just that you seem so certain you won't."

She gives a small shrug. "He knows me better than anyone. It wasn't love at first sight or anything," she continues. "I mean, when we started dating, it was just fun, you know? Movie dates and parties and making out in the back of his truck." She laughs, but then something else drifts across her face, something more somber. "But when my dad got sick, Blake was just amazing about it—"

"Wait. What?" I sit up in surprise. "When was this?"

"Last year. We didn't tell anyone," she explains, "and he's in remission now, so . . ." She trails off. "But Blake, he was, like, a rock. I expected him to back off, you know, because I was being all emotional, but he was so supportive."

"Really?" I suddenly feel bad for all the times I wrote Blake off as a dumb jock with zero depth.

"I know he doesn't seem like it," Kayla adds, as if reading my thoughts. "But away from all the guys, he's really sweet. He dropped all that player crap, was there whenever I needed to talk. Or just cry. That's when things got real." She smiles—the calm, secure smile of a girl in a long-term relationship. "I knew I could count on him."

"That's great," I say quietly.

"He even did a stupid home karaoke version of 'Can't Take My Eyes Off You' on my birthday, to cheer me up," she adds, grinning at the memory.

"Like in *10 Things I Hate About You*?" I laugh. "I haven't seen that movie in . . . I don't know, forever!"

"What?" Kayla cries. "You were the one who made me watch it every month all through sixth grade."

"You're exaggerating," I tell her, then crack a smile. "It was every other month." I pause. "You know, I bet I still have all that stuff stashed away," I say, leaping up. "Come on!"

We head back inside, this time going to the storage closet under the stairs, aka the Cupboard of Doom.

Kayla blinks as I tug on the overhead bulb, illuminating approximately ten years of clutter crammed into boxes, spilling off every available shelf.

"Whoa. Hasn't your mom cleared this out yet?"

"It's her guilty little secret," I answer, scrambling up onto a broken chair and reaching perilously for the back of the top shelf. "Every time she opens the door, she chickens out." I stretch as far as I can, fingertips nudging a shoe box closer. "OK, got it!"

I clamber down, holding my trophy aloft.

"What's in there?" Kayla asks.

"Only every teen movie we ever used to watch." I grin, pulling off the dusty lid. The DVD boxes are stacked inside, remnants of my childhood I packed away when Garrett came around and deemed them teen-girl trash: *Josie and the Pussycats, Clueless, Bring It On . . .*

"What are they doing locked away in a dark corner?" Kayla demands. "These are classics! I have them out on my main shelf."

I laugh. "I'm sorry. I was wrong to deny myself all these years."

"Hell, yes, you were." Kayla pauses. "You're free tonight, right?"

"I guess. . . ."

"Perfect! How about a sleepover movie marathon?"

"Sleepover movie marathon?" I repeat slowly, as if it's a foreign phrase, but Kayla only beams at me.

"Trust me, this is going to be the best!"

The Anti-Him

What does he hate? What stuff makes him rant or rage or just curl his lip in disdain? Books, music, TV shows, food? The collected works of Amanda Bynes, peanut M&M's, fries with mayonnaise?

Go out and try it all—everything and anything. Fill your world with the stuff you've been avoiding to keep his good opinion. It might suck, just the way he always said, but it might also be made of awesome.

Embrace the teen movie experience. Bring on the peanutty candy joy! He has crappy judgment about suitable romantic matches, so why trust his taste in anything else?

CHAPTER EIGHTEEN

Six hours, two bags of chips, and a quart of rocky road later, I'm kicking myself for having put away my childish things for so long. Sure, the movies I watched with Garrett may have been insightful meditations on the nature of the human condition, but they were severely lacking in spirit fingers, and while those dour black-and-white Swedish films may win all kinds of prestigious awards, they don't leave you with a radiant glow of possibility and girl power the same way the kick-ass story of a wannabe roller-derby girl does.

So what else have I been missing out on? Inspired, I spend the next week devouring Kayla's movie collection, and soon I'm hungry for more.

"What else?" I demand from LuAnn, wielding my pen and a growing list of new must-sees. I'm using a lull at work to assemble a new curriculum: the education of Sadie going full-speed ahead.

"Um . . ." She considers. "How about some TV shows? *Gilmore Girls, Veronica Mars, The Vampire Diaries* . . ."

"Do they have makeovers and spontaneous musical numbers?" I ask hopefully.

She laughs. "No, but they're good—trust me."

"Ooh, have you got *Empire Records* down?" Aiko asks, clearing the next table. "It's way old, but great."

"Yes!" LuAnn cries. "And read Elaine Dundy, and Lorrie Moore, and Emma Forrest, too."

I make diligent notes as they banter suggestions back and forth. It's not that I like everything I've seen—the appeal of teen horror movies goes way over my head. Same for macho sports movies, and that whole "she takes off her glasses and suddenly is the most popular girl in school" thing—but the point is I'm *trying* it. If I've learned one thing from this crash course in mainstream culture (besides the fact that smushing marshmallows into vanilla pudding is all kinds of delicious), it's that appearances can be deceptive. Don't write off a book (or person, or movie) just because it has a pink, sparkly cover.

Soon, I have pages of suggestions from everyone— all of them just dying with jealousy that I get to experience these wonders of the world for the first time.

"All of the *Battlestar Galactica* reboot? Aww, man . . ." Jules says wistfully. He pushes a handful of shaggy brown hair out of his eyes. His face is dusted with three-day-old stubble. "I spent some of the best years of my life with that show."

LuAnn and Aiko join me at the table for our traditional downtime break. "My feet are killing me," LuAnn moans, sinking into a chair next to me. The lunch rush is over, and now there's just a smattering of students and our usual WiFi leech camped out around the room, sun filtering through the slatted blinds.

"That's because you wear heels." Aiko grins, sticking her sneakers in the air. LuAnn pushes them away.

"But these shoes are so pretty. . . ."

We all pause to admire the strappy sandals, adorned with little red bows. "They are cute," I agree.

"Beauty is pain." LuAnn sighs. "Oh, well." She pushes a plate of smushed pastries toward me. "Eat."

"What are you, my mother?" I laugh. LuAnn is like my personal Goddess of Nutrition, always insisting I'm but one skipped meal away from wasting to nothingness.

"Were those actually broken?" I ask, surveying the plate of suspiciously fresh goods.

"They are now!" Aiko pops a chunk of double-chocolate cookie in her mouth.

I pause. "Guys . . . I can't get in trouble with Carlos again. I'm on permanent probation after my meltdown."

"Relax." LuAnn laughs. "Like he cares about a few crumbled cookies. As long as nobody drags him into work—ever—he's happy."

Aiko nods. "Anyway, he's been in a weirdly good mood recently. The other day he wandered in and announced coffee on the house, because his song got licensed for some car commercial again."

"Which song is it, anyway?" I ask.

"You know, *I'm feelin' free.* . . ." Aiko hums a few bars.

"No way! That's him?"

"Yup."

"Wow." I pause. "What's he doing here then? Instead of out in Hollywood or something?"

She shrugs, pulling out a sketchbook. "Says he hates the industry, it's full of snakes and liars."

"He just wants to find a girl," LuAnn adds, her voice syrupy with sarcasm, "spit out a few kids, and live in a cabin in the woods somewhere. Rock 'n' roll." She pushes her half-eaten salad toward me. "Here. Greenery. Vitamins. Try them."

"This has fruit!" I say, holding up a blueberry as evidence.

"You'll get scurvy."

"Patronizing, much?" I retort.

LuAnn shakes a carrot stick at me. "I think I liked it better when you were a scared li'l newbie, kid."

"Yeah, well, those days are gone." I smile, getting up to go deal with some new customers. "Deal with it."

And they are. As I bustle around behind the counter—fixing teas, whacking the Beast into submission—I can't help feeling a warm glow of contentment. The easy banter I have with LuAnn and the others isn't something I can take for granted just yet, but I'm more relaxed with them now. I thought it would never happen, back when I was bumbling around doing everything wrong (and leaping three feet into the air every time Garrett texted me), but finally I feel like I'm really part of the group and not a scared newbie outsider.

Imagine, me with actual (cool, stylish, awesome) friends! There I was thinking that missing out on lit camp was dooming me to a summer of depression and loneliness, when really, it was the best thing that could have happened to me. Just think what I would have done if I'd been accepted: absolutely nothing at all. Nothing new, I mean—just the same mix of pining after Garrett and burying myself in thick old books, only this time, in some forest up in New Hampshire. No coffee shop, no hanging out with Kayla, and definitely no *Bring It On* (1, 2, 3, 4, *and* 5).

"Hey, Sadie," Josh calls from the kitchen. I poke my head around the corner and find him balancing four different plates on the tiny countertop, his hat askew. "Can you do me a huge favor?"

"That depends. . . ."

"Grab the trash for me? Pretty please? I'm nearing a disaster of epic proportions."

I look at the bins, piled high with gross remains. "What're the magic words?"

"Cinnamon rolls." Josh grins at me. I laugh; his rolls are legendary. He bakes them from scratch, only on Mondays, and by nine a.m. every last one is sold out.

"OK, OK." I wrinkle my nose and reach for a garbage bag. "But I want two. Fresh from the oven!"

"Yes, ma'am." He salutes me with a pair of tongs.

I grab the rest of the bags and push out through the back door into the alley behind the building: a charming, narrow passage of trash cans and empty cardboard boxes. There's a whiff of rotting food in the air and a smattering of cigarette butts in the corner, courtesy of Denton and Jules, who are always ducking out here to puff away. I grimace, edging farther down the alley toward the street to find space for the bags.

"I was thinking maybe we could get away this weekend." I hear a male voice ahead, and then Dominique's unmistakable French accent. I stop. I didn't know she was in today.

"I told you, I have a test. I have to study."

"So study with me." The guy's voice is low, intimate.

"Sure, and then get an F." She laughs.

Dominique. Laughing. With a guy?

I edge forward. She's not dating anyone, not as far as I know, but Dominique is nothing if not secretive. So has she been carrying on some illicit affair all this time, sneaking out for romantic rendezvous?

I look around at the day-old coffee grounds and sandwich remainders. OK, so making out in broad daylight in the dirty back alley is hardly romantic. But the million-dollar question is, who's the guy?

I creep closer, spurred on by the prospect of genuine grade-A gossip, until I can see them both, nestled between two stacks of old boxes. I can't see his face yet, but he must be something special for her to risk staining her perfect khaki pants in this mess.

"Come on," he urges, nuzzling her neck, his back still to me. "I promise I'll quiz you for your test."

"I can't. You know I want to, but . . ." She pulls him closer and kisses him softly. "Next time—I promise."

"I'll hold you to that." The guy kisses her again, turning slightly, and suddenly I see who it is.

Carlos!

I gasp, dropping the trash bags. Dominique springs back and sees me.

Silence.

For a split second, we stare at each other across the rotting remains—of lunch and their attempts at privacy. Then Carlos turns around, too.

"Um, sorry!" I cry quickly. "Just . . . putting the trash out. Carry on with . . . whatever!" I back away and scurry inside, slamming the door behind me.

Carlos! My mind reels at the impossibility of what I've just witnessed. But he's, like, *ancient*. Thirty-five, or something like that. And sure, Dominique is twenty-two, but that's still a whole person in age between them. Plus, she hates him! Loathes and despises him—anyone can see. When she's not bitching at him, he's threatening to fire her. Just last week they had an epic fight, so loud that LuAnn had to lock them in the office to keep them from scaring the customers.

At least, that's what we *thought* they were doing back there.

I hurry back to the table, where Aiko and LuAnn are still lounging. "What's up?" LuAnn asks, looking over. "You're all flushed."

I open my mouth to spill the gossip, but something makes the words fade on my lips. Dominique looked so panicked when she saw me, as if this is a secret that really matters to her.

"Nothing," I lie, sliding into a seat. I don't know why I should protect her, but some instinct makes me want to. "I guess it's just hot out."

LuAnn turns back to her task at hand, upending her purse to spill bottles and packets all over the table. "I've got Advil, aspirin, Tylenol . . ." she tells Aiko.

"And a serious problem?" I laugh, picking up one of the painkiller packages. "Is there something you want to tell us?"

"Not me." LuAnn giggles. "Her."

Aiko sighs. "Mama's got a headache."

"And you just happened to knock over a CVS?" I ask.

"Nope, I just stay prepared. I get the worst cramps," LuAnn explains.

"Cramps! Eww!" Jules joins us in time to hear that last part. He drags over a chair and sits on it backward. "Can't you keep your lady talk down? You'll freak out the customers."

We girls all roll our eyes in unison.

"It's called the wonder of the female body," LuAnn tells him. "Deal with it."

"We have body hair, too," Aiko adds. "And we burp, and fart, and—"

"La, la, la, not listening!" Jules covers his ears. "Help me, man!"

I turn. Josh has emerged from the kitchen. He

stretches, yawning. "Don't look at me. I have three sisters. Our bathroom is overflowing with tampons."

"Traitor."

"See? We're harmless." LuAnn waves Josh over. "Come. Sit."

"You do that a lot." I press my fingertips onto the now-empty plate to claim the last few crumbs. "Order us around, like we're dogs."

"Ruff!" she barks.

Josh falls into the chair next to LuAnn as if he would curl up on the floor if there were nowhere else to sit. He reaches back to massage his shoulder, and without a word, LuAnn positions her chair behind him and begins giving him a neck rub.

"Me next!" Jules cries. Aiko elbows him.

"No, me, me!" The others clamor for the next spot in line, but I watch, curious. Josh has his eyes shut, blissed out, and suddenly, I wonder if there's something going on between them. If they're more than just friends. LuAnn is affectionate with everyone—even forcing hugs on Dominique—but she seems so relaxed with Josh. . . .

But we all are. There's something about him that puts me at ease. Josh is goofy, sure, but with this relaxed pace about him. We can be going crazy in the café, with orders stacked up, but he just works through them without a glimmer of panic. I like that.

"So who's in for Saturday?" Josh asks, looking around the table.

"God, yes, one of you has to come," Aiko adds quickly. "Please?"

"For what?" I ask.

"Only the greatest display of masculine aggression ever!" Josh grins at me.

"Football?" I venture. "Monster trucks?"

"Greco-Roman naked wrestling?" LuAnn suggests.

"Nope!" Josh laughs. "Ice hockey!"

"Oh."

"Exactly." LuAnn echoes my tone.

"Isn't that a winter sport?" I ask, looking out at the seventy-degree summer's day.

"It's some exhibition match thing. Come on," Aiko begs. "Help me, please. I'm the only girl going. I'll drown in testosterone."

"Sorry, hon," LuAnn says, sounding anything but. "I'm all for sweaty men folk waving their big sticks around, but I draw the line at blood. Try Sadie."

Aiko turns to me.

"I don't know. . . ." I hedge. "I've never really been into sports. . . ."

"But you're trying new things!" Aiko exclaims. "That's what you told us, right? And this is new. Go crazy — you might just like it!"

"She's right." Josh grins. "You said you'd try anything."

I slump lower. "I did, didn't I?" I try to think of a way out, but that wouldn't be in the spirit of new adventures. "Fine," I tell them. "I'll come. It could be fun."

"Famous last words." LuAnn laughs.

STEP 8:

Embrace the Unexpected

You used to have everything planned out, right down to your prom dress (blue, **his** favorite color), the route of your postgraduation road trip (eating your way through the barbecue of the South), and the song that will be playing when you guys finally kiss (Jeff Buckley's "Lover, You Should've Come Over"). You've spent so long planning your blissful joint future that you can't even begin to imagine what your life is going to look like without him.

So stop trying.

Let stuff simply unfold, for once in your life, without spinning all those hopeful romantic fantasies. The less time you spend dreaming up a world of happily ever after, the more time you'll have to actually live—no evers or afters required.

CHAPTER NINETEEN

Despite LuAnn's ominous words, I'm feeling pretty upbeat as we head to the game the next day, bundled up in sweaters against the chill of the stadium and armed with vast coolers of snacks. "It's like a winter picnic," I tell Aiko as we shuffle along the bleachers to our seats. "That's fun, right?"

"Just wait for the action," Jules interrupts, a disturbing gleam in his eye. Denton is with us, an arm slung over Aiko's shoulder; Josh has brought what looks like six bags of potato chips, and even Carlos has come along — "To keep an eye on you kids," he says, cracking a beer and stashing the rest of them away out of Jules's reach.

Aiko snickers. "Like he's not pretending he's twenty-two all over again," she whispers to me. I watch him, wondering what his deal is with Dominique. Is keeping it secret his idea or hers? And is it something real, or—eww—just a casual hookup thing?

"Ooh, they're starting!" Aiko leaps to her feet to get a better view. Hulking guys in fifty pounds of padding are skating around, getting ready for kickoff. Or hit-off. Or whatever it is they do to start this game. The stands are full, foam fingers waving everywhere, and the organ jingle climbs another level, pumping the crowd with rowdy enthusiasm.

"This is so cool," I say, beaming. Aiko laughs. "I don't do sports!" I explain. "I've always been more into the stationary arts. Sitting. Reading. Napping."

There's a foghorn blare, and then the players whip around on the ice, sticks at the ready, moving so fast I can barely keep track of the tiny black puck thing. It whooshes around, flicked back and forth at lightning speed.

"I love it!" I exclaim happily. "It's just like ice dancing, only—"

SLAM! CRACK!

Before I can finish my naive comment, a player smashes face-first into the Plexiglas barrier. Blood splatters. The crowd roars.

"Are you going to take that?" Aiko screams, suddenly baying along with the rest of them. The player turns around and hurls himself straight into the guy who pushed him. They fall to the ice and throw punches blindly until their teammates come to split them up.

"OK." I breathe, battling a powerful wave of nausea. "It's all over."

But then the teammates start brawling, too.

"Oh, boy." I crouch down in the parking lot, resting my forehead on my knees. I can still hear the yelling of the crowd, a thunder in the stadium behind me, but it's nothing compared to the queasy storm in my stomach right now.

"You OK?" Josh hovers beside me. He must have drawn the short straw on babysitting me.

"Uh-huh," I manage, trying to sound upbeat. "Fine. I just didn't know his arm was going to . . . pop like that when that goalie dislocated it."

Josh laughs. "Don't worry. That kind of thing, they can pop right back in."

"Oh," I murmur, feeling another wave of nausea. "Great."

"Here."

I lift my head enough to see a soda cup in front of me.

"It's supposed to calm your stomach," Josh tells me. "Or at least, that's what they always say."

"Thanks." I cautiously begin to slurp. Back inside, another roar goes up. I can only imagine what brutal fist-icuffs are going down right now. "Sorry you're missing it. I just wasn't expecting it to be so . . . bloody."

"It's cool. You've seen one broken nose, you've seen them all."

I nod slowly. "That's . . . not at all comforting."

The old wives' tale about soda must be true, because slowly, the nausea ebbs away until I feel stable enough to stand. Josh helps me to my feet. "Better?"

"Uh-huh," I murmur, not actually sure. "But, I, um, think I'll give the rest of the game a pass. You go back," I tell him quickly. "I can just hang out here until it's over."

"No, I'm good," Josh reassures me. "They're not my teams, anyway." He pauses, hands bunched in his front pockets. "I can give you a ride home if you want."

I brighten. I was resigned to loitering, alone in the parking lot, through another forty minutes of blood-filled hockey action. "Are you sure?" I double-check, still feeling guilty about dragging him away from all the fun. "You don't have to. I mean, I don't want you to feel like you're stuck looking after me or anything. . . ."

"Who's stuck?" He grins, jamming his baseball cap on so that tufts of hair stick out over his ears. "I just have to make a tiny detour first."

I follow Josh to his truck, a rusted red old pickup. He climbs easily into the driver's seat and leans over to open the door for me. I clamber up, with decidedly less grace. "Sorry about the mess," he says, sweeping some empty soda cups aside. He starts the engine and yanks it into gear.

"It's cool. I'm all about the mess." I look around, disoriented to be so high off the road. "This is great," I tell him as we head out of the parking lot. "It's like you can crush everything in your path."

Josh laughs. "Almost. Although, I had a run-in with an SUV last year, and we barely made it out unscathed.

Isn't that right, Dolly?" He pats the steering wheel affectionately.

"Dolly?" I laugh. "What kind of name is that?"

"A great one!" he protests, but when I keep giggling, he explains, "When I got her, the radio was jammed. She would only play this classic country station. I fixed it in the end, but the name stuck."

"Dolly," I repeat, amused. Such a feminine name for such a hulking great mass of metal—the total opposite of Garrett's Vespa, Vera. "Why do guys do that?" I ask. "Name their vehicles."

"Ownership." He grins. I reach over and punch him lightly. "What?" he protests. "It's true! And it gives us something to swear when we break down out in the middle of nowhere." He grabs a cable hanging from the old-fashioned cassette player and plugs it into his iPod. "Ready to rock?"

"I don't know about that." I get comfortable, slipping off my sneakers and propping my bare feet on the dashboard. "But I could maybe manage a leisurely roll."

He hands me his iPod. "Go crazy."

I pick some old-school Springsteen, and we turn onto the highway, beginning to wind through the sprawling woodlands of the Pioneer Valley. I love this part of the country. Sure, western Massachusetts can be frustrating if you want entertainment—and live a painfully car-free existence—but when it comes to twilight filtering through the leafy canopy or dense, lush hillsides, we can't be beat. Out past Sherman, the towns are farther apart: small, white clapboard hamlets buried in the woods, marked by church spires and town ponds, signs for homemade honey for sale along the side roads, and farm stands with fresh eggs and corn.

"So, your first hockey game didn't turn out too great."

It's only when Josh speaks up that I realize I've zoned out, watching the world speed by in the soft evening light. "At least I tried it," I say, trying to look on the bright side of bearing witness to three nosebleeds and one shattered cheekbone. "That was the point, right?"

"I guess." He glances over at me. "How's it working out for you, this trying new things kick?"

"Good," I answer slowly, feeling self-conscious. He hasn't been a part of my Getting Over Garrett squad, but he has to know what's been going on. By now, even regular customers like Mr. Hartley must know what's going on. "Do you think I'm crazy?" I suddenly ask. "It must seem weird, me running around with this plan of mine. . . ."

Josh thinks about it, which isn't really reassuring, but then he shakes his head. "No more crazy than the rest of us. I mean, at least you know what you want, and you're trying to get there." He shrugs, shoulders rolling beneath his faded blue T-shirt. "Most people just sit around complaining."

"Yeah, I did plenty of that." I sigh at the thought. "A couple of years' worth."

"So, don't worry about what people think," he says, easy and relaxed. "As long as it works for you."

"You're right." I smile back, relieved. "And it is working. Well, except for today," I correct myself. "Note to self: no sports. Ever."

Josh laughs. "Come on, I bet we can find something more your speed. Bocce, maybe. Or table tennis."

"Right, because I'm in a retirement home." I laugh, relaxing back into the old, faded bucket seat. My bare feet are up on the dashboard, the nails still painted with remnants of sparkly pink polish from Kayla's sleepover. I'm struck suddenly with how much things have changed this summer. Changed, or grown from nothing at all. I'm riding here alongside a guy I didn't even know a few weeks ago, my life filled with friendship and new adventures I'd never even considered.

Sure, I may have wound up huddled on the asphalt outside a major sporting event, fighting not to hurl, but I went. I showed up! Old Sadie wouldn't have deigned to attend in a million years, not when she was locked so securely in her bubble of a world.

Maybe the path to that extraordinary life I wanted is just a lot more meandering than I figured.

"About this 'tiny' detour . . ." I say, a half hour into the drive. "I'm not complaining, I just think we should have a plan, you know, if you're going to be transporting a minor across state lines."

Josh laughs. "Not much farther now. I'm just seeing a guy about a thing."

"Cryptic." I fix him with a look, but he just shrugs.

"That's me, international man of mystery."

"You mean, the kitchen-boy act is just a ruse, and secretly you're off fighting spies and evil scientists between shifts?"

"Gee, my cover is blown." He turns off the road into a dirt parking lot, a series of buildings just visible through the trees. "Here we are."

"Here being . . . ?"

Josh shakes his head. "I don't want to jinx it. But if it works out, I'll tell you everything, OK?"

"Deal."

Josh arranges to meet me in twenty minutes, then disappears off on his mysterious mission. I don't mind, because he's deposited me at what might just be the cutest bookstore I've ever seen: nestled under the beams of an old converted mill, overlooking the falls. I haven't been on a quest for used books since Garrett left, but this place feels like home right away, even without him. The sound of water rushing outside, the dusk light fading through the old paned windows . . . It's pure bliss. There's even a resident cat, strolling by occasionally, letting me tickle its chin.

I browse the stacks until I can't carry any more choices, then settle in at the little coffee shop next door to whittle down my short list, surrounded by bearded college undergrads and burly biker types. I'm so deep in a collection of vintage kids' ballet stories that I barely hear Josh's voice. "Is that a cinnamon roll? Traitor."

I look up as he folds himself into the chair opposite, a

stern expression on his face. I hurry to swallow a mouthful of the offending pastry.

"Just keeping tabs on the competition," I protest quickly. "And they've got nothing on you."

He breaks into a smile. "I'm kidding. And, sure they don't."

"Modest," I tease. "Anyway, no more delays." I push my plate aside. "I can't stand the suspense. What's the big secret? Did everything work out?"

Josh suddenly looks bashful. In fact, if the light wasn't already rosy from the stained-glass panels in the window, I would swear he's blushing. He reaches for a sugar packet and begins to tear it open. "I, uh, came to talk to the guy next door. Did you take a look around?" I shake my head. "Right, I forgot, the books. Anyway, he's got this great restaurant. Nothing fancy, just simple, fresh stuff. They even grow a bunch of the produce on a farm nearby—the whole local-food movement."

"That's cool," I say, even though I don't really follow.

Josh makes tiny circles in the sugar crystals with his fingertips. "So . . . I came to see about working here. An apprenticeship," he explains. "Not just the stuff I do at work, but real training." He stops, and then a huge grin spreads across his face, as if he just can't hold it back. "And . . . he said yes. I got the job."

"Josh!" I leap up. "That's amazing! Congratulations!" I hug him across the table. "So you're going to be a chef, for real?"

"Maybe. We'll see. It doesn't pay much, and I'll be

working crazy hours, but . . . I don't know, I think I could be good at it." Josh looks at me, hopeful, as if he's waiting for agreement.

"Of course you will," I insist. "We'll miss you, though. When do you start?"

"Not for another couple of weeks. His summer intern goes back to culinary school in the fall."

"Is that something you'll need to do, then?" I ask, curious. "Go to cooking school?"

"I don't know. I'm not thinking that far ahead." He's still grinning, clearly thrilled. "For now, I'll just see how this works out."

"It will be great," I declare. "I can just see you in one of those floppy white hats, whipping up amazing meals and yelling at all your kitchen underlings."

He snorts. "I think I'll be the one getting yelled at for now. And I won't be anywhere near the real food—just chopping stuff and cleaning up."

"But it's a start," I insist. "You'll be winning Michelin stars in no time. That's the award, right?" I check. "That all the fancy restaurants have?"

He nods. "But I want to be more of a James Beard guy. It's the award they give for the best chefs in America," he explains. "The ones who really push the boundaries and put a whole modern spin on things."

I'm amazed. "You never said you were into this stuff. You always complain about being stuck in the kitchen back at work."

Josh shrugs again. "Sure, because I'm grilling sandwiches for the millionth time. This is different. Will—the guy in the restaurant—he's doing amazing stuff with meats and herbs and—" He seems to catch himself, stopping with a shy smile. "Sorry, I get kind of carried away when it comes to cooking."

"No, it's great." I look at him, at the energy in his expression. The casual act is gone, and instead, there's something focused and full of excitement. "I've never seen you like this."

Josh coughs, and suddenly that goofy smile is back. "There I go, ruining my bad reputation."

"Sure, you're a regular rebel without a cause." I laugh. "Now, how about we get something to toast this news of yours?"

Brace Yourself

There's a reason you didn't block off contact with him entirely. And that reason is friendship—or at least, the dream of a happy, healthy friendship, unencumbered by the crippling weight of unrequited love. The utopia of BFFs, the (ahem) platonic ideal of emotional maturity. It's getting closer every day, but the question is, are you ready for it?

I don't mean kind of, almost, nearly ready. I'm talking immune-to-his-charms, cool-and-collected, ready-to-hang-up-in-a-heartbeat kind of ready. Because you haven't done all this work just to turn around and hurl yourself at his feet again, pleading, "Love me! Love me!"

Asphalt hurts. But not as much as abandoning your dignity.

CHAPTER TWENTY

"I'm bored." Kayla collapses next to me after Sunny Dayze lets out. I'm perched on the bench in front of Totally Wired on my break, peeling an orange and watching people on Main Street meander past. There's a soothing calm to it, I've found: the slow strolling and absent errands that used to fill me with disdain and frustration are now kind of charming, after a manic morning serving coffees in the café.

"That's new." I offer her an orange segment. "Usually you're exhausted and/or homicidal. Which, you know, isn't the best thing when you're working with kids."

"But they're so inane." She sighs. "It's all, 'Kayla, look at my crayons!' and, 'Kayla, I made you a bracelet!' Please. Come back when you can pee on your own."

I laugh. "And somehow, every mom in town thinks you're God's gift to child care."

Kayla bats her eyelashes at me. "As long as they tip at the end of summer!"

We sit side by side in the sun, enjoying the last orange sections. "Fall's coming," Kayla says. "I can feel it in the air."

"You lie," I tell her. "Fall isn't coming, because if it does, that means winter's on the way, and I refuse."

"You refuse?"

"Yup. I'm not allowing it this year," I declare, folding my arms. "Wet mittens and runny noses and ugly snow boots, and waiting in the cold for the bus. It's just not going to happen. I forbid it. It's staying summer forever."

Kayla giggles. "Good luck with that, holding back the seasons."

"Hey, they're always telling us we don't know what we can achieve if we set our minds to it." I shrug. "So, I'm setting my mind to this."

"Aww, I like winter," she muses. "Fires and hot chocolate and snuggling up with . . . well"—she stops—"snuggling in general."

I shoot her a sympathetic look, but Kayla fixes a smile on her face. "Anyway, you won't be standing around in the cold in the mornings, you'll be riding in with me."

"Well, in that case, winter is allowed this year," I decide. "Just for you."

LuAnn's peeling red Civic screeches into a spot just across from us. She hops out, dressed in a crazy polka-dot dress, with ballet slippers tied crisscross all the way up her calves. "Hey!" She waves over to us, walking straight out into the street. A minivan slams on its brakes and blares its horn, but LuAnn just bounces over to us, beaming.

"I thought up another step for that plan of yours!"

"You did?" I remain noncommittal. LuAnn's previous suggestions for the "Getting Over Garrett" file have so far included transferring to an international school somewhere glamorous and European, making out with twenty-four boys in twenty-four hours, and staging an intricate voodoo witchcraft ceremony to peel his essence from around my soul. "That's sweet," I tell her. "But I'm doing fine for now."

"She's hardly even talked to him this week," Kayla agrees.

I turn to her. "You've been keeping tabs on me?"

"Duh." She rolls her eyes good-naturedly. "Do I need to remind you about a certain Slushie incident? For the sake of my wardrobe, I need to know if you're in panic mode."

"No panicking," I tell them both. "I'm good—I promise."

"But you could be better!" LuAnn cries. "If you just had—drumroll—snap bracelets!" She produces a handful of thin rubber bands. "See? You put them on, and then whenever you think about Garrett, you snap them." She demonstrates on my bare wrist. I reel back in pain.

"Owww!"

"It's negative reinforcement," LuAnn declares, eyes lit up with a sly gleam. "Eventually, you associate Garrett with pain and stop thinking about him."

"Um, no," I tell her firmly, peeling them off. "Don't you think it's a little extreme?"

LuAnn shakes her head. "You said it yourself: you can't underestimate a broken heart."

"It's OK." I laugh. "Really. I don't need to resort to physical harm—I promise."

LuAnn doesn't look convinced. "It can sneak up on you at any time," she warns, tucking the rubber bands away. "One minute you're fine, and the next—bam! You're weeping in the corner in three-day-old sweatpants, with nothing but a pack of Hostess Cupcakes to fill the emptiness and longing inside."

I blink. "Thanks for the warning," I tell her slowly. "I'll let you know if I change my mind."

"Sure thing!" She heads inside, skirts fluttering.

I turn to Kayla. "Um, let me know if you ever see her with a cattle prod, OK?"

The rest of the afternoon slips by without any more crazy ideas from LuAnn—except her attempts to play Lady Gaga on the stereo, which are quickly overridden by five different customers and an executive decision from Dominique.

"Some of us are trying to work," Dominique informs LuAnn, striding behind the counter and snatching the offending CD from the player.

"You're not even on today. You don't get a say!" LuAnn objects, rushing to save her pop mix from the trash. I edge back, out of the way.

"I have six chapters to learn before my test tomorrow."

Dominique stalks back to her corner table: a makeshift fort of textbooks and wide-ruled notebooks. "I need quiet!"

"But Dom—"

"Just play something else," Carlos calls from the back office, where he's been locked away, scowling at the books. He scoots his chair into the doorway and tells LuAnn, "The customers are always right, remember?"

"Fine," she answers with a grin, reaching for another CD. "You asked for it."

A moment later, Carlos's hit song starts playing; LuAnn sings loudly along. *"I'm feelin' free . . ."* she warbles. *"Like a bird in the sky . . ."*

"LuAnn!" Carlos warns her. She pivots away, turning to the next customer.

"You like this song, don't you?"

"Uh, sure." The middle-aged man blinks, then begins nodding in time with the beat. "I heard it on TV, that car ad."

LuAnn shoots Carlos a triumphant look and keeps singing. *"I'm flyin' so high . . . Freeeeee . . ."*

Carlos retreats, slamming the door behind him. I sneak a glance at Dominique, still full of questions about their weird back-alley makeout setup. She hasn't said a word to me yet about my unfortunate discovery; she's just been breezing through her shifts with the same icy detachment as ever. Does she care that I've kept her secret, or is she so far above petty gossiping that she wouldn't even care if I told? I watch her: head bent over those law books, a pair of chic, wire-rimmed glasses on her nose.

She looks studious and reserved, like the last person to be having a scandalous affair with her boss, but perhaps that's the point.

Dominique looks up suddenly and catches my gaze. I turn away quickly, embarrassed to be caught staring.

"I don't know why he's so touchy," LuAnn says. "Anyone would think he's ashamed of selling out. I'd sell out in a minute," she adds, "if it meant I got a check in the mail every month."

I laugh. "What happened to artistic integrity?"

"Screw artistic integrity," she shoots back. "Mama needs to pay rent."

The door dings behind us.

"So what does a guy have to do to get some service around here?"

I turn. And there he is, a crumpled button-down shirt half tucked in to brown corduroy pants; his beat-up leather satchel slung across his body. He approaches the counter, a familiar grin on his face.

Garrett.

"So, what's the coffee of the day?" His grin broadens as he leans on the counter.

I gape, frozen in place with a pair of muffin tongs in one hand and the other clutching a coffee mug for dear life.

Garrett. Back. Here.

My mouth drops open in shock. How is this possible? I had a whole countdown planned: his return date circled in red on my calendar at home—the calendar I haven't looked at in weeks, I realize. The one currently buried under a mountain of trashy romance novels and teen movie DVDs. "I . . . I don't . . ." I stutter, helpless.

LuAnn gives me a weird look. "That's our Somali roast," she says, stepping into the breach. "It pairs really well with our almond torte, if you'd like."

Garrett turns to me. "What do you think, Sadie?"

"You guys know each other?" LuAnn brightens. "Why didn't you say?"

Finally, my brain engages. "Garrett," I manage. "He's back. I mean, you're back."

"Surprise!" Garrett laughs. Before I can even think, he circles the counter and enfolds me in a massive hug. "I can't believe it. The past six weeks have felt like a whole lifetime."

I stay still, motionless in his arms.

Sure, I knew this day would come—but not yet! I was supposed to have time to strategize, to put a whole emergency plan in place before I was faced with this momentous occasion.

"Hi!" I finally manage, disentangling myself from his arms. Up close, he's painfully familiar—the way his hair falls into his eyes, the perfectly sculpted cheekbones, the smudge of birthmark just above his right ear. There's newness, too, though: a fuzz of blond stubble on his chin, tan lines on his wrist. "What are you doing here?" I manage. "I mean, you didn't say you were coming home!"

"Just got in." He exhales. "I spent six hours crammed up against a Hell's Angel named Bubba, so God knows I need a shower, but I just had to come by and see you first. Man, I missed you."

I blink up at him, reeling. Then I remember LuAnn, standing just two feet away from us. Aiko has arrived, too, watching us curiously as she ties on her apron.

I leap back. "I'm going to go get you some of that torte!" I exclaim. "You go sit down. Relax."

"It's OK. I don't want to keep you. I just wanted to say hey." Garrett's still smiling, seemingly unconcerned by my babbling, clumsy performance. "But let's hang out later. We could do a movie tonight. *Annie Hall* is playing in Northampton."

"I don't know. . . ." I try to think straight. "I was going to—"

"No excuses," Garrett says, cutting me off. "Come on, it's my first night back in town! You know how you love Woody Allen." He gives me a mock puppy-dog look, and right away, everything rushes back to me—the late nights, the road trips. The way he can look at me like I'm the most important person in the world.

"OK," I agree. "Tonight. I'll see you then."

"Great!" he says. "Pick you up at seven!"

I watch him lope away, still reeling from the change, from a ringtone on my phone, a face in photographs, a memory to this, flesh and blood, and back in town.

"Emergency staff meeting, *now*!" LuAnn announces. "Dominique! Aiko!"

She grabs my arm and drags me back toward the office. Carlos looks up in surprise as we barrel in.

"Sorry, we need the room," LuAnn announces. "Shoo."

"Shoo?" he repeats, looking at her with a mix of amazement and disbelief. "This is my office!"

"And we need to borrow it!" she replies. "Pretty please? You can go cover the register. It's a girl thing," she adds. "Let me find those tampons for heavy flow. . . ."

He leaps up. "Uh, sure. Take your time." Carlos bolts so fast, he almost trips on his unlaced sneakers.

LuAnn laughs. "Every time . . ."

But the humor of men's predictable aversion to girl talk is beyond me right now. I sink into Carlos's seat, still dazed, and soon, LuAnn, Aiko, and Dominique are lined up opposite me. LuAnn holds out her phone. "I have Kayla on speaker, too."

Kayla's voice comes through, tinny on the tiny speaker. "So, what happened?"

"He's back," LuAnn says. "Just came right in like nothing had happened."

"Some nerve." Aiko tuts.

"He looks like an idiot to me," Dominique adds, studying her nails.

Something about the way they're lined up, united against him, fills me with a warm glow of friendship. I'm not alone in this.

"Thanks, guys," I tell them, finally taking a deep breath. "It's sweet of you to back me up, but . . . Garrett isn't the enemy here. He never did anything wrong. It was all me."

"Still, he hurt you!" LuAnn protests, eyes wide with outrage.

"But he's my friend. That was the whole point of getting over him," I remind them. "To keep him in my life. That means you're going to have to be nice to him."

Silence.

"I mean it," I add, wondering if LuAnn is going to spike his coffee or spit in his food.

Finally, she sighs. "Fine, we'll be nice." Aiko nods in agreement.

Dominique shrugs. "Sure, whatever."

I exhale. "OK, then." After a moment, Kayla's disembodied voice comes through the speaker.

"But how do you feel?"

They all look at me, expectant.

"I . . . I don't know," I say slowly. "I think I'm still in shock. I mean, I've been so focused on not thinking about him, I didn't really plan for this part." I look between them, lost. "What do I do now?"

"We need new rules," LuAnn says immediately. "For having him back. Like, no spending time alone together. And definitely no hugging."

"No romantic situations of any kind," Aiko agrees. "No candlelight, sunsets, or places playing the Yeah Yeah Yeahs' 'Maps.'"

"You should stand him up a few times," Dominique offers. "Make him see he can't take you for granted anymore."

"New rules . . ." I nod slowly.

"It'll be OK." Aiko gives me a reassuring pat on the shoulder. "You can do it!"

"She's right," LuAnn agrees. "You've come so far. This is, like, the last hurdle. It'll be no problem now."

I take another breath, and slowly, my confidence returns. They're right. I *will* be OK. I'm a million miles away from the wretched, lovelorn Sadie I was when I saw him last, and there's no way I'm going to regress now, not after all the sweat, tears, and spilled coffee I've put into getting over him. The guide has gotten me this far; I just need to adapt it to suit this new reality!

"I'm ready," I announce. "I can do this."

"Atta girl." LuAnn grins.

"But Sadie . . ." Kayla's voice comes through. "Be careful, OK? Don't go falling for him again."

"No way," I swear. "He surprised me today—that's all. We're just going to be friends."

Dominique sighs. "Sure, you are."

"Show a little faith," I tell them. "I can be strong!"

Brave New (Platonic) World

Someone once said that the definition of insanity is doing the same thing over again and expecting a different result. Remember how you used to send silent prayers to the Gods of Requited Love for a divine intervention every time you hung out with him? And did said intervention ever occur?

It did not. Clearly, the old approach didn't work out so well. So it's time for some new rules.

Start with no touching. Add no romantic locations, no long midnight drives, and most definitely no innocent tickle fights on his bed. There is no such thing as innocence once your heart has been broken into a million anguished pieces, just remember that.

CHAPTER TWENTY-ONE

And I am strong. When Garrett picks me up that night, wearing that slate-gray T-shirt that usually sends me into paroxysms of delight, I barely even glance at his newly tanned forearms. I'm so careful to keep a safe distance between us that I nearly fall off the back of the Vespa because I'm not holding him tight enough, and when we get to the movie theater, I suggest we see a new— incredibly loud, extremely unromantic—action movie instead of *Annie Hall*.

"You're kidding, right?" Garrett laughs as we stand in line for tickets. The lobby is crowded with groups of teenagers and couples on dates, the smell of buttery popcorn wafting in the air. "That stuff is such trash."

"It'll be fun!" I argue. More fun than two hours of watching Woody Allen and Diane Keaton debate the fraught intricacies of male-female friendship, anyway. "Give something new a chance."

Garrett gives me a look. "What did they do to you this summer?" he teases. "The Sadie I knew would never even think about watching aliens blow stuff up."

The Sadie he knew also would have walked over hot coals rather than have him think she was silly or uncultured, so I simply give him a smile and shrug. "Maybe she expanded her horizons a little. Come on, I'll buy the popcorn!"

"OK, OK," Garrett says. "You win. But only because I've missed you so much." As if to underscore his point, he pulls me into a hug.

Hugging is definitely up there on my danger list, so I carefully disentangle myself from his arms. As I step a safe half-pace away from him, I catch sight of a flash of red hair out of the corner of my eye. I turn, searching the crowd of moviegoers. Is that . . . LuAnn?

"What's up?" Garrett asks.

"Nothing. I just thought I saw someone. . . ." I check again, but there's no sign of her. "Anyway"—I turn back to him—"tell me about camp. I want to hear everything."

Everything except this mythical Rhiannon, who is most definitely on the danger list, but Garrett must have learned from my constantly shutting down his every mention of her, because he doesn't utter her name. "The classes! Sadie, it was amazing. I had this poetry professor, you would have loved her. . . ."

We get tickets and snacks, and head inside, Garrett

still waxing rapturously about his various literary triumphs. "It was incredible. I wish you could have been there. They had so many amazing teachers and guest lecturers," he says. "I feel like my writing has gone to a whole new level."

"That's great," I tell him, checking for our row.

"Sorry," he apologizes quickly. "I don't want to rub it in; I know how disappointed you were."

"No, it's fine," I reassure him. "It actually turned out for the best."

He squeezes my shoulder. "It's OK—you don't have to pretend with me. I know summer must have sucked, stuck in Sherman. But I talked you up to everyone, so next year, you'll be a shoo-in, I'm sure."

"Thanks," I say slowly, distracted by a glimpse of blue-tipped pigtails farther up the aisle. But when I look again, they're gone. I must be imagining things. I shake my head to clear it. "That's really sweet. I'm not sure if I'll apply next year, but . . ."

"What?" Garrett stops dead in the middle of the aisle. "Sadie, you have to. You can't let the rejection get you down—it's part of life for us writers. Think of Kerouac or Cummings; they were turned down by dozens of publishers before they got their breaks. You'll make it," he insists. "You just have to keep trying."

It wasn't exactly what I meant, but hearing Garrett gush about "us writers" makes me realize: aside from my recovery steps, I haven't written all summer. I settle into the worn velvet seat, wondering how I didn't notice until now. But maybe writing was always something I did more to bond with Garrett than for myself.

"Sadie?"

I look over. "Sorry?"

"I was just asking what else you've been up to," he says, getting comfortable in the narrow seat. "Working at the café seems . . . fun. I mean, if you're going to be a minimum-wage drudge, it seems like the best place," he adds.

"I like it," I tell him, scooping a handful of popcorn. "It took me a while to fit in, but now we're all friends. A bunch of us went to a hockey game, and—"

"Wait, hold up," Garrett stops me, shocked. "You went to . . . a hockey game? As in meatheads in jerseys, trying to kill each other on the ice?"

"Sure. It was fun." I grin at the memory. "Well, until the fighting, and all the blood. But, aside from that . . ."

Garrett reaches over, takes my face in both hands, and turns it from side to side. "Who are you, and what have you done with the real Sadie?"

I duck away—no touching!—and give a small laugh. "I guess I've changed."

"Clearly." He studies me again. "I go away for a few weeks, and look at you. New hobbies, new look, new hair . . ."

"At least mine isn't crying out for a cut."

"Don't you start too. I've already been hearing about it from my mom!"

"She's got a point," I say. "And that fuzz on your chin . . . Did they not have razor blades up in the woods?"

He strokes his patch of wannabe facial hair pro-
tectively. "You don't like it? I think it makes me look
older. . . ."

"Sure." I giggle. "If by older, you mean all of
nineteen!"

Garrett clutches his chest. "You wound me so! And
there I was, counting the days till we'd be together. . . ."

I stick my tongue out at him. "What were you
expecting, a ticker-tape parade?"

"Of course not." He makes that puppy-dog expression again. "Just a small brass band . . . some of the high-
school baton twirlers . . ."

"Dream on." I settle back in my seat as the lights go
down and the theater begins to quiet. "Now, settle down
and enjoy some alien destruction."

I've made it.

That's the thought that dances through my head
as various buildings are blown to fiery smithereens on-
screen. I've made it. The work and tears have all been
worthwhile, because sitting here with Garrett feels just
like old times. Only better. Because instead of spending
the entire show with my hand placed hopefully on the
armrest between us, waiting for him to accidentally brush
against it, or secretly studying his profile in the glow of
the movie screen instead of actually watching the film
itself, I can relax and just be me. No wistful wondering,
no anguished hopes. Just us, together, friends.

The way it should be.

"It really was a masterpiece." Garrett laughs as we

emerge from the movie theater. It's cooler now, a chilly breeze slipping through the air, and I pull my cardigan more tightly around myself as we pause outside the lobby.

"Such depth, and that dialogue . . ."

"You loved it!" I nudge him. "You didn't look away once."

Garrett coughs. "Only because I was riveted by how awful it was."

"Sure, that's your story." I laugh. "But I bet you'll be first in line when the sequel comes out!"

"Never," he declares. "And I still can't believe you made me watch that. Your standards are slipping in your old age."

"Says the senior." I grin. "If I'm old, then you're just about stumbling towards the grave."

We start walking, but I quickly stop, struck again by the strange feeling that somebody's watching me. I spin around. Nothing.

"Sadie?" Garrett waits just ahead, illuminated by a streetlight.

"Coming!" I start walking, but I take only a few steps before turning again. This time, I see them: Kayla, Aiko, and LuAnn, skulking behind a group of teenage boys, trying to stay out of sight. Unfortunately for them, their outfits don't exactly spell inconspicuous. LuAnn is dolled up in a trench coat and sunglasses, while Aiko and Kayla have on these all-black quasi–cat burglar ensembles.

I march over.

"Um, hi, Sadie!" Kayla exclaims brightly, lowering the flyer she's been pretending to read. "What a coincidence! We were just catching a movie, and—"

"Save it!" I cut her off. "I can't believe this. You're actually following me!"

"Not following," Aiko objects, twisting a pigtail. She's wearing black spandex leggings under clompy black boots, with a cropped black satin bomber jacket. Real casual for a night out at the movies. "More, keeping a friendly eye on things."

"In case you need rescuing," LuAnn agrees, her eyes wide with concern.

"Like, a backup squad!" Kayla grins.

I look at them, a mismatched set of PI's-slash-spy-movie-wannabes, and can't help but burst out laughing. My friends are kind of insane.

"Where did you even get those outfits?" I ask, gasping for air.

"You like? I styled everyone myself." LuAnn does a little twirl. "Undercover chic, I call it."

"You look . . . very film noir." I grin. "But isn't the point of undercover to, you know, blend in to the crowd?"

LuAnn rolls her eyes. "But the crowds here are so boring!" She looks past my shoulder and hisses, "He's coming!"

Garrett is indeed heading in our direction, looking curious. I don't blame him. "Act normal, please," I beg.

"Normal? Us? No problem!" Kayla adjusts her fake plastic spectacles as Garrett reaches us.

"Hey." I gulp, suddenly nervous. It feels like two halves of my life are suddenly colliding here.

Garrett looks at the group, clearly waiting for an introduction.

"Oh, right!" My voice comes out strangely high-pitched. "This is LuAnn, and Aiko. You saw them at the café yesterday. And you know Kayla already."

"Hey." Garrett nods to them, his expression warm and friendly. "I'm Garrett."

"Garrett," LuAnn repeats darkly, as if he just introduced himself as Satan. I shoot her a desperate look.

"Hey," Aiko adds in a grudging tone.

Garrett looks less confident at the cool welcome. "Great to meet you all. Uh, Sadie's been telling me so much about the café, I feel like I know you all already."

"Really?" LuAnn raises her eyebrows. "And we haven't heard a single thing about you. How do you guys know each other?"

I cough. Garrett looks back and forth between us, still thrown. "We've been friends a while now. Best friends," he says, and smiles at me. I look away.

"Oh. Weird!" LuAnn replies. "But I guess Sadie is friends with so many guys, it's hard for us to keep track."

"She is?" I can feel Garrett's questioning gaze.

"Oh, sure, they're always in the café," LuAnn continues merrily. "Sam and Pete were mooning over her so much, we had to bar them. Too distracting for the customers."

"Why don't we go get something to eat?" I exclaim brightly, before LuAnn tells Garrett I have boys throwing themselves at my feet twenty-four hours a day. "Herrell's is right up the block."

"Sure, I could go for ice cream," Garrett agrees. Immediately, the girls pile on.

"Perfect."

"Let's go!"

"Now, Gary, was it?" LuAnn links her arm through his and steers him up the street with a dangerous gleam in her eyes. "You're a sophomore, right?"

We cram into a corner booth, surrounded by glass jars of candy toppings and children ingesting way too much sugar. But although this is officially the best ice cream around, I can only swirl my Oreo Smoosh-in around in my cup, still tense over the mixing of my new friends and old. Garrett seems relaxed enough, chatting with the girls about school and camp, but I'm all too aware of how easily this could all come crashing down with one stray comment from, well, anyone at the table.

"So you're the next literary master?" LuAnn slurps her ice-cream float through a thick straw and stares at Garrett.

He laughs. "I don't know about that."

"Come on, don't be modest," she teases. "This camp sounds so *exclusive*."

"Garrett is really talented," I interject. "He's won all kinds of prizes."

"But I'd keep writing, even if I hadn't," Garrett adds, bashful. "You have to do it for love, not money, like the real greats."

"What about dating?" Aiko asks brightly. "Those places can be a full-on party, right? Or do you have a girlfriend?"

I choke on my Oreo crumbles. "Aiko!"

"What?" She gives me an innocent look, biting into her maraschino cherry. "I'm curious!"

"We want to know *all* about you," LuAnn agrees. I glare at them.

"Just ignore them," I tell Garrett. But he waves away my concern.

"It's fine. I . . . uh, was with someone at camp," he tells them. "But we broke up."

I whip my head around. "You didn't tell me that."

Garrett looks uncomfortable. "You said . . . you know, that you didn't want to hear about that stuff."

My mind races. So he's not with Rhiannon, after all? How, what, who . . . ?

I take a breath and try to act casual. "What happened?" I take a tiny spoonful of ice cream, as if this is only vaguely interesting. "I thought she was 'the one.' "

"Garrett's right," Kayla interrupts, giving me a warning look. "You don't want to hear about it. Do you, Sadie?" There's a loaded pause, and all three girls stare at me, full of meaning.

I cough. "No, you're right," I say, sinking in my seat. "It doesn't matter."

"Anyway, that's all ancient history now," Garrett tells me, slinging an arm over my shoulder. "It's why I didn't say anything."

"Hey, Garrett," LuAnn says loudly, pulling his attention away from me. "Could you be a doll and go get me some napkins?" She gestures helplessly at the girls on either side of her. "I'm kind of trapped."

"Oh, sure." Garrett gets up. "I'll be right back."

The moment he's out of earshot, LuAnn grips my hand. "What did we say about touching?" she hisses.

I pull away. "It was a friendly hug!"

"Sure, but I count three friendly hugs, an arm squeeze, and a hand pat in the last hour alone," she retorts.

"And that's not even including what we couldn't see in the theater with the lights down low," Aiko adds with a knowing look.

"Exactly!" LuAnn nods. "That was another thing, no dark rooms!"

I laugh at their concern. "It's OK, guys. Can't you see? Everything's OK. Normal. *Platonic*. There's nothing to worry about."

"Really?" Kayla checks, concerned. "Everything's not rushing back, being around him again?"

We all look over to where Garrett is gathering an armful of paper towels for us, and some tiny cups of water, too. He's as cute as he ever was to me, but there's something different now—as if I'm seeing him from farther away, not so bound up in longing and hopeless romantic dreams.

Like I've been telling myself all summer: he's just a boy.

"Really," I swear. "Even if he hugs me a hundred times, I'll be OK."

· · ·

We make it through the ice-cream break without any more passive-aggressive digs from LuAnn, and soon, Garrett's Vespa is idling to a stop outside my house.

"You know, you've changed," Garrett says as he walks me to the front door.

"Oh, right." I touch my curls, self-conscious. "The hair. I figured it was time for a change."

"No, not just that." He pauses, studying me. "You seem . . . I don't know, different from when I saw you last."

I shrug. "Different good or different bad?"

He pauses. "Well . . ."

"Garrett!" I shove him. Off balance, he stumbles backward.

"OK, OK! Different good." He laughs. "I don't know how to describe it."

"What?" I tease. "You, lost for a good description? No similes, metaphors, long comparisons to Whitman or Hemingway—hey!" Now it's his turn to push me. I skip ahead, laughing. "Camp has clearly drained you of all your literary prowess."

We pause by the door. "It's good to be back." Garrett smiles down at me. "I really did miss you out there."

"I missed you, too," I say quietly, and despite everything, it's true. "Anyway, I better go." I back away, pretty sure that lingering on the dark front step is up there on LuAnn's list of risky behavior.

"Sure. Right." Garrett grins. "I'll see you . . . when?"

"Not sure." I open the door. "I'm working, and then hanging with Kayla, so . . . maybe over the weekend?"

He blinks. "But that's ages away."

I laugh. "You've managed six weeks without me. You can last!"

I close the door behind me, overwhelmed with relief. I may have dismissed Kayla's concerns as if they were nothing, but part of me has been scared that they might be true. After all, it's one thing to say I'm over a guy when he's safely out of range—over state lines and far away—but back, here in front of me, laughing, talking, touching . . . How would I fare then? Would I crumble in the face of his cuteness? Melt inside all over again at his literary musings?

No!

I skip upstairs, buoyed by my success. Sure, Garrett is just as charming as he always was. And, yes, maybe my stomach *has* been skipping with exhilaration all evening, but why shouldn't it? This was an important night—the testing of my resolve. And I was victorious! Not filled with pangs of desperate longing, not left feeling rejected and miserable. No, for the first time, it felt like we were . . . equals. Two friends, hanging out—not one guy with a girl trying to mask her slavish devotion.

I don't need him anymore.

The list of anti-crush commandments is still pinned up above my desk: a record of my summer, right there in black and white. I take it down, remembering each painful event. The Slushie incident, my Totally Wired meltdown . . .

I rip the list in two, feeling a surge of achievement.

I'm freed from the shackles of longing, set loose from the bonds of my despair. Sadie Elisabeth Allen—a prisoner of unrequited love, no more!

CHAPTER TWENTY-TWO

"Are you feeling OK?" Josh finds me sitting outside the café at 6:45 the next morning, basking in the early sun. "Sick? Delirious maybe?"

"No, why?" I blink, baffled.

"Because you're never early!" Josh begins unlocking the half dozen bolts on the door. "Hmmm, maybe you've been taken over by aliens. No, wait—you're really an evil Sadie-shaped cyborg!"

"That's not fair!" I protest, following him inside. "I'm never late. Well, hardly ever," I add.

"Sure." He grins and flips on the lights. "But on time isn't early."

"So, maybe I'm feeling good today." I pirouette to stash my bag in the lockers. I could hardly sleep last night, I was so happy my first big test with Garrett had passed without faltering. Now freedom is sparking through my veins, filling me with the sweet energy of independence. Which reminds me . . . "Didn't someone promise me two fresh cinnamon rolls?"

"Now I get it." Josh pulls upended chairs down from the tables with a clatter. He's wearing a faded blue sweatshirt over jeans; his hair is still hanging in wet strands. "They only ever love me for my baked goods."

"We start with the baked goods," I console him. "But then we come around to you, too."

"Wow, way to build a guy's ego."

"Who needs building?" I laugh. "You're doing just fine all on your own."

We slip into our morning setup, now a well-practiced routine, until the counters are gleaming and full sugar shakers adorn every table. "See? This is why I'm never early." I slump against the register, surveying the calm, empty café. "There's nothing left to do now until opening."

"Nothing except watch me work my magic." Josh beckons me through the hatch.

I gasp. "But I thought your recipe was top secret!"

"I figure I can trust you." He shrugs. "And if you tell, well, I know half a dozen places to hide your body."

I scoot around to the kitchen. "Just a word of advice: you might not want to mention that to girls. On dates, or, you know, even just in casual conversation."

"Wow, that explains it." Josh hits his forehead with his palm. "I've been wondering why they back away, looking scared. I figured I just had crazy BO or something."

I whiff the air nearby. "No, you're good."

Ever since the hockey-game-slash-bookstore outing, Josh and I have fallen into an easy friendship, more comfortable around each other than before. I guess nearly vomiting on a guy's sneakers will do that for you.

He points me to a corner, between boxes of coffee beans and a perilous stack of spare plates. "Over there. And don't touch anything."

"I won't—I promise." I hop up on the countertop, eager to watch the baking master at work.

"You should count yourself lucky." Josh pulls on his baseball cap and his apron—a black full-length thing covered with band graffiti and random doodles in Wite-Out. "Many have tried to glimpse this magical process, yet none have succeeded."

"Until now." I swing my legs against the cabinet doors in time with the indie rock song he has playing on the tiny kitchen boom box. "Are you excited about the new job?"

"Sure." He shrugs, assembling flour and butter and all kinds of sugary goodness. "I guess."

"Right, I forgot—you're too cool to get worked up over anything."

"No insulting the chef!" He flicks some flour at me. I laugh.

"Still, we're going to miss you around here."

Josh gives me a shy smile. "I'll miss you, too. All you guys," he adds. "Well, except Dominique."

"Aww, she's not so bad," I protest.

He blinks. "Since when?"

"I don't know. Maybe she's grown on me," I say.

"Or maybe I'm just immune to her icy glares by now. Anyway, I think there's more going on with her than we know. She just doesn't show it—that's all."

"That's true about everyone," he argues, sifting and mixing with sure, expert movements. "But I don't walk around making small children cry."

I laugh. "Not until you talk about hiding bodies, at least."

"OK, you're up." Josh gestures me over. Somehow, he's folded the dozen ingredients into a sticky dough with barely a glance.

"Really?" I clap my hands in glee and hop down. "I better warn you, though, I even burn toast."

"It's foolproof—I promise." He waits while I wash my hands, then shows me how to roll the dough into a sheet and sprinkle pecans, cinnamon, and butter on top. "Then you fold it up like this, and smush it into whirls in the pan."

"*Smush.* Is that a culinary term?" I tease, studding the dough with plenty of sugar until there's no bare surface left to be seen. I roll carefully. "Doesn't it need the sticky sauce on top?"

"That's from the butter and sugar," Josh explains. "It melts in the oven."

"Butter." I sigh happily. "Oh, how I love it so." I finish and present my handiwork. Josh high-fives me.

"Now, you bake."

"I'm actually baking something," I marvel, watching as he slides the pans into the oven. "And that was so easy, too. I thought you toiled in here for hours to make those things!"

"Ah, but you can't tell anyone how simple it is." Josh grins. "You promised."

I pause as the track switches on his mix CD, a familiar melody bursting out of the tinny speakers. "What is this song? You played it in the car before."

"The Thermals," he replies. "You like them? They're playing in Northampton in a couple of weeks." Josh pauses. "I could get tickets, if you want. . . ."

"Sure, sounds fun," I reply, scrubbing my hands clean in the sink (since I'm guessing that licking the sugar off wouldn't be the classiest move). "Maybe we make it a group thing? I know Kayla would like them, and maybe Garrett, too."

"Garrett?" Josh stops clearing the baking ingredients.

"You know, my friend-slash-former-obsession?" I make a face. "That's right, you weren't here yesterday. He's back from camp."

Josh doesn't say anything, he just goes back to cleaning the countertop, so I add, "LuAnn and Aiko went kind of crazy over it, but I'm fine. I mean, we're friends. Anyway, I'll ask about the gig."

"Sure." Josh shrugs. "Could you . . . ?" He gestures for me to move out of the way. "I need to get to . . ."

"Oh, sorry!" I scoot back into the doorway. "Do you want me to do anything else?"

"No, you're good." Josh looks up briefly. "You know, you should probably get out front, in case of customers. . . ."

I blink, thrown. "OK, right. Let me know when the rolls are done."

"Sure." Josh turns away again. "The oven buzzer is pretty loud, you'll hear it."

A customer arrives out in the café, so I don't have time to dwell on Josh's weird mood swing, but it must be the day for it, because everyone who walks through that door all morning seems to have a dour scowl on their face, even with the sweet, sweet scents of cinnamon and sugar wafting through the air. When I get back from my lunch break, Aiko is slouched behind the register, morosely flipping through a zine.

"Not you, too!" I cry. "What is it with today?"

She sighs. "Denton's pissed at me because I said he looked like a hipster douche in his new sunglasses."

"Ouch."

"Yeah, well, it's true. And Dominique hasn't shown yet, and LuAnn has barricaded herself in the back office for some reason and is refusing to come out."

"Is she OK?"

"No idea." Aiko shrugs. "She practically knocked me down bolting out of here. I thought I'd check in a minute."

"I'll go." I quickly order the Beast to make LuAnn's favorite mocha drink. "Anything sugary left?" I ask Josh through the hatch, but he has the music turned up and can't hear me.

At least, I hope he can't. Like I said, mood swings everywhere.

The office is locked, so I tap lightly on the door. "LuAnn? Is everything OK?"

No reply.

"I've got you a coffee," I say, tapping again. "With extra whipped cream and marshmallows."

There's silence, and then I hear the lock slide back. The door opens a crack, and LuAnn peeks out. "Caffeine?" she says hopefully.

I hold the mug back, just out of reach. "Not unless you let me in."

There's a pause, then the door opens wider. I slip inside as LuAnn goes and slumps in Carlos's desk chair and spins it back and forth. She looks miserable.

"What's up?" I ask gently, handing over the mug. "Aiko said . . ."

"That I freaked out?" She exhales, tugging the sleeves of her orange cardigan over her hands. "Tell her I'm sorry."

"Hey, we've all done it!" I grin, but she doesn't crack a smile. "Does that mean you're not coming out?"

"It depends." She wavers. "Is he still there?"

"Who?"

"*Him,*" she says, and I can hear the capitalization in her tone. It takes me a moment to get there, but then I realize what she means.

"Oh," I breathe, wide eyed. "You mean . . . ?"

"Yup."

"Let me check." I open the door and peer down the hallway into the main café space. "What does he look like?"

"A lying, cheating asshole," LuAnn says, still spinning in the chair.

"I'm going to need something more to go on," I tell

her, surveying the floor for possible candidates for the man who broke her heart so thoroughly she's still reeling years later. "OK, there's an older guy in a Hawaiian-print shirt. . . ."

LuAnn snorts. "Give me some credit."

"Fine." I move on. "Those guys are way too young, and that one looks like he's over fifty, so that leaves . . ." I stop, landing on a kind of cute, scruffy guy with dark hair. He's wearing skinny jeans and a vintage-y T-shirt, and is sitting on one of the couches up front with his arm slung over some girl's shoulder. Some young, pretty, adoring girl.

Bingo.

I turn back to LuAnn. "Does he know you work here?"

She nods sadly.

"What an ass!" I glare across the floor, as if I could pull a Matilda and ignite something out of sheer fury. "Bringing her here, like a trophy. Tacky."

"Very." She sighs. "But he doesn't see it like that. He wants us to be friends."

"Ugh!"

"Ugh," she echoes, but she doesn't sound outraged or vengeful, just . . . worn out. I know all too well how that feels. Not everyone can wind up happily platonic like me and Garrett.

I wait with her a moment, but I can see customers beginning to line up by the front counter. "I have to get back out there," I say reluctantly. "Are you going to be OK?"

"Sure." She musters a smile. "I'll just wait it out, plotting all the ways I could kill him."

"Well, as long as you're being productive!" I give her a quick hug. "And if it makes you feel any better, you're so much prettier than she is."

LuAnn smiles, a real one this time. "It shouldn't, but it does."

The rest of the day passes uneventfully enough. LuAnn's ex leaves, she emerges from hiding, and Dominique breezes in to replace Aiko on the afternoon shift—not that her Ice Queen glares help lift the mood at all. One potential customer even turns right around and walks out after taking in the tables full of depressed patrons and the miserable staff.

"You guys need to do something!" I hiss. "We're not going to make any tips if you keep moping around like this."

"Mneah." LuAnn just shrugs, barely looking up from the fashion magazine she's leafing through.

The doorbell dings, and Kayla walks in, her red shirt covered with an array of kid-related stains. "What can I get you?" I ask, relieved. Kayla will cheer them all right up; she's practically the Goddess of Perkiness.

"A ticket down to New York?" She exhales in a long, pathetic breath. "Blake left today. Athletic orientation."

"Aww, Kayla!" I round the counter and give her a hug. "I'm sorry. When will you see him again?"

"Not for another few weeks." She looks forlorn. "We decided he should get settled and bond with the guys, you know? Instead of driving back to visit me every weekend."

"That sounds sensible," I say, trying to stay upbeat.

"It sucks." She looks at me, genuinely upset. "I mean, we knew this was coming. It's just . . . It hurts. I don't know what's going to happen next."

"Sure, you do." I steer her to LuAnn's table. "You'll call, and text, and time will fly by. You guys are solid, remember? Made to last. Tell her, LuAnn."

"Love is a lie." LuAnn looks up from her magazine. "It's all doomed to end."

"LuAnn!" I turn to Kayla. "Don't listen to her. You and Blake will be fine."

I go get them some drinks and pastries, but by the time I get back, Dominique is camped out with them, too, denouncing all men as fools.

"You can't build your life around them," she says, stone faced. "Because it may seem all sunshine and roses, but what happens when you realize it's not anymore? What have you sacrificed by then?"

Kayla looks stricken.

"That's enough," I say, slamming the plates down. "No more moping, from any of you. This is a mope-free zone!"

Silence.

"I'm serious!" I exclaim. "Since when am I the functional, emotionally-balanced person here?"

Kayla makes a face. "OK, now I just feel worse."

"No," I tell them. "No bad, no worse. You had the good sense to intervene when I was going crazy, so now it's my turn. We are going to do something fun tonight, and nobody is going to talk about their boyfriend." I look at Kayla. "Or ex-boyfriend." I stare at LuAnn. "Or . . ." I turn to Dominique, but trail off at her panicked expression. "Or any other guy. OK?"

"Sadie . . ." Kayla sighs. "I don't know. . . ."

"Sure, you do. Fun!" I demand. "Who's with me?"

More silence, broken only by the sound of my cell phone. "I mean it," I tell them, backing away. "Start thinking about what we can do." I answer my phone. "Hello?"

"Sadie?"

"Hey, Garrett." I find a quiet corner. "What's up?"

"Nothing much," he says. "Getting settled back in. You have no idea how great it is not to be taking communal showers anymore!"

I laugh. "What, you don't miss bonding with your fellow man—one big group of sweaty towels and shared soap?"

"Er, no," Garrett says firmly. "Anyway, what are you up to? I thought we could get together tonight."

"I'm at work right now," I tell him as I watch the girls across the room. They don't look like they're planning a night of fun and debauchery—that's for sure. "And I can't hang later, I'm doing something with the girls."

"Come on," he says, dragging the words out temptingly. "You see them every day. I only just got back!"

"Garrett . . ."

"We could get takeout," he continues. "Go for a drive or something."

I feel the smallest tug in my chest, the muscle memory of response from all those times I would drop what I was doing to see him. Every time. And look how that turned out. "Sorry," I tell him, my tone brisk. "Things are hectic until the weekend. I told you. But we'll do something then, OK?"

"But Sadie . . ."

Across the room, Dominique scrapes her chair back, about to bail. "I have to run. Call me later." I hang up and quickly call over to them, "If you all haven't agreed on something to do by the time I get back, you're taking my morning shifts for the rest of the week."

"But—" Dominique starts, but I'm already heading to serve the next customer.

"Morning shifts," I call back. "Seven-thirty, bright and early. Get thinking."

Moving On, aka Other Guys

They exist. Honestly, they do. Guys who aren't **him.** Who might actually like you back and, *gasp,* do something about it.

(Pause to recover from the shock of it all.)

The sooner you start interacting with those other guys, the sooner you'll see that he isn't your sole chance of romantic happiness in the world. And that these Other Guys might actually be cute, and fun, and maybe even a better match for you.

After all, they actually notice you're alive.

CHAPTER TWENTY-THREE

We hear the party before we even arrive: the faint thud of bass echoing through the trees, and laughter drifting out in muffled bursts. My anticipation grows. By "fun," I figured a movie night or five-dollar bowling at the lanes outside of town, but LuAnn knew about a party happening a couple of towns over, and by some miracle, they all agreed to come.

Dominique slows her car and turns down a dirt road marked with a chalk X on the dry earth. "*Deliverance* much?" she mutters as we emerge into a clearing filled with other cars and beat-up pickup trucks.

I'm too busy squinting at my makeup in a compact mirror to reply, but luckily, LuAnn seems to have snapped out of her funk. "Hush, you." She prods Dominique with her lip-gloss wand. "If you didn't want to have a good time, you shouldn't have come!"

"I don't remember having a choice," Dominique replies, but she puts the car in park, swipes LuAnn's lip gloss, and turns the rearview mirror to check her reflection.

"So, whose party is this again?" Kayla asks. She's next to me in the backseat.

"Some college guys, I think," LuAnn replies. "One of those come one, come all things. I heard about it from a couple of people."

"But if it sucks, we're leaving," Dominique says quickly, teasing out her hair. "Designated driver's prerogative."

"At least walk through the front door before deciding the party's beneath you," LuAnn says with a laugh as we clamber out of the car.

Kayla falls back beside me as we follow a path through the dim trees. "Do you think my outfit is OK for a college party?" she whispers. She's wearing jeans and a plain blue T-shirt under a zip-up hoodie. "I'm not really dressed up."

"We're in the woods in western Massachusetts," I tell her. "There is no underdressed out here. If anything, I'm the one OTT."

"No way," she reassures me. "You look the cutest in that dress."

I hope so. I'm wearing the vintage red outfit I bought in the city, since Kayla nixed every other option of mine as too "Old Sadie." We told our parents we were going to a party at LuAnn's and that we'd be home by midnight, no problem. I hope the Gods of Completely Necessary

Partying are on my side. It's the first time I've ever had to lie to my mom about my whereabouts, but I figure it's for a good cause. After all, she should be happy I've made it to all of seventeen years old without sneaking off to illicit parties with my friends. She should be happy I have friends at all.

My cell phone buzzes in my pocket, and I startle, wondering if Mom can somehow sense my sneaking around. But instead, it's just Garrett. Again.

Last call for pizza. I ordered veggie, just for you.

"I don't get it. That's the fifth time he's texted tonight." I sigh, tapping out a quick response. "I know he's been away, but how come he's being so . . . I don't know, full-on?"

Kayla smirks. "Of course he's being full-on. You don't need him anymore. Guys can sense that," she adds, as we head deeper through the woods. "It's like they have a radar for it. TJ dumped Lexie last year by text, and then the minute she moved on, he started hanging around again, wanting to get back together. They always want what they can't have."

I shake my head. "Garrett's not like that. And anyway, we were never together."

"But you were always around whenever he called," Kayla points out. "Now you're busy. His tiny man-brain can't process it."

Before I have time to wonder if Kayla could be right, we round a corner and finally emerge into a clearing by the house.

"Awesome." Kayla grins, taking in the bright lights

and mass of older, infinitely cool people clutching plastic cups and beers; talking, dancing, and most definitely *not* moping around over boys.

"Classy." Dominique sighs, deadpan.

"What were you expecting?" LuAnn asks with a grin, leading the way up the front steps. "Wine and cheese?"

I follow, taking in the scene. The house is a log cabin, the kind Thoreau would have hidden away in to write his odes to the joy of nature. But tonight, the only odes will be to the joys of alcohol and loud music. Lights blaze into the dim woods, and people have spilled out onto the porch. There's something in the air—and not just the waft of smoke that might not be entirely nicotine based. No, this is more. Possibility. Adventure. Or, at the very least, some excellent people watching.

I turn to Kayla, excited. "See? Way better than sitting at home, waiting for Blake to call."

"OK," she agrees, looking more cheerful than when she slumped through the doors of the café this afternoon. "You were right. This is pretty great."

LuAnn drifts off to say hi to some people, and Dominique promptly disappears, so Kayla and I wander through the house, trying not to look like gawky high-school kids. We find some sodas and a couple of Popsicles from the freezer and set up station on the edge of the living room, midway between the "hang out and talk" zone on the back porch and the designated dance area inside. A hipster-looking kid in neon shades is iPod-DJing, sitting cross-legged on the coffee table, while kids shuffle and shimmy and even full-on dance in the crammed living room. There are couples everywhere—no real PDAs, but normal party fun: guys and girls talking, laughing, having fun. Together.

I watch them as if they're a foreign tribe.

"Do you think . . . ?" I start to ask, then stop, embarrassed. "Never mind."

"What?" Kayla turns to me.

"I just . . . You know how in the plan, you guys talked about me needing to find some other guy—just for fun?" I add quickly, seeking refuge in my Popsicle. "Well . . . maybe I'm ready for that."

Kayla lets out a little shriek of excitement. "Really? You think? Because I wanted to say something, but I didn't want to be pushy or anything."

"Since when has that ever stopped you?" I tease.

"I can be cool!" she protests, laughing. "But you want to? Find a guy, I mean."

"Maybe." I shrug. "Not for an actual relationship or anything, but maybe to try and . . . I don't know, flirt. Not that I'd even know how," I add quickly. "See, this is the problem! I've spent so much time loving Garrett, it's like I missed these crucial training years, when everyone else learns how to hang out and flirt and hook up."

"And now we get to make up for lost time!" Kayla squeezes me with a hug, "I'm so proud of you!"

I laugh, blushing. Admitting my complete inexperience when it comes to dating is kind of humiliating, but Kayla doesn't seem fazed. In fact, she's practically bouncing with excitement.

"So, what kind of guys do you like?" she demands,

then immediately answers herself: "Wait, we know that already. Tall, intellectual, pretentious. OK, so for tonight, I think we need the complete opposite. The anti-Garrett."

"A short, dumb jock?" I say, dubious. She shakes her head.

"No, we can do better than that. . . ." Kayla scopes out the party, eyes narrowed with concentration.

"You know, you look like one of those sharks on the Discovery Channel," I tell her, amused. "Hunting for prey."

"Your prey," she corrects me as a guy with cropped blond hair and stubble passes by. He's twenty, maybe, wearing this faded red T-shirt that hugs his back. I pause, watching the muscles ripple as he reaches to hand his friend a beer.

"And we have a winner," Kayla murmurs beside me.

I turn. "Who, him?" I blink. "No way. He's old, and cute, and . . . so far out of my league!"

"Oh, no!" Kayla shakes her finger at me, scolding. "Don't even start with that. You're cute, and awesome, and your hair looks great tonight."

"Thanks." I soften. "But what do I even say to him?"

Kayla shrugs. "Anything. 'Cool shirt.' 'Great party.' 'Do those pants have secret pockets?'" She takes a look at my nervous expression and laughs. "Guys aren't some weird foreign species, Sadie. They're people. You can talk to people! You do it all the time at the café."

It's true, I do. But as I look back over at this guy, I'm suddenly reluctant. "You know what? Maybe we should wait a while, until I'm more relaxed, and—"

"Nope!" Kayla links her arm through mine and begins to drag me purposefully out onto the porch toward that group of guys. "What have you got to lose?"

I don't know, my self-respect? My dignity? Then I realize that I lost those things weeks ago, scrambling on the coffee shop floor.

"Nothing, I guess," I agree, and head after her to go make a complete fool of myself.

Or maybe not. Red T-shirt guy's name turns out to be Oliver. He's nineteen, training to be a forest ranger, and to my amazement, after ten minutes of basic get-to-know-you chatting, he has yet to turn and flee into the dark night. In fact, he's smiling at me, easy and relaxed. "So you're in college around here?" he asks, leaning against one of the porch posts.

"Just graduated high school," I lie. I try to sound casual, "I'm taking the year to work and travel before deciding on college."

"Cool." He nods, blue eyes smiling down at me.

Kayla clears her throat. "I'm going to go get a drink!" she exclaims brightly. "But I didn't see where the bar is." She flutters her eyelashes at Oliver's friends. "Could you guys show me?"

There are murmurs of agreement, and before I realize what she's doing, Kayla has ushered them inside, sending me a swift wink as she closes the screen door behind them.

I'm left alone with Oliver.

"So, forest ranger . . ." I perch on one of the chairs,

trying to look casual, as if I do this all the time. Sure, I flirt with older boys—men!—every weekend. What of it?

"Does that mean you're an expert at building fires and all of that?"

The words are out of my mouth before I realize how inane they sound. *Smooth, Sadie. Real smooth.* But Oliver doesn't seem to mind. "Sure, but mainly we try to educate people about not building them. The risk of wildfires, and stuff like that."

"Right," I say quickly. "Of course. Fire, bad." I take a sip of my soda, still feeling lost. I shouldn't be so uncomfortable. I've spent hundreds of hours—maybe even thousands—just hanging out, talking to Garrett, but that feels like a whole separate universe: one where I felt at ease in my own skin, instead of glancing down every five seconds to check that my bra isn't showing.

"I've always been into the outdoors," Oliver continues. "Like, when I was a kid, I was always running around, climbing trees. My parents took me camping a lot. It was great."

"Mmm," I murmur.

He sits on the bench beside me. "The thing people don't realize is what a complex ecosystem the forests are," he says. His face is tanned and animated with enthusiasm. "We've got to try and minimize our footprint."

"Like tiptoeing," I joke, but he stares at me blankly. "Kidding," I add. OK, so, his sense of humor is somewhat lacking, but he is still blessed with those muscular arms. . . .

Oliver pauses a beat, then casually puts one of those arms over the back of the bench. "So, are you into the outdoors much?"

I pause, trying to decide if lounging in my back yard qualifies. "Kind of." I err on the side of vagueness.

Oliver brightens. "Oh, yeah? What kind of stuff?"

"You know . . ." I wonder guiltily if pretending to be a nature girl is the same as pretending to love Dostoyevsky novels and morose British music. Probably. But then my gaze falls to the ground and the point becomes moot, because he's wearing sandals—those leather thong kind that German tourists wear, usually over socks. But Oliver isn't wearing socks, and I can see his bare feet even in the dim light: they're covered in dirt, as if he's been hiking through the forest all day.

I swear I see something . . . wriggle, between his toes.

"Sadie?"

I know I told Kayla I wanted to try flirting with other guys, and I'm sure Oliver here is nice—heroically defending our great forests, with nothing but a backpack and those miraculous arms—but something about the sight of those grubby toes, and the dark, mysterious growths lurking in between. . . .

"Actually, I hate nature," I say suddenly, dragging my eyes back up to his.

"What?" Oliver looks like I've just admitted I like setting forest fires in my spare time, but before I can take it all back, I realize I don't want to.

"I mean, not nature—I don't hate that," I correct myself. "But being out in it. All the bugs and dirt and branches. I mean, going to bathroom in the bushes is just, eww, you know?" I grin, feeling strangely liberated by all this honesty. The plan was right—it may start small, with an innocent comment about camping, but before you know it, I'll be stranded out in the middle of the Pioneer Valley, huddled over a damp campfire with a poison-ivy rash on my butt.

Oliver blinks, those pretty blue eyes staring at me. "I'm fine looking at trees and flowers," I add. "But behind plate glass. Preferably with air-conditioning."

"Huh." He withdraws his arm.

"Anyway, it's been fun talking to you!" I bounce up. "Um, see you around?"

I head back inside, feeling strangely triumphant. Sure, the objectively hot guy thinks I'm an evil, nature-hating girl now, but for some reason, that feels better than pretending to like things I don't. I'm done smiling and nodding along just for some guy's sake.

Especially if said guy is housing fungus on his feet.

"Well?" I find Kayla perched on one of the window seats, watching the party. She bounces up expectantly. "How did it go?"

"It didn't."

"Why not? He was into you—I know it." Kayla peers past me. "Look, he's still there, you can go try again." She pushes me back toward the screen door, but I stand firm. "*Saaadie.*" She keeps pushing. "You can't keep pining."

"This has nothing to do with Garrett!" I protest. It's true, the Gods of Unrequited Crushes have finally been vanquished. For once, Garrett is the last thing on my mind. "Kayla, I swear. I talked, we flirted, but . . . I didn't like him enough, OK? I mean, I'm all for moving on," I add, "but can I move on to a guy who doesn't have mud between his toes?"

"Mud?" She screws her face up. "Eww, OK, that's gross!"

"Exactly." I look at the knot of people around us, suddenly feeling an itch of energy in my veins. "Come on, let's dance!"

We lose ourselves in the middle of the tight crowd for a while, and I forget everything except the thump of bass and quick beats of all these songs I've never heard before. I don't ever dance at parties, but tonight it's different; everyone here is into it, oblivious. Girls are dancing alone, eyes closed; burly guys in vintage shirts throw themselves into the music; and Kayla and I are unnoticed in the middle of it all. Nobody knows who I am, and nobody cares. There's something freeing about that. I spin around, dizzy, clutching onto Kayla as we laugh until my lungs hurt.

I tug her out of the crowd for a moment to catch my breath. "Have you seen LuAnn or Dom anywhere?"

"Nope." She shakes her head, hair falling loose from her usual ponytail. "Not all night."

"Oooh, seating!" I spy a free corner of couch and head over to claim it. Kayla follows, and soon we're crushed between an amorous couple and three long-haired hippie chicks passing a menthol cigarette around. "Maybe I should call Oliver over," I say. "There are Birkenstocks aplenty around here."

"Are you sure you don't want to go try again with him?" She asks, still dubious. "Because he really was cute, and mud washes off. . . ."

"I'm fine, really," I reassure her. "It was good practice, but we weren't meant to be. I don't even compost."

Kayla giggles. "Sorry. I was kind of pushing you onto him."

"No, I needed it. I can't avoid dating forever. And at least you have a future as a brothel owner ahead of you, if college doesn't work out." I grin.

"Sure, my parents will love that." She laughs, but then pauses, sounding almost wistful. "I guess part of me wants to live vicariously through you," she adds slowly. "Since I haven't kissed anyone aside from Blake."

I blink. "Ever?"

"Ever." She nods, blushing. "We got together freshman year, remember?"

"Weird," I say. The hippie chicks leave, murmuring something about a drum circle, so I scoot over on the couch to claim their space. "I mean, good weird," I add. "That you found each other and all."

She nods slowly, curling up in the corner. "Sometimes I wonder what life would be like if we hadn't."

"What do you mean?"

"It's not that I don't love him or anything," Kayla says quickly, playing with the fringe on a couch cushion. "But I don't know. . . . Sometimes I try to think who I'd be, without him."

"You mean like me trying to figure out who I am without Garrett?"

"Right. And we're happy, me and Blake," she says quickly, as if to even mention otherwise is girlfriend sacrilege. "But I think about it. Like, would I have run track, if practices hadn't clashed with date night? And would I have made different friends?" She's wearing a contemplative look I don't think I've seen on her before.

"I like the Laurens and Yolanda and everyone," she continues slowly, "but I started hanging out with them because we were all one big group—Blake and his friends, and then us girls, because we were dating them." She bites her lip. "That's how it's always been: me and him together. And now I'm picking colleges to be near him, and . . . I just wonder—that's all."

She gives me a shy smile, and although I know she doesn't wish she'd never gotten together with Blake at all, I understand what she means. If I hadn't met Garrett, what would my life look like now?

"They never tell us what happens after happily ever after," I say. "I had to add a whole new section to the website. . . ." I trail off, realizing what I've said, but it's too late.

"What website?" Kayla asks.

I blush. "Um, remember those lists we used to make? About the top couples, or most romantic movie characters?"

"Sure." She smiles. "We filled whole notebooks with that stuff."

"Well . . . I kind of took it to the next level." Feeling like the biggest loser on earth, I tell her about my database. "I don't do it anymore," I say quickly. "It kind of faded out this summer, without my Garrett stuff fueling it on."

"I think it's cute!" Kayla laughs. "And, OK, maybe a little dorky."

I groan, covering my face with my hands.

"Aww, it's OK, it just shows you're a romantic at heart." Kayla nudges me. "Just be careful with that. Real-life relationships . . . they're not like they are in books and movies. Life is, well, it's a whole lot messier." She sighs.

I'm wondering what to say to that when LuAnn appears in front of us, breathless. "There you are! I've been looking all over for you."

"We've just been enjoying the scenery." Kayla winks. "And it's cute!"

"Uh-huh." Distracted, LuAnn looks back toward the living area. The volume has risen even more—raucous with music and the sound of the crowd cheering at something. "We might have a problem."

I pause, still distracted by Kayla's last comment. "What kind of problem?"

"A Dominique-shaped one."

There's a sudden whoop from the other room. Kayla and I exchange a look, then we quickly follow LuAnn to the scene of the commotion.

"Yeah, baby!" some guys are yelling. "Get it *on!*"

We push our way through the dense crowd until I can see what's causing such joy: Dominique, a bottle of tequila in one hand, grinding up against any guy in a ten-foot radius. The preppy cardigan is gone, and she's sweaty and disheveled, breaking out in hysterical giggles.

Dominique. Giggling.

"What the . . . ?" I blink, wondering if my Popsicle was spiked. I must be hallucinating, because the Dominique we all know and loathe would never make an ass of herself in public, let alone give a stripper a run for her booty-shaking money.

But no. It's her. And she's utterly wasted.

"What happened?" I ask, fighting to be heard over the braying pack of assholes.

"I don't know!" LuAnn yells back. "I left her for, like, twenty minutes."

"She works fast." Kayla gazes at her with a strange look of admiration.

"What should we do?"

LuAnn shrugs. "I don't know. She's legal. I guess just make sure she doesn't do anything crazy?"

"Crazier than this?" Kayla yells.

That's when Dominique whoops, "Who wants body shots?" A great roar goes up from the crowd.

And then she takes off her shirt.

CHAPTER TWENTY-FOUR

LuAnn and Kayla deal with the re-clothing Dominique situation while I go call for rescue. But forty minutes after Garrett says he'll come get us, there's still no sign of him.

"Where are you?" I press my cell phone to my ear and try to block out the party noise. Garrett's voice is distant on the other end.

"See, *now* she wants to hang out!" Garrett teases, but I'm not in the mood.

"This is an emergency, Garrett." I try to stay calm. "Kayla and I need to get back home before her parents ground her forever!"

"I know, I know." He laughs, as if amused by my panic. "Don't worry. I got caught up here, but I'm on my way."

"You said that ages ago!" I exclaim.

"Relax. I'll be there," Garrett promises. "I just have to—"

"You know what? It's OK," I say, catching sight of a guardian angel in jeans and a gray sweatshirt, emerging from the dark woods. "Josh is here. LuAnn must have called him."

"I told you, I'm on my way—"

"It's fine. See you later." I hang up, going down to greet Josh. "Thank you so so so so much," I tell him fervently.

He shrugs, nonchalant as ever. "Where's the party girl?"

"She's sleeping now, thank God." I nod toward Dominique, fully clothed again and passed out cold with a sweater tucked under her head. "For a while, she wanted to go on a night hike in the woods."

"So you knocked her out just to avoid physical activity?" Josh jokes. I manage a smile.

"You know me so well."

He peers at her. "Is she going to be OK?"

"I don't know—I've never inhaled half a bottle of tequila." I exhale, worn out. "Thanks again for coming. LuAnn was drinking, and we have to be back before curfew."

"No problem." He shrugs again, as if I haven't dragged him out of bed and into the back of beyond. "Where are the others?"

"Looking for Dom's purse and keys."

"Then I guess it's time to get her in the truck." Josh assesses her quickly. "Which end do you want: top or bottom?"

"Just take an arm and drag. That's what we've been doing."

We manage to hoist Dominique into an upright position. "Wha . . . ?" she murmurs, squinting as we carefully maneuver her down the steps. "Stop spinning."

I meet Josh's eyes over her head. "Remind me to never drink. Ever."

We manage to get her down the path to his truck with no more than a few minor bumps. Sliding her into the backseat is a bit trickier, but Josh is surprisingly strong; he lifts her all on his own and gently sets her down on the bench seat. She slumps, unmoving, and begins to snore. It would almost be cute, if there wasn't drool dribbling down her chin.

"I'm sorry," I apologize again. "I had no idea she'd let loose like this."

"What happened, anyway?"

"I don't know. It was like she was possessed. A completely different person." I sigh, leaning against the truck. "She's usually so controlled."

"Those are the ones you have to watch for," Josh says. "I knew this math whiz in high school—never says a word all year, then downs ten beers at a party and starts yelling the value of pi to fifty places."

"Those math guys, they know how to party."

We wait in the dark, the lights and noise from the

party drifting out to us in faded bursts—the sound of people having the time of their lives. I sigh. "I guess nothing turned out the way I expected tonight."

"Why not?"

"I thought it would be a fun, girl-bonding thing. No boys allowed—I know, right?" I laugh at my foolish optimism. "And then Dom decides to stage her one-girl strip show, and I tried flirting with this guy. . . . They all say I need to move on," I explain quickly.

He raises an eyebrow. "How's that working out for you?"

"It's not. The flirting, I mean. The moving on is fine. Good, even." I laugh, self-conscious. "Sorry, I'm kind of incoherent. It's been a long night."

There's the light of a cell phone glow through the trees, then Kayla and LuAnn arrive.

"Angel!" LuAnn launches herself at Josh in a hug. "Sweetheart! Darling! You're a doll, helping us out like this."

He laughs. "Yes, yes I am. Feel free to reward me with massages and undying devotion."

"You know, I might just do that. You're saving our asses here. Or rather, these two cute underage asses," LuAnn corrects herself. "I only had a couple of beers, so I'm going to wait here a while, then drive Dom's car back. Can you take Dom home with you tonight?" She directs that last one at me.

I nod reluctantly. "I can stash her in my bedroom and try to sneak her out when Mom's at Pilates."

"Then we have a plan." LuAnn claps. "It's been a blast, ladies."

There's a groan from inside the truck, then Dominique sticks her head out the door and vomits onto the ground.

"And there's my cue." LuAnn backs away. "Laters!"

We stay until Dominique has evacuated the entire contents of her stomach, then head home. We pull into our street with minutes to spare before Kayla's curfew. "Sorry I can't help," she apologizes, leaping out of the front seat. "I'll call tomorrow, OK?"

We watch her sprint up to her door, the lights all on.

"What about you?" Josh asks, turning to look at me in the backseat, with Dominique's head on my lap. "How do you want to work this?"

"Um . . . Can you try and get her in the back door while I distract my mom up front?"

"Sounds like a plan."

I gently shake Dom awake. "Come on, hon, we need to go inside now."

"Then bed?" she yawns.

"Yup. Well, my floor," I correct myself. "But it's comfy—I promise. You just need to help us get you inside."

Josh opens the back door. "You go ahead. I've got this."

"Are you sure?" I glance toward the house. It's dark except for the lights in my mom's study. With any luck

273

she'll be deep in project work still, or even sleeping in her chair like she does sometimes after a long day. "The stairs are right next to the kitchen, then my room is first down the hall."

Josh nods. "We'll be fine, won't we, Dom?"

"Meugh."

"See?" Josh grins. "We'll launch evasive maneuvers while you get on with phase one: distraction."

"Yes, sir!" I salute. "Go in T minus five?"

"T?"

"I don't know," I admit. "They just always say it in the movies."

"Then T minus five it is." Josh salutes back. "Over and out."

I leave him to hustle Dominique into a standing position while I let myself in the front door.

"Hey, Mom!" I yell loudly. "I'm home!"

I go to the kitchen and unlock the back door, then hurry straight to her office before she can come out to see me for herself. She's working at her desk, the radio playing on low. "See?" I present myself in the doorway. "Right on time, like I promised."

She smiles. "Did you have a good time?"

"Yup." I nod quickly. "It was fun." I sneak a look back toward the kitchen. Josh is in the hallway, guiding Dominique toward the stairs. There's a thump, and a faint "Ow" as she stumbles against the wall. I leap forward. "Ooh, I like this song." I turn it up loud.

"You like the Bee Gees?"

"Sure!" I grin, frantic. "Seventies stuff is totally in right now. They're so uncool, they're cool again."

"I remember when they were just plain cool."

"Five million years ago," I add. "So what have you been doing?"

"Just some accounting stuff." Mom makes a face. "I always put it off until the last minute."

"What?" I act shocked. "Ms. Organization lets things slide?"

She laughs. "I'm still human, honey."

"So you claim." I check the hall again. Josh is creeping back out. He gives me a thumbs-up, then slips out the back door. All clear. I exhale, relieved.

Mom moves her papers to one side. "There was actually something I wanted to talk about. . . ."

"Tomorrow!" I tell her, already backing away. Lord knows if Dominique is busy vomiting all over my bedroom floor right this instant. "I'm super tired. I just need to crash."

"All right, then. 'Night, sweetie." Mom smiles. "I'm glad you had fun."

I scoot upstairs, praying to the Gods of Trusting Motherhood and Obedient Drunk Girls that Dominique keeps quiet. Having to explain why there's a wasted girl—well, woman—in my room would take powers of persuasion way above my level and probably get me grounded for life with a side helping of lectures about bad influence and peer pressure.

I crack open my door. Dominique is sitting on the bed, sipping a glass of water.

"Hey," I whisper. "You're awake."

She grimaces. "Barely. My head hurts."

"Just keep hydrating. I'll get you some blankets." I cross to the closet. "The floor is actually pretty comfy once you're down there."

She stays quiet while I arrange pillows and my sleeping bag into a cozy little nest, but when I look up, I find she's kicked off her shoes and snuggled up under my comforter.

I guess I'm the one on the floor.

I turn out the lights and try to get comfortable, shifting around on the pile of quilts, but just when I find a halfway decent position and prepare to slip into blissful unconsciousness, Dominique's voice comes, quiet from the other side of the room.

"I'm sorry. I . . . I know I wrecked everything."

"No, it's fine." I sigh, rolling over. "Are you going to be OK? There's a wastebasket there, if you need to . . . you know."

"Thanks." She's silent for a moment. "Listen, about Carlos . . ."

"I haven't said anything," I reassure her quickly. "I mean, I don't really know what's going on. It's none of my business."

"Thanks." Then her voice twists. "It's not serious or anything."

I don't know what she wants me to say, so I don't say anything at all.

"I mean, what am I supposed to do—stay in this town with him and serve coffee for the rest of my life?"

She sounds wrung out, miserable. "I didn't work this hard just to give it all up. I have a plan!"

There's another long silence. Slowly, her breathing gets even, and I roll back over, ready to sleep. Then she whispers again.

"But I love him."

The plaintive note in her voice haunts me even as I listen to the sound of my mom's footsteps on the stairs. My heart stops for a moment as they pause outside my door, but then they head onward to her room, and I slowly exhale.

But even though the immediate danger has passed, I find I can't sleep. My head is whirling with thoughts about Kayla and Blake, LuAnn and her ex, Dominique and Carlos, and, yes, even my wretched history with Garrett. Now that everything's quiet—except for Dominique's gentle snores from across the room—I keep coming back to it all. But no matter which way I look at everything, I can't get past this strange contradiction that seems to lurk behind everything we do. Because no matter what, or who, we end up choosing, all of us feel like we've failed somehow.

Kayla feels guilty for planning for a future with Blake; Dominique feels guilty that she won't with Carlos. LuAnn dropped everything to make it work with her guy, and I'm filled with shame every time I think about how I did the same thing, building my life around Garrett without even realizing it and then working just as hard to take that version of my life apart, piece by piece.

So how are we supposed to win? On the one hand,

the world tells us that capital-*L* Love is epic, and all-conquering, and the meaning of everything, but on the other, it drills us with this message that we shouldn't make any sacrifice or effort to pursue it, because that would make us weak, unempowered, desperate, silly girls. But it's not silly to want that connection, and it doesn't mean that we're weak just because we want to share our lives with someone. I didn't even lose my mind over Garrett—no giggling or blushing or writing his name in my notebooks—it's not that simple. Everything I did, I thought I was doing it my way: being independent and grown-up, getting by in school, living my life.

I just wanted him to love me, too.

I exhale, worn out. I thought it would be easy once I was done with the plan: no urge to check my messages, no obsessing over what he's doing and with whom. But the problem won't just disappear now that I'm over Garrett. I realize that now. This isn't about him; it's something deeper than that. It's about who I am with him. With anyone.

What happens with the next guy?

I'm going to want to be loved by someone else one day; I'm going to long for him the same way I did for Garrett. More, maybe. So what's stopping me from doing the exact same thing—molding myself around him without even realizing because I'm so desperate for that connection? It won't change just because I'll get older; LuAnn and Dominique are proof of that. They still feel that pull to subsume themselves in somebody else's life, to go all or nothing for the sake of a relationship. And if they do, then they risk losing themselves, but if they don't, well, they lose him instead. But it can't be that simple a choice, can it? There has to be some middle way where I stay myself, in the world I choose, but get love, too.

There must be.

Old Habits Die Hard

So, you're officially over **him**—finally free from romantic agony, loose from the clutches of miserable, lonely woe. You did it. And doesn't it feel wonderful?

But even though you deserve a party—a celebratory circus, a ticker-tape parade—for your awesome achievement, be warned. The specter of unrequited love can strike at any time, reducing even the most fearless, independent woman to a weepy wreck.

Don't let it happen again. You were strong enough to strike it down before; you'll be smart enough to avoid it the next time around.

Love isn't pain. Heartbreak isn't noble or romantic. You deserve better, so don't ever forget.

CHAPTER TWENTY-FIVE

Dominique is gone when I wake up, with nothing but perfect hospital corners on the bedding and an ache in my neck to show she was ever here at all. I trip downstairs, wondering how she went off the rails so spectacularly. Maybe Josh is right, and it really is the quiet ones you need to worry about—the ones with years of rebellion stored up tight, just waiting to burst forth in new, self-destructive ways.

Mom is waiting in the kitchen, with a plate of . . .

"Are those pancakes?" I say, shocked. I hop up on the counter and take in the spread: turkey bacon, syrup, even fresh juice. "Like, not from a box or anything?"

She laughs, depositing another batch of pancakes onto the platter, fresh from the pan. The scents of butter and vanilla waft through the sunlit room. "You make me sound like a lost cause in the kitchen."

"No!" I say, loading my plate with deliciousness. "Well, it's never really been your number-one strength," I admit with a grin. "But these are great. What's the occasion?"

She leans against the counter, already dressed for the day in a smart business outfit, polished and professional. "Well," she begins, sounding almost cautious, "I thought we could have that talk. . . ."

"Mmm-hmm?" My mouth is full of pancakey goodness.

"Your father called last night." Mom presses her lips together. "He has . . . a proposition for you. For, us really."

"Oh." I stop, the free breakfast not seeming so free anymore. Dad has kept sending his usual postcards and short e-mails from his tour, but his bailing on my birthday still lingers, uncomfortable at the back of every breezy phone call. "Where is he this time?" I ask slowly.

"California, for now. He's doing some session work." Mom uses that same neutral tone for whenever we talk about Dad, as if we're discussing the weather or a TV show. She has a stack of books in her study about positive postdivorce parenting and how important it is to remain impartial in your children's relationship. "But he'll be going to Europe for a couple of weeks over Christmas vacation," she adds. "And . . . he wants you to go along, too. To make up for his canceling these last months."

I blink. "Europe?"

Mom nods, her expression still unreadable. "He's

playing some shows in London, and then Berlin, Rome . . .
I have the itinerary, he e-mailed it to me."

"Would you . . . ? I mean, would I be allowed to go?"
I ask breathlessly, already picturing the quaint cobbled
streets of Paris, snow falling softly on the River Seine.

Europe!

"If that's what you want, then, yes, we would work
something out." Again, Mom stays neutral, hands
wrapped tightly around her mug of tea. I pause my fantasy of *macarons* and *chocolat chaud* for just a moment.

"You don't sound too thrilled," I tell her. She gives a
small shrug.

"I don't think it's the best idea—you crammed in a
tour bus with a bunch of musicians. But . . ." She exhales.
"I want you to spend time with him, Sadie. He's your
father. And if the only time he has is this, then so be it."

That wasn't a no. Which means, it's a yes.

I leap up. "Mom! Thank you!" I squeal, burying her
in a hug.

She pulls back. "Before you get carried away, just
think about it, please?" Mom fixes me with a look.
"Think about what it would actually be like. You know
how focused he gets, especially on tour. It's your decision," she adds. "But don't go rushing into it. Think
about it for a few days before we talk to him."

"Yes, fine, I'll think," I tell her, but the decision was
made the minute she said "Europe." What is there to
think about? "And thanks for breakfast." I grab another
pancake to eat on the go. "You're the best!"

．　．　．

I'm still bouncing when I get to work, just imagining the adventures I'll have. Garrett will be so jealous. He's always talked about taking a trip abroad and tracing the footsteps of the great American expat writers who used to hang out in the coffeehouses of Berlin and Paris. He said we'd go together, after high school or when one of us did a college semester abroad, but now I'll be the one venturing out there before him.

"You seem happy." Josh leans against the counter, his red T-shirt emblazoned with a cute cartoon zombie. "Was the mission a success?"

"Yes, sir." I salute. "Mission complete. We really owe you one, Mom had no idea what happened." I move closer, distracted by the familiar-looking illustration. "Is that one of Aiko's designs?" I ask.

"Yes!" Josh grins, tugging at the shirt. "She finally caved to LuAnn and started selling them online. What do you think?"

"I like it. Very undead chic." The doorbell dings behind us suddenly, and I turn to see Dominique sashay in, her shirt crisp and her jeans fresh—not a sign that merely eight hours ago she was stripping for a room full of strangers. She looks past us as if we don't exist, breezing through to the back of the café.

Josh and I exchange a look. "Not it," he says quickly.

"Hey!"

"You snooze, you lose." Josh backs away, grinning. "And someone has to be alive to open up!" He crosses to the front of the café to flip the closed sign while I brace myself for battle.

Here goes nothing.

I find Dominique clearing out her locker: stuffing old time sheets and notes into a trash bag. "Spring cleaning?" I approach gingerly, not sure quite how to act now after her drunken revelations. She looks up.

"No," Dominique answers simply, pulling a cardigan from the lockers and folding it neatly into her shoulder bag. "I'm quitting."

"What?"

"The café, Sherman . . ." Dominique gives me a tired smile. "I'm applying to transfer to another school. Out West maybe, or Chicago. I'm done here."

I look around. The café is almost empty, nobody except Josh to witness this huge development. All the times she's threatened to quit, nobody actually thought she'd go ahead and do it. "B-but . . . Carlos," I stutter. "I mean, what did he say?"

"What could he say?" she replies with a shrug. "I left a note. He'll be fine."

She turns back to the locker and checks it one last time. She's utterly self-contained, and something about her pose—so studied and careful—reminds me of that poem they always drag out in lit class, the John Donne one, about no man being an island. But Dominique is. She is a vast territory, walled and guarded.

"Um. Good luck, I guess," I offer, feeling useless. She finishes packing, but before she leaves, she reaches out and puts her hand lightly on my arm, the kindest gesture I think I've ever seen her make.

"*Merci,*" she tells me quietly.

"For what?"

"You changed. This summer, with that plan of yours . . ."

I don't follow. "What do you mean?"

There's another pause, and for a moment, I think she's just going to snatch her hand back, deliver a dead-pan bon mot, and leave, but once again she surprises me. "I don't like who I am with him," she answers. "How he makes me feel. Last night . . ." She swallows and shakes her head, stronger this time. "You were right. I don't have to be this girl. I can do something about it."

And then the wall is back up: she straightens and gives one last look around. "Tell the others . . . Well, tell them whatever. It won't matter to me."

She stalks away, the door closing behind her with a final *ding*.

Without Dominique on shift, I'm run off my feet for the rest of the morning, dashing around to keep up with orders while I try to deconstruct her cryptic comments. Just taking off and leaving town, transferring schools, lit-erally running away from Carlos? It seems so extreme to me, yet more drama from our most dramatic staff mem-ber. Ex-member now, I guess. But as much as I'm shocked by her sudden departure, a part of me understands it, too. That plaintive note in her voice, coming through the dark last night; the glimmer of self-loathing on her face today. She wants to escape the woman she's become around him, any way she can.

"I called LuAnn; she'll be in ASAP." Josh hauls an

armful of dirty dishes into the kitchen, backing through the swinging doors.

"Thank you, thank you, thank you!" I call, trying to juggle three different drink orders for five different kinds of coffee. I hit the Beast, say a short prayer, and turn to the next customer to apologize. "Sorry, we'll just be a moment—"

"Hey, Sadie." It's Garrett. He gives me a lopsided smile, his hair still falling long enough to tuck behind his ears. "What's up?"

"Garrett, hi!" I turn back to the counter, trying to remember which jug is soy and which is two percent. "Could you hold on, like, ten minutes? We're kind of slammed right now. . . ."

"I know, but I wanted to say sorry about last night." He takes a hand from behind his back and holds out a bunch of daisies. "I got so caught up with this new poem, I lost track of time."

The flowers are tied with string, obviously hand-picked. I always loved daisies. I soften. "Thanks, that's sweet. But we really are crazy right now."

Josh appears next to me. "I can take the register if you pour."

"Perfect." We sidestep around each other in a well-practiced ballet while Garrett waits on the other side of the counter.

"Oh, before I forget . . ." Josh pulls a CD from his back pocket and slides it over to me. *Sadie's Mix* is written on the front in scrawled Magic Marker. "I burned you some of those Thermals tracks."

"Um, thanks," I say, my focus pulled in three different directions. "That's great. I'll take a listen later."

"Anyway." Garrett coughs. He looks back and forth between me and Josh. "Sorry. I guess this isn't a good time."

"Not really!" I froth milk with one hand while Josh passes me a fresh mug. "I just had someone quit on me," I explain to Garrett. "And the lunch crowd will be here any minute. . . ."

"Why don't I help?" Garrett brightens.

"No, it's fine." I turn back to the drinks in front of me, and then stare at them, lost. "Crap. Was it soy in the mocha or in the latte?" I ask Josh.

"The latte."

"Double crap." I pour the drinks out and start fresh, pausing to wipe my sweaty face with the edge of my apron.

"I'm serious," Garrett says, still loitering there on the other side of the counter.

"About what?"

"I'll help," He tells me. "I pulled mess-hall duty all summer, I can handle it."

I pause. Normally, I'd turn him down flat, but today . . . ? I eye the debris scattered around the café, a vast wasteland of dirty plates and coffee rings on the tabletops. "Are you sure?"

"Positive. You need me." Garrett laughs. He reaches over the counter and uses his thumb to wipe cappuccino foam from my cheek. "Just tell me what to do."

"Um, it's kind of the scut job," I start cautiously, "but if you could bus tables . . ."

"Already done!" He backs away, grinning. "I'll be the best table wiper you've ever seen!"

And he is. Well, good enough, anyway. Garrett fetches, carries, wipes, and cleans for the rest of the morning, until our rush dwindles to a steady stream, and LuAnn finally arrives to take over Dominique's vacated post.

"Well, well, well. What do we have here?" She leans against the counter, watching Garrett clean tables out front. He's found an apron and slung a dishcloth over one shoulder, happily playing the part of busboy for the day.

"What? Oh, right. Garrett offered to help out."

LuAnn smirks. "And how does Josh feel about that?"

"Josh?" I pause. "He's fine. We needed the help."

"Are you sure about that?" LuAnn nods across the room. Josh is trailing Garrett's route, checking every table after Garrett is done. "It's cute the way guys get so protective of their territory. I'm surprised he doesn't just pee all over the place."

"LuAnn! Eww!" I bat her with the dishcloth.

She laughs. "I'm just saying. . . ."

"Well, don't. At least not where customers can hear you."

She props her chin on one hand and bats her eyelashes at me. "You know, maybe it's not the café Josh is feeling protective about. . . ."

"What?" LuAnn gives me a meaningful look. "Oh,

no, no way," I tell her firmly, feeling heat rise in my cheeks. I turn away, busying myself with the pastry cabinet. "Now you really are being crazy."

"Am I?"

"Yes," I say firmly. "Now, can we please focus on what we're going to do about Dominique?"

For the next few days, Dominique's scandalous departure is the only gossip in the café. Carlos takes the news with a nonchalant shrug, then proceeds to go AWOL for the week, apparently crawling every bar in the state until Josh and Denton go scrape him off the floor of a karaoke joint in Boston, clutching the mic and belting out his one big hit. I don't know what to think; their relationship was way too clandestine for me to know if he meant it or was just playing around with her, but when Friday rolls around and he spends an hour flirting with a table of blond coeds—regaling them with tales of music festivals gone by—I get the feeling Dominique made the right call. If he loved her, he would have gone after her, or at least spent more than a few days mourning her loss before hitting on the next pretty young thing to cross his path.

"Penny for 'em." Josh collapses against the counter next to me on Saturday morning. I jolt. "Your thoughts," he adds. "You've been spaced out all shift."

"Oh, it's nothing." I shrug. "Just contemplating the meaning of life, love, the universe . . . You know, the usual."

"Nothing big, then." He glances over to the front of the café, where Garrett is camped out at the window table with a book and his battered notepads—same as every other day this week. "That guy sure drinks a lot of coffee."

I laugh. Garrett has become kind of a fixture in here: working on his poetry, chatting to the staff on their breaks, waiting patiently for me to swing by and hang out. "He shouldn't put his feet up on the seats like that," Josh adds, giving the Beast a smack. "You know how Carlos gets."

"Come on . . ." I give him a look.

"What? I'm just saying. Customers bitch about that kind of thing all the time."

"Fine, I'll go tell him." I start to edge out from behind the counter, but Josh turns, suddenly bumping into me.

"Sorry." He looks awkward, realizing he's trapped me in the narrow space. "I, uh—"

"It's OK." I step the other way, but he does, too. I laugh. "You want to pick left or right?"

"My left or yours?" He grins back.

"I don't know. We could vote."

"But what if it's a tie?" Josh replies, forcing a serious expression.

"Good point. We could be here all day."

"On the count of three . . ." Josh decides.

"Wait!" I stop him, giggling. "Which way am I going again?"

Finally Josh takes me by the arms and physically moves me to the side. "There."

"Why didn't you just do that five minutes ago?" I call, heading across the café.

"What? And miss our meaningful debate?" Josh calls back.

I arrive at Garrett's table, still laughing. "You don't have to stay here all day," I tell him, pushing his feet off the chair and sliding in beside him. "You must be bored."

"Not at all." He leans back. "It's fun, watching you in action."

"Sure, because wiping tables is a spectator sport," I murmur, but he just gives me that grin.

"But we're hanging out. Kind of." He drums his ink-stained fingers on the tabletop and shoots me a bashful look. "Remember, I've been starved for Sadie time all summer."

I smile. I may not be hanging on his every word anymore, but I can't deny the glow I get from him wanting to see me—choosing to loiter over a cup of coffee all day just for five minutes of my time, here and there. "So what's the plan for the rest of summer?" I ask. "We've only got a few weeks left before school starts."

"Plan?" he teases. "Next thing you'll be making lists and plotting us a schedule."

"Why not?" I protest, embarrassed. "At least that way we won't forget anything. We should go into Boston—get stocked up on books and stuff for school." I pull my order notebook out of my apron pocket and begin to make a list, but when I look up, he's laughing at me. "What?"

"Nothing, it's just—what happened to order being the enemy of creativity?" He reaches over and flicks my pencil. "You'll turn into your mother if you don't watch out."

"And what would be so wrong with that?"

Garrett laughs. "Only that you've been complaining about her for years. Decades even. Maybe you were right all along," he adds, teasing. "Maybe the pod people did brainwash her. And now they've come for you, too!"

"At least pod people get things done," I inform him lightly, flipping my notebook closed. "Instead of being scatterbrained and late for everything all the time. Like *some* people!"

"Guilty as charged. I'm sorry," Garrett apologizes. "I promise I won't be late tonight."

"What's tonight?" I steal a corner of his cookie.

"I'm taking you out. It's a surprise." He grins at me, but I waver.

"I don't know. . . . I was maybe going to hang with Kayla. . . ."

"But I already organized everything!" Garrett gives me the puppy-dog look again. "Come on, you'll have the best time—I promise."

A big surprise? I have to admit, I'm intrigued. "OK, I'm in," I decide.

"Great! I'll pick you up at eight."

CHAPTER TWENTY-SIX

"Not the blue—it's too sexy." Kayla folds her arms, keeping a careful watch as I delve through my wardrobe that evening, hunting for something to wear for this big surprise.

"What?" I hold up the plain shirt, confused. "How is this sexy? More importantly, how is *anything* I own sexy?"

"I'm just saying, you don't want to give him the wrong idea." Kayla presses her lips together.

"Sure, because everything in my wardrobe has thus far filled him with longing and desire." I hurl myself down on the bed in exasperation. "This is the thing about surprises: they don't help you figure out a dress code!"

Kayla shifts out of my way. "You shouldn't even care," she points out. "Not if you're as over him as you say you are."

"Of course I'm over him." I sit up, determined to get this fashion crisis resolved before Garrett shows. "Maybe the vintage dress, the red one? If it doesn't stink of smoke from the party."

"Sadie . . ." Kayla drags my name out. "Just listen to yourself! You can't do this again."

"Do what?" I bound back over to my dirty laundry hamper and pluck the dress out. I sniff it carefully, then hold it out to her. "What do you think? I've got some perfume somewhere, to cover the cigarettes."

"Sadie!"

I sigh. "Stop worrying, Kayla. I'm fine."

"No, you're not," she insists. "I've seen you, fluttering around him in the café."

"Fluttering?"

"He's flirting with you," she continues, stern faced. "And you're falling for it! After everything we've done . . ."

"A, he's not flirting," I tell her, stripping off my T-shirt and pulling the dress over my head, "and B, even if he were, I'm not falling."

"What about yesterday?" Kayla shoots back. "You were sitting there, laughing with him for, like, half an hour."

"So? That's not a crime." I check the mirror. "Ack, I'm going to need a different bra." I cross to my dresser and rifle through the drawers for something seamless. "Look, Kayla, it's really great that you're looking out for me, but you don't have to—I promise. He's my friend, remember?

"Yes, and we all know how that worked out last time around."

I turn. She's looking at me with this accusatory expression, as if I've already committed grave crimes against girlhood. I feel myself start to get defensive. "What do you want me to say? That I'm never going to see him again?"

She shrugs. "Maybe that would be the smart thing."

"Why?" I exclaim. "Because I enjoy his company? Because we're hanging out?" I take a breath, trying to stay calm. "Look, I know you never liked him, but he's my friend, and I'd appreciate it if you could give him a break."

"You want me to just stand back and watch while you drape yourself all over him again?" Kayla asks, her voice dripping with unfamiliar sarcasm. "Sure, why not?"

"I'm not draping!" I protest. "But I like Garrett, and I want us all to be friends. Is that really too much to ask?"

"Yes, Sadie, it is." She gets up. "Because what you wanted was to get over him. And you did! You were actually thinking for yourself, instead of wandering around like a little Garrett clone."

"Gee, thanks." I glare, tense now. "Says the girl who's planning her whole life around a boy—at sixteen!"

Kayla's expression hardens. "Not my whole life, my college town," she spits back. "Because unlike you, I know about real relationships, not just fantasies in books and movies!"

I gasp. "That's not fair! And this is a real relationship—a real friendship. Garrett cares about me."

"Right." Kayla rolls her eyes. "You finally don't adore him anymore, so now he wants to reel you back in. Yup, that sounds like a great friendship to me."

I back away, shocked by this sudden venom. Kayla is the perpetually upbeat one, the ultimate cheerleader, and here she is, full of bitterness and vitriol. Out of nowhere! "You know what? I don't have to listen to this," I tell her.

"Oh, no, not when you could be listening to *him* instead." Kayla clasps her hands together and bats her eyes. "Garrett, tell me about that boring book again. What's that? You want me to drop everything to hang out? Sure, let me trail you around like a pet poodle!"

"Screw you!" I yell.

She grabs her cardigan. "Enjoy your date. And yes, that dress smells like a freaking ashtray!"

Kayla storms away, her footsteps harsh on the stairs. Then the door slams and I see a flash of her blond hair through my front window as she hurries back across the street. I turn away and catch my breath.

Where did that come from?

Kayla is the last person I'd expect to flip into bitch mode, but the things she was saying. . . . She must be jealous, I decide, quickly stripping off the dress again and grabbing a plain white T-shirt. Jealous, that's it. After all, Blake is away at college now, and with Garrett back, I haven't been so free to hang out with her. But even so, that's no excuse for saying those things!

I hurry to get ready, and by the time Garrett arrives,

I'm waiting on the front step in jeans and a cute jacket, my hair carefully styled into bouncy curls.

"Hey, you look great." Garrett greets me with a hug. He looks dressier than usual, sporting a dress shirt and cords, his hair combed into something resembling a neat style. I look past him to the gleaming car parked by the curb.

"Where's Vera?" I ask, shocked. "Did she finally give up on you?"

"No, she's good. My parents lent me theirs for the night." Garrett grins proudly, spinning the keys on his finger. "They said it might rain, and I didn't want you getting wet."

"Ooh, fancy." I follow him to the car, where he hurries to the passenger side to open the door for me. "Remember the time we got caught in that hailstorm?" I ask, sliding into the leather seat. "I thought I was going to freeze to death."

"Not this time." He closes the door behind me, then walks around to the driver's seat. "Tonight, we ride like kings!"

We drive a half hour out to Northampton, where Garrett insists on covering my eyes as we make our way—very slowly—from the corner parking lot to some mysterious destination.

"Can I look yet?" I ask, his hands still over my face.

"Hold on." He steers me forward.

"But we—ow!" I exclaim as I trip on a hard step.

"Sorry!" Garrett keeps his hands in place, maneuvering me down a flight of stairs. "OK, now you can look!" He uncovers my eyes. "Ta-da!"

I blink. I'm standing in a dark, dingy basement-café-slash-bar. Through the dim lights I can make out some faded, torn couches, with a bunch of college kids sitting around a small stage area. The smell of something not entirely legal wafts in the air.

This is his big surprise?

"Over here." Garrett leads me to a table in the corner with a red-and-white checked tablecloth and a single rose in a chipped vase. "It's a poetry night," he announces, clearly thrilled. "Some of the guys from camp told me about it. They should be here later."

"Oh . . . awesome," I say slowly, taking a seat in one of the rickety chairs.

"You want a drink? Soda?" He asks eagerly. I nod. "I'll be right back."

He goes to the bar, while I scope out the room and try to shake the niggling feeling that's been stalking me ever since he arrived to pick me up. I know I'm not exactly experienced in this department — OK, not *at all* experienced — but I know Garrett, and I've seen him at work when it comes to other girls. The borrowed car, the dress shirt, the special table . . .

It can't be a date, can it?

"One soda for the girl with the amazing hair." Garrett returns, pulling out the chair across from me. I take the glass and gulp down a long swallow, remembering what

Josh said about it settling your stomach. For some reason, mine is suddenly twisting in a strange dance. Garrett seems totally at ease, but now that that thought is in my mind, it's all I can focus on. Is this a date? Does he want it to be? Does he think *I* want it to be?

But the biggest question of all is, *do* I want it to be?

"I'm glad we got to do this." Garrett smiles at me. "You've been so busy since I got back, I feel like we haven't had any time to ourselves. You know, just us." He pushes back a lock of hair—the one that's always falling in his eyes. Despite the cleanup, he still has faded ink on his fingertips, and something about the familiar gesture makes me take a breath. What am I doing? I'm overthinking this; there's nothing wrong with us hanging out and talking, the same as we've always done.

I relax. "Me too." I smile. "Anyway, I have all this news. You'll never guess what my dad said—"

"Here they are!" Garrett suddenly bounces up, waving across the room to a group of college-age kids who just came in. They wave back but stay on the other side of the room, where they claim a couple of the moth-eaten couches. "I'm just going to go say hi," Garrett says. "I'll be right back." He heads across the room and greets them with backslaps and handshakes.

I sip my soda and wait. The room is filling up now, the crowd full of guys in army jackets, with dreadlocks and/or goatees, while the girls all seem detached and disdainful in that "dark eyeliner and piercings" kind of way. A few of them shoot me curious stares, and I feel painfully young in my plain outfit, wishing I hadn't let Kayla talk me out of that vintage dress.

Kayla . . . I'm starting to feel guilty about our fight now, and the things I said to her. I didn't mean to snap, but the way she was talking about me and Garrett. . . .

I look over at him, but he's pulled up a chair and is talking enthusiastically with his new friends, showing no sign of getting back to me anytime soon. I waver, uncertain, but as the minutes stretch out, I start to feel even more conspicuous, sitting here alone. Finally, I scrape back my chair and approach his group. A boy with one of those Russian army coats is in the middle of talking about Hemingway and how he's the ultimate male writer.

"Absolutely," Garrett agrees, leaning back in his seat. "Although, that braggadocio was always more myth than man."

"I knew you'd say that," the girl next to him mutters darkly. She's got her hair bobbed in a sleek flapper style, and her carefully painted eyeliner disappears into two winged tips. "Never mind what a rampant misogynist he was. What about the five wives he left in his wake?"

I hover awkwardly for a moment. Finally, Garrett looks up. "Oh, sorry—everyone, this is my friend Sadie."

"Hi." I wave. They all nod back before resuming their spirited debate.

"But you can't write off an artist because of his personal life. What about D. H. Lawrence, or Polanski?"

"God forbid we measure the content of their souls as well as their creative output."

I wait a while longer, then go and drag over a chair from the next table. Garrett scoots over to make space for me. "So, were these people all at lit camp with you?" I ask quietly.

"Just Alex, and Charlotte there." He nods. "But we all drove down for the slam night a couple of weeks ago and met everyone else."

"You came down for a visit?" I repeat, confused. "You never said."

He looks back at me. "Oh . . . I mean, I didn't come to Sherman. It was just a crazy road-trip thing." Garrett pats my knee. "Hey, look—they're starting."

I open my mouth to speak, but he turns his chair to face the front. The lights get even dimmer, and the Russian army coat guy takes to the small stage.

"Hey, everyone. Welcome to our open mic night. We've got some great artists lined up, so let's get things started with Malachi and his poem in sixteen parts: 'The Decay of Being.'"

I blink. He can't be serious?

But he is. There's applause, and then one of the goateed guys walks slowly onstage. He's dressed all in black, except for a square of red handkerchief in his shirt pocket. "Thanks, Logan." He nods solemnly, unfolds a thick wedge of pages, and reaches for the mic. "I wrote this poem about my breakup with my girlfriend." He pauses and squints out into the audience. "Luna, I hope you feel my pain."

And thus begins my torture.

After sixteen verses, five haiku, and three more epic odes to love unfulfilled, the last reader finally lopes off-stage, and I let out a long sigh of relief. Have my prayers to the Gods of Terrible Amateur Poetry finally been answered?

"Don't worry—we're not finished!" Logan bounds back, dashing my hopes beneath his battered army boots. "We'll be right back after a short break. Feel free to discuss the work and chat with the writers!"

The lights go back up.

Garrett turns to me. "Wasn't that first one provocative?"

"You mean, the one where he imagines his ex-girlfriend's bloody death?" I venture, blinking.

"Right, the imagery was so powerful."

The rest of the group murmurs in assent, besides Charlotte, of course. "Typical," she spits. "Another example of shock-machismo torture, literally silencing women through death."

Garrett ignores her. "You know, you should read here sometime," he tells me. "I can't wait to see what you've been working on this summer."

"Um, actually I haven't done much writing," I admit. "Any, really."

"Sadie! You have to be disciplined," Garrett scolds. "I got up at dawn every morning and worked for an hour, just freewriting. My professor told me about it, you really get the creative muscles working."

Another guy with ratty dreadlocks nods. "If you don't take it seriously, you can't call yourself a real writer."

"True artists have to live, breathe, *bleed* for their art," Charlotte agrees solemnly.

I let out a snort of laughter. I try and cover it with a cough, but clearly, my drama skills are about as good as Malachi's self-editing skills, because when I look up, they're all staring at me.

"You find that funny?" Charlotte asks archly.

"Well, I—" I start to speak, but Garrett interrupts me.

"Sadie's starting out," he says to them apologetically. He pats me on the knee again. "She's just a sophomore."

I stop.

"Her work shows a lot of promise," he adds. "She didn't get in to the program this time, but maybe next year. Right, Sadie?" He gives me a smile—full of encouragement—but I just stare at him, confused. Garrett's support always meant the world to me, but now I can't help wonder if he was always so . . . patronizing.

Dreadlock guy laughs. "Man, I wish I could be young and naive again."

"Right," Garrett agrees. "Trust me, Sadie. You'll learn soon enough that you have to suffer for your art." He looks past me to the stage area. "Oh, great, they're starting again."

The rest of them all turn eagerly to hear the next round of poets, but something in Garrett's expression makes me stop.

He looked past me. The whole time he was talking

about me—talking *to* me—he never once really looked at me.

How many times has that happened? I find myself wondering. How many times have I sat, waiting, while he catches up with somebody else, somebody more important?

I feel a shiver, cold on my spine.

"Garrett," I murmur. He doesn't turn. "Garrett." My voice is louder this time, and he tears his focus from the stage. "I think I'm going to get out of here," I whisper, reaching for my purse.

Garrett frowns. "What? But Sadie—"

"Stay if you want," I tell him softly. "I can call my mom for a ride."

I slip away, hurrying up the stairs and emerging back onto the street, lit with the neon glow of streetlights in old-fashioned lamps. I don't know why I need to leave so fast, but something in me is itching, uncomfortable, and I can't stay in that place—with those people—a moment longer.

"Sadie, wait!"

I turn. Garrett jogs down the street and comes to a stop a few steps from me. "What's wrong? Are you feeling OK?"

"Sure, I'm fine," I tell him, confused. He's staring at me with such concern, I wonder if I've got it all wrong. As if reading my mind, Garrett moves closer and reaches out to touch my arm.

"I'm sorry I got distracted with those guys," he says,

giving me an apologetic smile. "I promise, the rest of the night, it's just you and me."

I pause. "Oh. You don't have to . . ."

"Sure, I do! What do you want? Name anything." Garrett makes a sweeping gesture, full of theatrics. He backs down the sidewalk, calling out, "The world is ours! Well, western Massachusetts, anyway." He beckons me after him, but I don't follow.

He stops. "Are you sure nothing's wrong?"

"I—"

"Because I'll make it up to you—I promise. Tonight, and tomorrow too, the whole day, we can do whatever you want." Garrett smiles at me again, as charming as he's always been. "I'll even let you take me to another one of those alien invasion movies. And I won't complain, not once!"

I stare at him, lost. This is what I wanted, isn't it: for Garrett to choose me over his other friends? But just as quickly as that thought comes, it's replaced with another, louder question.

Why am I doing this all over again?

Waiting for him to choose me. Getting swayed by all his charm and focus. This is exactly why I wanted to get over him, to feel like we were partners, instead of just Garrett and his desperate, pining friend. I spent my summer carefully cutting out my feelings for him, tracing around the outline of my heart because I was so desperate to keep our friendship together, the same as before.

But it can't be. And more than that, I don't want it to. Not if "the same" means waiting around for him, having him treat me like the girl I used to be instead of the person I am today.

I feel a rush of calm, cool and easy in my veins. "You know what? I'm beat," I tell him. "Can you just take me home?"

Garrett's face falls. "But, are you sure . . . ?"

"Another time, maybe." I try to smile. "It's been a long week."

"There was something I wanted to say," he begins. "This wasn't exactly how I pictured saying it, but—"

"Can it wait?" I ask, turning to head back to the parking lot, but before I even have time to think, he closes the distance between us, takes my face in his hands, and kisses me.

CHAPTER TWENTY-SEVEN

This can't be happening.

I stay frozen in place, his lips on mine, trying to make sense of the impossibility. Garrett moves a hand to my waist and pulls me closer against him. Dazed and reeling, I go. His lips are soft on mine, his skin faintly rough and unfamiliar against my cheek, and for one blissful moment, I sink into it.

Everything I've been waiting for—all those sleepless nights imagining this very moment—has come to this. Now. Here.

The kiss deepens, slow and sweet. I barely move. I barely even breathe. *This is Garrett,* I tell myself, giddy. *This is Garrett, kissing me.* My heart swells with triumph.

I finally made him love me.

At last, Garrett pulls away. "Hey," he whispers, tucking a strand of my hair behind my ear. He smiles down at me. "I've been waiting forever to do that."

"What . . . ?" I'm dizzy, clutching the front of his shirt for balance. "I mean . . . Why?" Garrett's still smiling at me, that special smile I've longed for for two entire years. The one that says, "You're the only girl in the world." The one I've seen given to Beth, to Julie, to a parade of other girls, but never to me.

Until now.

"Don't you know?" He pushes his hair back in a nervous gesture, almost bashful. "I love you, Sadie. I think I always have," he adds earnestly. "But I was just too stupid to see it. I didn't realize . . ."

Love. He said he loved me. I stare at him in amazement. But for some reason, the words dance just out of reach, like a language I can't quite understand.

What does that word even mean to him?

"What?" I ask again, stronger this time. "What didn't you realize?"

"Well, how great you are." Garrett laughs. "And how great we could be together." He traces my lips with his fingertip, then kisses me again. We're closer than we've ever been before, so close I can feel his breath, taste the faint bitterness of coffee from his mouth. But for some reason, Garrett suddenly feels like a stranger to me, a foreign body pressed against mine.

I stay frozen in place on the sidewalk, aware of everything around me. Farther up the street, a group of people emerge from a bar, laughing; couples wait in line outside an Italian restaurant; a boy with scruffy long hair plays guitar on the corner, the faint strains of Jeff Buckley drifting down to us. And Garrett, here against me, but feeling farther away than any of them.

I pull away, that first blissful swoon I felt dissolving now, leaving something else—something cooler, more solid—in its place. A simple question. "What happened with Rhiannon?" I ask softly.

Garrett frowns. "What do you mean?"

"What went wrong?" I take another step back, watching him carefully. The haze is clearing; I can see things for what they are now. "It was only a couple of weeks ago that you were in love with her. You said she was the one. And now, you love me?"

He shakes his head. "It's not like that. I mean, yes, we were together," he says, stumbling. "But when she ended things, it made me see what had been right in front of me all along!"

I exhale, disappointment washing over me. "She broke up with you." In the two years that I've known him, Garrett is almost never the dumpee. He's always the one in control.

Garrett flushes guiltily. "No. I mean, yes, she did, but then I realized, you know—what we have. How special it is. You never let me down, Sadie; you're always there." He takes my hands in his, full of emotion. "Don't you see? We're meant to be together!"

I stare back at him, his words hitting me with painful force. I never let him down. I was always there for him. And he's right: I was.

But not anymore.

"I'm sorry," I tell him, pulling my hands away. "It's too late. I can't do this."

The smile slips from Garrett's face. "I don't understand."

Of course he doesn't.

"You're not in love with me, not really," I explain, realizing it for myself even as the words slip out. "You just love the way I always made you feel. Like you were the center of my world. Because you were." I shrug, helpless. "I would have done anything for you."

"I'd do anything for you, too!" Garrett says, confused. "That's why this is meant to be!"

"No," I say, understanding for the first time the great distance between who I used to be and who I am today. "I don't love you. I did," I add. "God, I loved you so much. But it's over. I'm not that girl anymore."

"Sadie . . ." He trails off, speechless. There's nothing for him to say.

"It's OK." I smile faintly. "You'll be fine. But I have to go now."

I reach up on tiptoes and press a kiss to his forehead, feeling one last pang of regret. However it turned out, Garrett was my first love, my best friend. But it's over now. All of it. The scene down there at the poetry slam proved it for sure. He sees me as some kind of adoring acolyte, a fan. But I'm more than that now.

"Take care," I tell him, and then I turn and walk away.

CHAPTER TWENTY-EIGHT

It's late by the time Mom pulls in to our driveway, but I don't feel tired at all. I'm still buzzing with a strange adrenaline, a mix of relief and pride and exhilaration all in one. Something ended tonight. Something finally finished for good.

"Do you want to tell me what happened?" my mom asks at last. She managed to show amazing self-control all during the drive home, but now she finally breaks. She looks over with concern. "Are you OK?"

I nod. "I'm fine. No, I'm better than fine," I correct myself, feeling a smile creep across my face. "I'm good."

"Oh." Mom is clearly thrown. She waits while we go inside and then broaches the subject again as she crosses the kitchen to the kettle for her ever-present cup of herbal tea. "And is everything all right with Garrett?"

"Not really." I give her a smile, slinging my purse on the kitchen table. "But that's OK, too."

She looks confused, so I reluctantly continue. "I just can't do it anymore. Being friends with him, or more than friends. . . ." I shrug. "I've spent enough of my life revolving around him. I had to stop."

"Oh, Sadie." Mom comes over and pulls me into a hug: swift and strong. "I'm proud of you, sweetie. I know how much he meant to you."

I blush.

"Don't look so embarrassed," she laughs, going back to her tea. "It's not easy to do, separating yourself from someone like that."

I pause. "Is that what happened with dad?" I ask slowly.

She looks up, surprised. "Not exactly," Mom begins, checking to see if I'm really going there. I've never asked what happened, not directly. They sat me down, of course, for that talk about how even though they weren't going to be together anymore, they both still loved me. But as for actual details, the breakdown of what went wrong. I've never asked, and she's never told.

Still, something about tonight makes me tell her, "I want to know." So she continues.

"Well, you know how he gets so caught up in his music, it's like nothing else in the world exists? Not even us." She pours the water carefully, a distant expression flitting across her face, and I can tell she's back there — in this house, all those years ago. She holds out a mug, and I take it and follow her to the back porch.

It's dark out in the backyard, so Mom lights the lamps, and we curl up on the long wicker couch with a blanket around our legs. "He was just starting to tour," she explains. "So I was on my own with you all the time, waiting for him to get back. And my art wasn't paying anything, and the bills were mounting up, and, well, there came I point when I had to decide." She gives me a tired smile.

"Decide to divorce him?" I ask.

"No, it wasn't even that." She pauses, thoughtful. "It was more about whether I was going to shape our world around him or make a life on my own terms—for the both of us."

I nod. After this summer, I understand exactly what she means. Even I can see that I've had to fold myself into pieces for Dad—making myself small enough to slot into the spaces he has around this show or that session. In twenty years, he's never put anything—or anyone— ahead of his music, and I doubt he ever will.

"I think you're right about Europe," I say at last. She raises an eyebrow. "I didn't think it through before, what it would actually be like," I explain. "But Dad will be in rehearsals all day, or on the road, and I . . . well, I'll prob- ably be waiting around backstage most of the time."

She smiles, full of regret. "I'm sorry. I wish it were different, but . . ."

"But it's just the way he is," I finish for her. Dad, and Garrett, and probably plenty more besides. They live their lives, and in the end, I have to choose to live mine, no matter how much I care.

We sit in comfortable silence a while longer, the crickets sounding out in the dark, and my exhilaration fading into pleasant tiredness. "Do we have any cookie dough?" I ask at last.

"Are you hungry?" Mom asks. "There are some leftovers, I think."

I shake my head. "I need to apologize to Kayla," I explain, feeling that guilt push through my fatigue. "And I figured it would go easier with baked goods."

She smiles. "I think there's some in the freezer. We'll whip something up in the morning. But now, bed." Mom pats my feet decisively. "It's late, and you've had a long day."

"The longest," I tell her, but before I get up, I pause, awkward. "Thank you," I say quietly. "For everything."

"Always."

The next morning, I drag myself out of bed extra early, bake two dozen sugar cookies from the pack of instant dough in the freezer, and decorate them with M&M's reading *I'm sorry.* I leave them on Kayla's front steps, along with a copy of *Grey Gardens* and twenty packs of my mom's gold stars.

"Is this your way of saying I was right about Garrett?" Kayla opens the door just as I'm nudging a cookie into place. I look up.

"Yes," I admit, shameful. "I nearly fell back into it again, trailing around after him. But you saw it coming."

"I'm smarter than I look." Kayla bites into a cookie, aloof. "My vast wisdom is often underestimated."

I laugh. She gives me a look. "Sorry," I mutter. "And I'm sorry for what I said, about you and Blake. I shouldn't have been so mean."

"You really can look wretched and pathetic when you want, you know?"

"It's a skill," I agree, waiting. Finally, she smiles.

"Fine, OK. Get over here!" She pulls me into a hug.

"Watch out!" I yelp, shifting us out of the path of cookies.

"Whoops." She grins, then settles on the front steps, still in her penguin-print pajamas. I sit beside her and try a cookie of my own. "And I'm sorry, too," she adds. "I was kind of a bitch. I just couldn't stand to see you fall back into the same old pattern again with him."

"Me neither."

"So, what finally made you realize he isn't your soul mate?" Kayla asks, perking up. "The flakiness? The pretentious angst? That hair?"

"All of the above." I laugh. "And when he decided to declare his love for me."

"What?" Kayla chokes on an M&M, but I shake my head.

"I'll tell you later. But can we not talk about Garrett for now? I feel like I've spent way too much of my life focused on him. Let's just say, that thing is done."

"Thank God." Kayla reaches for another cookie. "So what now?"

"I don't know. Work, I guess." I shrug. "The rest of summer. School."

"Gee, you make it sound so fun."

I laugh. "Well, what did you have in mind?"

"Um, how about more beach time? And some parties. Ooh, and a road trip!" Kayla lights up. "The brat camp finishes next week, and then I'm free! Broke, but free."

"You should come work at Totally Wired," I suggest, reaching for another cookie. "We've got an open slot now that Dominique's fled the state. I'm going to keep some shifts even when school starts, which means we could work together. I'll put in a good word for you."

"You really think they'd hire me?" Kayla asks hopefully. "Because that would be the best. If I have to wipe up after another leaking kid, I think I'm going to start shoving corks somewhere corks aren't designed to go."

I laugh. "There's wiping, sure, but no bodily fluids," I promise. "And Carlos is still permanently hungover, he'll say yes for sure—if we ask really loudly."

"Yay!" Kayla claps. "OK, I have this family thing with Aunt June today, but you want to hang out tonight? I could call the girls and do a movie slumber party thing?"

"Sounds great," I say. Just then, a familiar-sounding engine cuts through the silence. Kayla looks past me and breaks out into a smug little smile.

"Helllooo."

"What?" I ask, turning. Josh's mud-splattered truck is pulling to a stop in front of my house. He climbs down from the driver's cab and nods over at us, tugging on his cap sheepishly. "What's he doing here?" I whisper.

"Duh." Kayla laughs. "Go on!" She's already pushing me off the step. "But you better tell me everything!"

"Kayla . . ."

"Everything." She grins, then gets up and disappears back into her house, leaving me with no reason to linger here. I take a deep breath and head back across the street, inexplicably nervous. "Hey." I stop beside the truck. "What's up?"

"Sorry to just show up, but you didn't answer your phone," Josh starts, running one hand over the top of his head, messing his hair even more. His skin is tan against the red of that zombie shirt, his eyes bright but bashful. "I was just heading out to the beach for the day, and I wondered . . . if you want to come."

He looks up at that last part, meeting my eyes with a look that is definitely not just platonic.

I feel a thrill. "You mean . . . like a date?" I venture, suddenly needing to know exactly what this is we're doing here. No more unspoken agreements and blurry lines. I need some clarity, this time around.

"Maybe," Josh ventures, starting to smile. "If you want it to be. Or it could be just date-ish."

"Date-like," I reply, relaxing. "Date-esque."

"A quasi-date," he agrees. We grin at each other awkwardly.

"Yes," I decide. "I'm in, but . . . would you wait, just five minutes? I need to grab my stuff."

"Sure," he keeps smiling. "Take as long as you need."

I bound inside, thundering up the stairs to assemble my beach bag in two minutes flat. Sneakers, sunscreen, my iPod for the drive . . .

There's only one thing left to do. I walk over to my computer and sit down. A few quick clicks and I have it up on-screen: the whole website, every perfect relationship, every great romantic couple. Years of work. A lifetime of dreaming. A shrine to something that I now know doesn't exist—not in real life. Not so neatly. No, Kayla is right: real love is a whole lot messier—and maybe a whole lot more fun.

I click again and type in my password. A window pops up.

Are you sure you want to delete the database?

I hit the enter key without hesitation and bound back downstairs, out into the sunshine.

ACKNOWLEDGMENTS

A huge thank you to everyone who works so hard to make my books a reality: to Kaylan, Liz, Tracy, Jenny, and the team at Candlewick; Mara and the Walker crew; to Rosemary Stimola, Tyler Ruggeri, and Elisabeth Donnelly.